LIVING
UPSTAIRS

■ JOSEPH HANSEN ■

LIVING
UPSTAIRS

A DUTTON BOOK

■   ■

DUTTON

Published by the Penguin Group
Penguin Books USA Inc., 375 Hudson Street, New York, New York 10014, U.S.A.
Penguin Books Ltd, 27 Wrights Lane, London W8 5TZ, England
Penguin Books Australia Ltd, Ringwood, Victoria, Australia
Penguin Books Canada Ltd, 10 Alcorn Avenue, Toronto, Ontario, Canada M4V 3B2
Penguin Books (N.Z.) Ltd, 182–190 Wairau Road, Auckland 10, New Zealand

Penguin Books Ltd, Registered Offices:
Harmondsworth, Middlesex, England

First published by Dutton, an imprint of New American Library,
a division of Penguin Books USA Inc.
Distributed in Canada by McClelland & Stewart Inc.

First Printing, September, 1993
1 3 5 7 9 10 8 6 4 2

Copyright © Joseph Hansen, 1993
All rights reserved

 REGISTERED TRADEMARK—MARCA REGISTRADA

LIBRARY OF CONGRESS CATALOGING IN PUBLICATION DATA
Hansen, Joseph
Living upstairs / Joseph Hansen.
p.   cm.
ISBN 0-525-93682-3
1. World War, 1939–1945—California—Los Angeles—Fiction.
2. Young men—California—Los Angeles—Fiction.   I. Title.
PS3558.A513L59   1993

813'.54—dc20   93-2716
                                                                                    CIP

Printed in the United States of America
Set in Copperplate and Garamond No. 3

Designed by Steven N. Stathakis

For Michael Nava

It IS A SUNDAY MORNING IN July. The year is 1943. Hoyt is dressing up. Not in this room, where trees reach in the windows. In other rooms. On the quiet. Nathan catches glimpses of him through half-closed eyes from where he lies drowsy under a rumpled sheet. Hoyt has put on the suit. They share the suit. It is dark blue, and they bought it on sale for twenty-five dollars. They are lucky to be about the same size. They could never have managed fifty dollars. Still, Nathan has worn it only once. Hoyt seems to need it most. He is coming into the room. Nathan shuts his eyes and pretends to be asleep. Hoyt kisses him lightly, leaves the room, and in a moment Nathan hears him softly open and close the door and go down the stairs outside.

Nathan jumps out of bed, runs to use the toilet and comb his hair, kicks into jeans and flaps into a shrunken flannel shirt. He straps on his old Mexican sandals, and he too goes down the stairs. Hoyt isn't hurrying at all. He is not much more than a block ahead of Nathan, walking down Highland Avenue toward Hollywood Boulevard, looking very nice. Nathan cuts across Highland at a run to snatch two bananas from a tilted crate in front of a small grocery and drop a dime into the palm of a startled stock boy. He stands there, keeping an eye on Hoyt and eating the bananas. He is always hungry, a lean and hungry twenty-year-old—twenty years old next week. He lopes east on Yucca Street and down McCadden.

He waits on the southwest corner of Hollywood Boulevard and Las Palmas for the streetcar, keeping back in the recessed doorway of the Suzie-Q nightclub. Hoyt is on the streetcar, all right. Nathan dodges autos, climbs aboard the long, barn-red car, and drops his dime into a glass-and-steel fare box. He sits in the rear, where he can keep an eye on the back of Hoyt's head. Hoyt has been close-mouthed and sad for almost a week now. It's not his way. Something is wrong, but he won't tell Nathan what. He is far away in his thoughts, and when Nathan gets through to him he only smiles wistfully and strokes Nathan's hair and tells him:

"Don't worry. I love you."

Nathan believes this. Hoyt is always going off alone. When they'd only just met, when Nathan had only just moved his books and clothes and typewriter into Hoyt's place, Hoyt said he had to go out sometimes, and Nathan mustn't ask him about that. And Nathan hasn't asked him. Nathan trusts him. If he couldn't trust Hoyt, he couldn't live. He has settled that in his mind. Hoyt loves him, and him only. As he loves Hoyt. But he has never seen him downcast before, and it worries him. Hoyt hasn't gone out anywhere this week. He's stayed home, read, listened to the radio, listened to records, slept, almost never talked.

Now, suddenly, Sunday morning, all dressed up, he's on his way someplace important. Where? Why? The idea of spying on Hoyt or anyone else is hateful to him, but if he and Hoyt are part of each other, he has a right to know. *Curiosity killed the cat*, his mother's voice says in his head. He thinks of Bluebeard's wife and those terrible doors. He imagines Hoyt angry with him, throwing him out, and winces at the thought. Hoyt is gentler with him than anyone he has cared about has ever been, even Frank, his father. If Hoyt should see him this morning and turn on him, Nathan would die, crawl up into the hills someplace and lie there in the sun and rain and wind until he died. Tears blur his eyes. He reaches up to pull the cord so the car will stop and he can get off at the next corner, but he doesn't pull the cord. He slouches down on the seat, bows his head, puts his hand over his eyes, and prays Hoyt won't look back.

It's a long ride. Not until the conductor calls "Westlake Park" does Hoyt get up. Nathan ducks down out of sight, a grandmotherly colored woman across the aisle watching him, surprised, distrustful. The car stops with grating wheels. Its middle doors slide open and bump shut. Nathan stays out of sight until the next stop, then lunges for the doors. Dropping down the steps, he looks back, and the colored woman is still eying him suspiciously. He jogs toward the park. But there seems to have been no hurry.

Hoyt has seated himself on one of the benches lining the paths that cut diagonally through the park's rolling lawns. He slips a book from his pocket, bends his head, and reads. Ducks quack, white among the green reeds of the lake. A couple of dressed-up little children throw them bread crusts. On a tree-shaded bench an old man feeds pigeons dry corn from a rumpled sack. The pigeons bob their heads around his shoes. It makes Nathan sad. Frank was feeding pigeons like that the last day Nathan saw him. He lights a cigarette, leans back against the window of a drugstore, and waits to see what Hoyt will do next.

Across the park somewhere a church clock strikes ten. By this time, Nathan is sitting on the sidewalk, clutching his knees, his back against the brickwork under the drugstore window. He has smoked all the cigarettes left this morning in the crumpled red-and-black pack. But now Hoyt hears the clock too and gets up off the bench, sliding the book back into his pocket. He makes a turn, but not toward Nathan. He cuts northward across a sloping lawn, across a sidewalk, across a street in the middle of the block.

Nathan pushes to his feet and follows, dodging cars, ignoring red lights. Hoyt goes into a two-story building with French windows fronting it, wrought-iron balconies upstairs. PARK MANOR, the sign says. Nathan hangs back, scared, lurks around, walks up and down, and finally, with a thumping heart, steps through the open door into a sort of foyer, with meeting rooms opening on both sides and to the rear. The doors are all of square glass panes. No one but a cleaning woman with a mop and bucket is in any of the rooms. But a distant voice—somebody giving a speech, it sounds like—comes down a wrought-iron railed staircase, and Nathan climbs toward the voice.

At the top of the stairs, to his right, the doors of a meeting room stand open. Next to the doors on an easel leans a sign on posterboard. EVA SCHAFFER MEMORIAL SERVICE. SUNDAY, JULY 13, 10:00 A.M. Inside the room people sit on long rows of folding chairs, their backs to him. From the doorway, Nathan scans the heads until he spots Hoyt sitting toward the front, where he faces a speaker's rostrum flanked by tall baskets of flowers, and a couple more easels, these with wreaths of flowers. There are also flags— one for the U.S.A., one for the USSR. And taped to the wall are large photographs of Lenin and Stalin. Nathan is surprised, but he tiptoes in and sits in the back row.

The man giving the speech at the rostrum has shed his jacket and rolled up his shirt-sleeves. He is handsome, square-jawed, with a big chest and muscular forearms. He is talking about the workers of the world, and he looks as if he is one of them—a longshoreman or a coal heaver or a lumberjack. He says that death cannot stay the power of the workers. For every one the bosses kill, two more will rise up to claim their right to decent wages, hours, working conditions, and, at last, ownership of the means of production.

The man says Eva Schaffer believed in the workers and the

workers' state and the coming overthrow of the capitalist system, the end to wealth and privilege for the few and poverty and starvation wages for those who create the wealth. She believed with every fiber of her intense being in the glories of the Soviet socialist system, and had taught and written and lectured tirelessly and selflessly to bring about the dawning of that same glorious new day in America.

A gray little man in a cloth cap nudges Nathan and peers up into his face. He whispers with a thick accent, "You know who that is? Gus Hall, that's who. Remember that." He wags a gnarled finger. "You can tell your children."

Nathan looks surprised and impressed and nods for the little man, but he doesn't know who Gus Hall is, and he seriously doubts he will ever have any children.

Gus Hall says we will miss our stalwart comrade Eva, but will close ranks and move forward in the struggle for world socialism. This is what she would have wanted. She would have expected nothing less from us today.

A big, bald-headed black man named Pettis Perry gives pretty much the same speech, salting it with exhortations to the Negro in America—though he is the only Negro in the room—to wake up and recognize who his friends are, his only true friends, the ones who will raise him to real equality with his white oppressors. Perry's voice begins to tremble with emotion. Too long the Negro has been trodden underfoot. Too long he has had to settle for the empty solace of religion, promising him pie in the sky bye and bye. Today, an army of brothers and sisters of all races is reaching out to help him break his shackles—the Communist party of the United States of America.

Then a fat, jolly-looking woman, Elizabeth Gurley Flynn, talks of women's place in the struggle to defeat fascism in the world; and though she could not, as Russian women do, take up arms alongside her brother soldiers in the war, yet our fallen sister Eva has been no less heroic a warrior in the people's battle to bring to an end the vicious capitalist power of Krupp and the other industrial monsters who created Adolf Hitler and turned him loose upon the world in a final, frantic attempt to destroy forever the hopes and aspirations of the proletariat and turn them into slaves.

It looks as if the Flynn woman might be the last speaker, and Nathan wants to get away ahead of Hoyt, so he leaves before she can finish, wondering why he stayed so long.

Hoyt is good at making cheap meals—chili and pinto beans, lentils and bacon ends, sauerkraut and wieners. Nathan is still stunned by that meeting and scrambling in his mind to figure out why Hoyt went there when he climbs the steps to the flat at noon. But he is hungry and thinking also about the thick split pea soup with chunks of Spam in it that's congealing in a big, chipped Mexican pottery bowl in the refrigerator. Hoyt douses it with curry powder and cooks it over a low flame for hours. Just thinking about it, Nathan can taste it. His mouth waters.

But when he steps through the open door into the hallway at the top of the stairs he hears Reggie Poole's voice, and looks at the door to Reggie's rooms. The door is ajar. He pushes it. The room has cheap new wartime furniture without springs. Its bookshelves are filled with the memoirs of duchesses and countesses and queens. Reggie, wearing his best suit, sits at an unpainted kneehole desk, smoking, and reading aloud from typed pages. He looks up with raised brows at Nathan, then smiles. "Ah, Nathan. Come in." He's a tall, fleshy man of forty-odd, with a strong nose and jaw and the carriage of a dowager empress. He sublets the front apartment—two rooms and a small kitchen—from Hoyt and Nathan, though he has never yet paid them any rent. "I met Private Schaffer on my way out to church, and I couldn't answer his question. Perhaps you can."

Nathan steps inside. A young fellow in U.S. Army tans sits on the couch, facing Reggie. He turns to look at Nathan with luminous brown eyes. He appears about twenty. He stands up. "Before the gas shortage, my mother used to live here," he says.

"Then she had to move downtown, but I lost her new address. It's floating around in the ocean with all the rest of my stuff. I got a telegram when she died, but I was too far away to get back fast. Not with all the fucking red tape. Anyway, when I got stateside, there's this letter saying there'd be a memorial service for her today. But they didn't know where, yet, and I just got to L.A. this morning, and nobody answers the phone number they gave me. Did you know her? Do you know where the place is?"

Nathan shakes his head. "I didn't know her." He does know about her memorial service, but he can't admit it in front of Reggie; Reggie might mention it to Hoyt. What use would telling it be now, anyway? It's over, isn't it? "Maybe my friend knows—Hoyt."

"When I heard you coming, I was hoping you'd be he," Reggie says. He hasn't a lot of use for Nathan. Nathan is too young. Hoyt is only twenty-six, but he's the one Reggie regards as in charge. Rightly. Nathan has no wish to be in charge of anything. Reggie asks testily, "Where is Hoyt?"

"I don't know," Nathan says. And to Private Schaffer, "I'm sorry about your mother."

Schaffer shrugs. "Thank you. But we weren't close. She didn't have a lot of time to be a mother. She had to warn the world about Hitler." He gives a short, wry laugh. "She was right, but for all the good it did, she could have been reading me bedtime stories."

Nathan looks at Reggie. "Is that your play?" Though he has of course never told Reggie so, Nathan privately thinks the play is silly. It's about an encounter in Paris at some future time when the Allies have the Nazis on the run—a chance meeting between Hitler and the French lady novelist Colette, of all people. It embarrasses Nathan.

"I was reading it to him to pass the time," Reggie says complacently, "until Hoyt came."

Nathan eyes him. "You think Hoyt knew Eva Schaffer?"

Reggie tilts his head. "I think you did. No one but you has mentioned her first name."

Nathan gulps. "Somebody must have."

"It's a good play," Schaffer says. "I enjoyed it."

"You see?" Reggie says to Nathan. "You think it's lowbrow claptrap, don't you? But it's going to be a hit, my child, you wait and see."

"It's exciting," Schaffer says. "I want to know how it comes out."

Nathan looks at him. "Maybe, but I'll bet you'd rather have been eating."

Schaffer looks at Reggie, embarrassed. "Oh, look, I—"

"Come on," Nathan says. "I'm starving."

Schaffer grins and picks up his duffel bag.

"I hope"—Reggie lays aside his play—"you have an iron digestion."

Nathan is in the hall. "You're invited too, Reg."

"Thank you." Reggie rises. "I have an engagement. Luncheon al fresco at Grady Sutton's in Beverly Hills." Sutton is a big, plump, effeminate comic actor who gets a lot of work in pictures.

"Thanks, Mr. Poole," Schaffer calls.

Reggie appears in his doorway, buttoning his collar, straightening his tie. "My pleasure. But let me explain one thing." He looks hard at Nathan. "The reason I didn't offer you meat and drink is because the cupboard is bare. Like most writers in Hollywood, I live on hope." His smile is thin. "It nurtures the spirit, but not the flesh."

Schaffer doesn't know what to say.

Nathan mumbles, "I'm sorry, Reg."

The big man closes his door behind him. His fingers flutter on Nathan's head placatingly; then he sways out into the noon sunshine and down the stairs, plucking up the crease of one trouser leg, like a fine lady in long skirts.

The main room of Hoyt's place—that's how Nathan thinks of it, though it has been his place too for eight or ten weeks now—has green-shingled walls, like the outside of the house, a threadbare rug, a couple of slumping overstuffed chairs, orange crates teetering on top of each other and crammed with books, a small boxy phonograph with record albums stacked on it, and drawings thumbtacked to the walls, Hoyt's drawings—mostly of Nathan, as a life class model, not quite but almost naked. But the only student in this life class is Hoyt, the only studio this room.

Schaffer drops his duffel bag. "This is great. Trees all around, books, records, drawings. I wish I lived here." He picks up a book from a chair, the book Nathan is reading. "*Dangerous Acquaintances.* What do you think of it?"

"Evil versus innocence?" Nathan says. "Simpleminded."

"Simpleminded isn't always foolish."

"I liked *The Red and the Black* better."

"That's because it *is* better," Schaffer says.

"I'll heat our lunch," Nathan says, and he does, hearing Schaffer wandering through the ramshackle rooms. Then they're both at the cluttered table in the kitchen, spooning up the fragrant, thick split pea mess and munching soda crackers and drinking milk.

"Does Poole know a lot of famous people?" Schaffer asks.

"I guess so," Nathan says. "But some of them are pretty far gone. Fay Bower—he has her over sometimes."

Schaffer blinks. His eyes have long soft dark lashes. "I guess I missed out on Fay Bower."

"A big star once," Nathan says. "Before our time."

Schaffer smiles. "He wrote for the movies?"

"A studio brought him out from college—Yale, Dr. Baker's famous playwriting class," Nathan says. "The one where Thomas Wolfe went? This was in the late twenties. They thought they needed literate writers because pictures could talk now. But Reggie only got screen credit on one picture—something about the candid camera craze."

"That puts it a few years back," Schaffer says.

"He worked on other stuff, I guess, but the studio cut back because overseas sales are off. They dropped him. He couldn't get in the service, but he's very patriotic, so he signed up for the merchant marine. A cook. A sea cook."

"Long Jane Silver," Schaffer says.

"You have something against homosexuals?" Nathan says.

Schaffer drops his spoon and stares. He has smooth skin, and a dark flush appears under it. He gives his head a quick shake, picks up the spoon, mumbles "No," bends his face close to the bowl, and quickly shovels in food.

"But his ship got torpedoed," Nathan says. "And swimming around in cold oily seawater for hours in the middle of the night decided him he wasn't cut out for war, so he came back to Hollywood."

"I wish I had that option," Schaffer says. "But when my ship got sunk, they just issued me a new rifle and said 'Carry on, Private.' " Schaffer frowns puzzlement at Nathan. "How come they didn't get you?"

Nathan shrugs. "Scars on my lungs. I told them it was only from pneumonia, but they didn't believe me."

"If you're eager to go shoot people," Schaffer says, "you can have this uniform and my ID. You go back in my place, and I'll stay here."

Nathan thinks to himself how surprised Hoyt would be. The picture of Hoyt crawling naked into bed in the dark tonight and finding Schaffer there instead of him excites him, so his cock begins to stiffen. He doesn't understand that. He smiles. "Sorry, but I'm not eager to go."

"Chance of a lifetime," Schaffer says. "Who knows when there'll be another war?"

"How come you're a combat soldier?" Nathan says. "Why aren't you in an office someplace, doing the thinking for some dumb colonel?"

"That's the Army way," Schaffer says. "If you can type, they give you a gun. If you ever read a book or thought a thought, they assign you to scrub out latrines."

"Who are you?" Hoyt stands in the kitchen doorway.

"Steve," Schaffer says, "Eva Schaffer's son."

Hoyt turns pale. "Jesus," he says.

"This is Hoyt Stubblefield," Nathan says.

Schaffer puts out his hand and Hoyt shakes it. He nods but doesn't speak. He wets his lips with his tongue.

"This is the last address I had for my mother." Again, Schaffer explains about getting back late. "Mr. Poole said maybe you knew her, maybe you knew about the funeral."

Hoyt looks at Nathan. "Are there any cigarettes?"

Nathan shakes his head. Hoyt digs in the suit and pulls out coins and lays them in Nathan's hand. "Will you run across and get some?"

He wants to talk privately to Schaffer, doesn't he? It doesn't work. "I've got cigarettes," Schaffer says and jumps up. "I don't smoke, but I know they're hard for civilians to get, and the PX is loaded with them, so I brought some with me to give away." He goes into the living room. Fasteners on the duffel bag click. He comes back and hands each of them a pack of Chesterfields. He says to Hoyt again, "Did you know my mother?"

Hoyt nods reluctantly. "Yes. She fixed it so I got this place when she moved."

"A friend, then?" Schaffer says.

Nathan is watching Hoyt curiously, and Hoyt avoids his eyes. "I took some classes from her," he says, lighting his cigarette with a paper match, holding the match out for Nathan to light his. "At the Workers' School." He shakes out the match. "She liked the questions I asked. We argued a lot. She was an intelligent lady. I'm sorry she's gone."

"Where's the memorial service going to be?"

"It's over," Hoyt says. "It was very nice. Everybody loved and admired her. Gus Hall came out from the East for it. Elizabeth Gurley Flynn. Your mother was important."

"They wrote she fell under a streetcar," Schaffer says.

"It's hard to get gasoline," Hoyt says. "That's why she moved downtown. To be near the school. She took streetcars. A lot of people have to."

"Must have been those damned high heels," Schaffer says. "She always wore very high heels because she was so short. She hated being short. But high heels can be dangerous. She fell a couple of times. Broke her wrist once." He looks at Nathan. "Why didn't you go with him?"

"I didn't know her," Nathan says, looking at Hoyt.

Schaffer asks, "But you live together?"

"It's the housing shortage," Nathan says.

Something amuses Schaffer. "You aren't friends?"

Hoyt says sharply, "It's not the housing shortage. Nathan just—never happened to meet your mother, that's all." He glares at Nathan. "Of course we're friends."

"I thought you must be." Schaffer gives them a dry little smile. "You've only got one bed."

Hoyt reads aloud from *Lafcadio's Adventures*, Nathan from his own novel. They listen to a Mozart quartet, and at four-thirty Nathan and Hoyt watch Schaffer climb aboard a bus at the Greyhound station, duffel bag over his shoulder. He sits by a dusty window and smiles out at them. The engine of the bus roars to life. Black smoke from its tailpipe fogs the vast brick room that smells of scorched tires and empty highways. The bus begins to back out to the street. Schaffer waves to them. They wave to him. It makes Nathan sad.

"We may never see him again," he says.

"Do you want to see him again?" Hoyt says.

"I mean, he could be killed," Nathan says. "They do get killed, GIs do. So I hear. Haven't you heard that?"

Hoyt turns and starts across the blue-and-white waiting room that is so full of people there aren't seats enough for them and they sit on the floor. Women, children, old people—and sailors, soldiers, marines. They look pale and tired. Some of them sleep, chins on their chests. Luggage lies everywhere to trip over. Hoyt pushes out the doors to the wide sidewalk. More people wait out here, knee-deep in suitcases and cardboard cartons tied with twine. Hoyt and Nathan edge between them and start on up Cahuenga for home. Hoyt's hands are in his pockets. He slouches along, frowning at the sidewalk. "Some do," he growls. "Some don't."

"Why don't you like him?" Nathan says.

"You like him enough for both of us," Hoyt says.

Nathan steps in front of him, looking hard into his face. He laughs. "I can't believe it. You're jealous. What happened to logic, coolheadedness, rationality?"

"I used them to observe you with him," Hoyt says.

"I like him," Nathan says. "But I love you, Hoyt."

Hoyt waits a minute, studying him. Then he counts the change from his pocket. "You want a hamburger?" he says.

Nathan says, "The Workers' School?"

"It's one of the places I go nights." Hoyt pushes the doors of the Owl drugstore. "Forget it, will you?" He walks down an aisle of glass showcases toward the lunch counter at the rear. Nathan slaps along after him in his old sandals.

"But you won't be going anymore, right?" he says. "I mean, wasn't it Eva Schaffer you went to hear?"

"I go to hear a lot of people." Hoyt sits on a red-cushioned swivel stool and moodily lights a cigarette. "The less you know about it, the less you can get hurt."

"What about you?" he says. "You can't get hurt?"

"It will be my own fault." Hoyt blows out the match and forces a smile. He cranes, looking along the counter for the waitress. "You going to have onions?" he says.

"I'm not going to have anything," Nathan says.

He wakes up early. It's a rule with him. Hoyt lies against him, an arm across him, dead asleep. Nathan edges gently away from him, totters to the bathroom, uses the toilet, and, since there is no shower, crouches in the old claw-footed tub, and with a length of red rubber enema tube runs cold water all over himself. The day is already hot, and the water feels good, and it clears his head. In the kitchen, he fills a kettle, washes out the dented drip pot, and spoons coffee into it—some brand nobody ever heard of, but good coffee is hard to come by these days.

Back in the bedroom, he pulls on clean briefs—ragged because they're not making them now on account of the rubber shortage—and goes into the next room, where Hoyt has his drawing and painting stuff and Nathan has a table for his typewriter. He sits down on a creaky kitchen chair there and reads through the pages from Friday. What he's turning into a novel is the play about his childhood he wrote two years ago. Novels don't need actors and directors and a theater—only paper and a typewriter ribbon. He rolls a new page into the machine and begins to rattle out words. He loses himself in what he's doing, and the shriek of the kettle startles him. He runs to turn the flame down and pour boiling water into the coffee pot. When he passes Hoyt on the way back to his work, Hoyt, who is supposed to be asleep, reaches out from the bed and grabs the limp elastic of Nathan's shorts.

"Doctor," he says, "is that you?"

"It's very early," Nathan says. "Go back to sleep."

"Doctor," Hoyt says, wide-eyed, alarmed, "I have this awful swelling. Look." He throws back the sheet.

"It looks okay to me," Nathan says. "It looks fine."

Hoyt yanks the waistband of the briefs again, and Nathan loses his balance and falls across him. Hoyt grabs his hand and guides it. "Feel how hard it is? That can't be normal. Isn't there some way you can reduce it?"

"Hoyt, it's my writing time. You promised—"

"How about massage?" Hoyt says. "Like this."

"I'd rather kiss it," Nathan says, "and make it well."

———

T. Smollett Books is on Hollywood Boulevard. Its tall, elaborate Spanish colonial front is already sun-struck this morning. It's going to be a scorcher of a day. Nathan turns a key in a padlock and another key in a Yale lock and slides back a bolt to one side and a bolt to the other side, and hoists up the immense door on its rusty armatures and twanging springs. He rolls a wheeled table of cheap, ragged bargain books out into the entryway between the show windows. He switches on the fluorescent lights that ping and wink high overhead and walks a half-block to the packing room at the rear of the cavernous place, where he finds a push broom. With this he sweeps out yesterday's dust and cigarette butts. He sweeps the empty sidewalk too. He works the crank that lets down the awning. And comes back inside to find Angus MacKenzie laying money in the drawer of an old spring-operated cash register.

"Morning, Mr. MacKenzie," he says, passing with the broom.

MacKenzie, a tall, stoop-shouldered man with crinkly pale-red hair growing low on his forehead, and a cigarette always smoldering at a corner of his mouth, grunts and says, "My car is out back, full of books." And it is, a dull-green 1937 Chevrolet sedan. It is so full of books the only room left was for Angus to drive. The car smells of old paper. Nathan unloads the books, carries them down the cement steps into the shipping room, out into the shop, and, armload after armload, up long flights of wooden stairs to the third floor, where, as far as the eye can see, mountains of books just like them loom up waiting for—what? Nathan doesn't know. He doesn't think Angus MacKenzie knows either. He doesn't think God knows.

By the time the car is emptied, it's ten-forty-five, the day has hardly begun, and he is tired. He takes off his shirt and tie and in the washroom splashes the sweat off. When he steps out of the little room, blotting himself with stiff, scratchy paper towels, Mr. Constance is standing by the shipping bench. Mr. Constance is a handsome man, always has a suntan, keeps himself in trim. If it weren't for the wrinkles, no one would know he is past forty. His brown eyes caress Nathan's naked torso, but he says only:

"Others occasionally need to relieve themselves, you know, Nathan."

"Not you, surely," Nathan says, flapping into his shirt again. "I thought you were above such things, Connie."

Mr. Constance answers by stepping into the washroom and slamming the door.

Now the deliveries come. The new books. From the publishers in New York, Boston, Indianapolis. The parcel post trucker is a lame, cheerful Negro with sweat running down his face from under his natty cap. He brings in carton after carton. There's supposed to be a shipping clerk, but they're always being drafted, and new ones are hard to find, so it's up to Nathan these days to crack the cartons open on the shipping bench, unpack the books, and check them against the packing slips, and the packing slips against the statements Angus MacKenzie has speared on a hook over the bench. He's busy with this when Constance comes out of the washroom, water slicking down his yellow hair.

"You'd have more stamina," he says, "if you didn't go in for so much degenerate sex. At the rate you and that Texas tumbleweed carry on, you'll be dead of dissipation before you're twenty-five."

"But what a way to go," Nathan says with a leer.

"No, now, listen to me," Constance says strictly. "I know what I'm talking about. I've been through it. I told you how miserable it made me. If Wilma hadn't rescued me in the nick of time, I'd have cut my throat. Get out of that life, Nathan. It's not natural, it's not manly, it's not mature." He leans in the doorway from the shop. Nathan, checking titles against lists, makes a face. Constance says, "Don't act the know-it-all adolescent with me. What I'm telling you is the wisdom of the ages. Perversion leads to misery and disease and death. And loneliness—oh, the agonizing loneliness! Nathan, find a good woman, marry her, have children. It's the only way to true happiness. It's nature's way. You're on the wrong track." Nathan gives him a long-suffering glance. The man's eyes brim with tears. "If you only knew the pain I feel, watching a handsome, well-bred, intelligent boy like you throw himself—"

"Mr. Constance," Angus MacKenzie calls from the shop. "Can you help this lady, please."

Constance leaves, and Nathan shuts his eyes, leans on the bench, takes deep, slow breaths. He doesn't believe in hitting people, but at times like this he comes close to it. He wishes he didn't have to work with Mr. Constance. For eighteen dollars a week it's hardly worth it. He wishes he'd kept his mouth shut when he'd first hired on here and the man seemed to want to be a friend, hinted he understood, invited confidences. He keeps staring at Nathan, keeps brushing up against him accidentally on purpose. If Nathan is busy wrapping books for a customer, or totting up figures on the adding machine, Mr. Constance every chance he gets will come up behind him and massage his shoulders, trying to get him excited. Old Connie is a fraud. Is there really a Wilma at all? A wife? If so, she must be blind and deaf.

It's Saturday noon. He has the rest of the day off. He has been paid. A short check—he had to borrow five dollars from Mr. MacKenzie on Tuesday. Hoyt's hundred dollars comes only once a month—from his family in Amarillo—and he and Nathan always run short before it gets here. Nathan wanders along beside the butcher counter of the supermarket across from where he and Hoyt live, trying to find bargains to add to the bags of onions, beans, and rice already in his cart.

"Ah don't know what's going to become of us," Rick Ames says, sidling up to him, a red-faced, big-bellied man with crinkly white hair, dressed in a tent-size faded red sweatshirt, baggy corduroys, tennis shoes. "If that old Hitler doesn't stop cutting up pretty soon, there won't be a scrap of food left on the shelves." He carries heavily laden shopping bags. Without looking, Nathan knows most of their cargo is wine. Maybe, as he claims, Ames was once a writer. Now he is a drinker. He has a way of peering sideways worriedly with his white-lashed, china-blue eyes into the face of whomever he's talking to. "Have you heard anything from New Yawk yet? About your novel?"

Nathan says wanly, "I check the mailbox twice a day. It doesn't help."

"Nevah mind," Ames says, and pats him with a puffy red hand. "Ah'm sure the news will be wondahful when it finally comes." He wanders off, splay-footed. "Don't forget to tell me. Ah believe in you."

Nathan silently wishes somebody believed in him who wasn't a has-been like Rick Ames, or a would-be like Hoyt. He doesn't know how exactly he got into this strange world. Maybe just by moving to Hollywood.

He ought to have stayed working at Joe Ridpath's shacky nursery in Fair Oaks, starting out at dawn, falling dead asleep at sunset in the cobwebby storeroom Joe gave him to sleep in, playing an old wreck of a banjo in the kitchen on Sundays while Ridpath sang the hillbilly songs he loved—"Old Joe Clark," "Sourwood Mountain"—and danced and clapped his hands, the dog barking and chasing around his dirty, shuffling bare feet.

Standing in the supermarket checkout line, ration book at the ready, Nathan smiles to himself. After the bruising months that preceded them, the eighteen uneventful ones with Joe Ridpath were good. Except he never had time to write, and in the end he got too lonesome. Joe was no one to talk to. Nathan owed him a lot —Joe had once saved his life. But he never read a book, or even a newspaper. He made good money and paid Nathan fairly, but in the end the boy moved on, maybe just to be able to get his nails clean.

He welcomed the chance of a job at the big, bright bookstore on Sierra Street when they offered it to him at Christmas. They knew him because he bought books there, and they'd talked to him and thought he was bright. Afterward, they'd asked him to stay on and offered him a raise, only he'd have had to sell paper clips and typewriter ribbons as well as books. So he came to Hollywood and T. Smollett Books, but after half a year he can face the days there only by believing he'll sell his novel soon.

Walking out of the market into the hot sunshine, sacks heavy in his arms, pockets light, he nearly runs into Stanley Page. Stocky, freckled, ex-convict, ex-drunk, ex–horse player, once the owner of a famous bookshop on Hollywood Boulevard, Page is now a literary agent. He lives around the corner on Franklin Avenue. As always, he is nattily dressed: cinnamon-brown suit, shirt with a red pin-stripe, dark red tie with a wide knot. He even wears a hat. What's incongruous here is that he has a baby in his arms. In a blue blanket.

"How you doing, kid?" he says in a raspy voice. "They bought your book yet?"

"Not yet, Mr. Page," Nathan says.

"Don't get discouraged," Page says. "You'll make it. You got a lot of time ahead of you."

"I'm aging rapidly," Nathan says. "Your friend Saroyan was a best-seller at twenty-three." He steps close to peer at the baby. It is very small. Its eyes are shut tight. So are its little fists. "What do you call it?"

"Bill," Page says. "Maud needed some sleep. Old Bill gets in a lot of roistering in the middle of the night. Like his old man."

"Like his old man used to." Nathan has heard legends.

"Yeah," Page grunts sourly. "Used to. If the old me met the new me today, he'd die laughing."

"Don't you like being a husband and father?"

"I bought it," Page says. "I don't welsh on a deal." He moves for the supermarket doors. "I was sent for pabulum. I don't know why. He spits out more than he eats."

Nathan climbs the stairs, carries the groceries to the kitchen, and stows them. It puzzles him, since he isn't a pretty girl, but the very butch butcher sold him ham hocks without asking for ration points. His mother used to cook ham hocks and lima beans, and Nathan thinks he knows how to do it. It will make a change for Hoyt, who always does the cooking. Nathan opens the sack of beans, dumps them noisily on the table, pokes around in them picking out pebbles, scrapes the beans into a big pot, runs water into it to cover them, and leaves them to soak. He dries his hands on the dish towel, turns, and a man is standing in the doorway. He is middle-aged, wears a pale suit, has a brush haircut.

"Jesus," Nathan says, "who are you?"

"Mumble," the man says, "FBI." He holds out a leather folder that flaps open and shows a badge. "Like to talk to you a minute, please."

"Not me," Nathan says, heart beating fast.

"Aren't you Dwayne Hoyt Stubblefield?"

"He isn't here," Nathan says.

"You want to show me your draft card, please?"

Nathan takes the dog-eared card from his wallet.

Mumble reads it, hands it back. "You live here?"

"Yes." Nathan puts the card away.

"This is Stubblefield's address," Mumble says.

"We share the place," Nathan says.

Mumble looks over his shoulder. "And Reginald Poole?"

"He rents the front rooms from us."

"I see." Mumble tries to smile. He needs more practice. "But you and Stubblefield live together? You're friends?"

Nathan has a wild impulse to tell Mumble exactly what he and Hoyt are to each other. He wants to upset Mumble in the worst way—like having to piss so badly you stand on one leg. But he controls himself, because he doesn't want to get Hoyt in trouble, worse trouble. He only says, "Yes."

"You share his interests?" Mumble asks.

"He's an artist," Nathan says, "I'm a writer. We both like the same things, yes—music, books."

"Yeah, you've got a lot of books." Mumble glances at the

room behind him. "Quite a few by Marx and Engels, I guess." His eyebrows waggle.

"I'm sorry to disappoint you," Nathan says. "Not a one. Your favorites, are they?"

Mumble's mouth twitches. "Funny," he says. "Heh-heh."

"Why do you care what we read?" Nathan asks.

"Your friend Stubblefield keeps company that suggests to us he might like those writers."

Nathan shrugs. "Then you know more about the company he keeps than I do."

"He doesn't bring them here?" Mumble asks.

"Marx and Engels?" Nathan says. "Never."

"His Communist party friends," Mumble says wearily.

"I didn't know he had any." That makes two lies, and Nathan doesn't like the way his truthful answers sound any better—as if he's trying to dissociate himself from Hoyt. "He doesn't bring anybody." There is Benbow Harsch, but if the suave, smiling Benbow is a Communist, then why wasn't he at Eva Schaffer's funeral? "Look, Hoyt isn't a Communist. Anyway, aren't the Communists on our side?"

"That's what they claim, but you know what they want? They want to overthrow the U.S. government by force and violence. That's what they want. And you're wrong about Stubblefield. He goes to all their meetings."

"I didn't know that," Nathan says.

Mumble studies him. "How old are you, Reed?"

"Twenty." Yesterday. Nathan forgot all about it.

"Dear God." Mumble shakes his head in pity, turns, walks away. He stops at the open door to the hall. He calls, "I'm old enough to be your father, and I'm going to give you some advice. Move out of here. Go home to your folks. Get away from Stubblefield. A man is judged by the company he keeps. And Stubblefield is bad company."

Nathan's fists bunch. He bolts into the living room, ready to

JOSEPH HANSEN

shout at the man. But he chokes the words back. Hoyt doesn't need any defense. So the FBI doesn't like what he is doing—does that make it wrong? Mumble hands him a business card. "Give that to Stubblefield, will you? Tell him I want to talk to him?" Nathan reads the card. The man's name is John F. Noble. "If I remember," Nathan tells him. "I forget a lot."

Nathan clambers down from the streetcar, waits in the island for traffic to pass, then dodges across Sunset to the northeast corner of Westerly Terrace. He stands on the sunny sidewalk, opposite the Black Cat Cafe on the northwest corner. It's a ramshackle place painted black. A cat is outlined in white on the side, winking an eye. The door is open, and jukebox music blares out of it, and male laughter. It's a gay bar. He has never been in one of those and he's curious about it. However, it's irrelevant now. He looks up Westerly Terrace. The narrow street climbs steeply, with many sharp bends. Benbow Harsch's rambling, multilevel house is almost at the top, and Nathan doesn't look forward to the climb on such a hot day, but John F. Noble has scared him, and he doesn't know where Hoyt is, and he needs advice, and Benbow is the only person he can think of to ask.

When, panting and sweating, he gets to the long outside staircase that mounts among brush and trees to Benbow's lofty front porch, he hears music. Someone is banging a piano hard. A Rachmaninoff prelude. Nathan's footsteps keep time to it as he climbs. The front door stands open. Nathan raps with his knuckles on the door frame, but nobody hears, and he goes inside. In the low-ceilinged living room, skinny little George Lafleur lies on a sofa with a faded slipcover, reading a volume of the *Encyclopaedia Britannica*. He is plowing through the whole set from A to Z to try to make up for having quit school at age thirteen. Benbow, with whom he's lived since then, is an educated man—maybe, as Hoyt says, overeducated. A beer bottle and glass stand on the rug where

22

Lafleur can reach them. He lowers the massive book and blinks. "Nathan," he shouts over the music, and cranes to look past the boy. "Is Hoyt with you?"

"I thought he might be here," Nathan shouts back.

"Thank God, no." George dumps the book, sits up, and holds out a hand. "Now is our golden chance. Come to bed with me."

Nathan one drunken night, trying to find his way out of this complicated house, opened the wrong door and got a vision of Lafleur in bed with a sailor, whose white togs were strewn across the floor. Lafleur, frail as he is, has a cock like the yardarm of a mighty ship. So had the sailor. The two of them in their sexual nip-ups looked as if they might be trying to club each other to death. Nathan likes Lafleur all right, but not his monster cock. He likes Hoyt's cock. It is average, if anything is average about Hoyt. But he wouldn't sleep with Lafleur anyway. He wouldn't sleep with anyone but Hoyt. He twitches Lafleur a preoccupied smile and walks on past.

"Thanks, but I need to talk to Benbow."

"Follow your ears," Lafleur says, and subsides on the couch and takes up the encyclopedia again.

Following his ears means going down a flight of stairs. There is a second common room down here, and in it now is a spinet piano. It's against the far wall by some open windows. A beefy man in his mid-thirties, with thinning dark hair, is pounding the keys. His back is turned. Nathan taps his shoulder. He finishes a phrase, then turns. He has a roman nose and bright eyes. He smiles. "Nathan. See my piano."

"It finally came," Nathan says.

Benbow stands up. "Sit," he says. "Try it."

Nathan sits and tries it. "My God," he says, and gapes up at Benbow. "What have you done to the action?"

"Made it as stiff as possible," Benbow says.

"I guess so," Nathan says.

"To strengthen my fingers," Benbow says, "my wrists."

Nathan tries to play Frank's favorite, "In a Mist." The piano barely makes a sound. He quits and gets up off the bench. "So you're really going to give up teaching philosophy to be a concert pianist?"

"That's how I feel today," Benbow says. "What brings you here on this glorious afternoon?"

"I'm worried," Nathan says.

"Will you have a beer?" Benbow moves off down the room.

"Okay, if you're having one." Nathan follows him into a kitchen. "But it's your advice I came for."

Benbow gets a brown quart bottle of Acme beer from a refrigerator, plunks it on a table in a sunshiny breakfast nook, brings down tumblers from a cupboard. "Sit down." He sits down himself, pries the cap off the bottle, pours beer into both glasses. "What's up?"

"The FBI is after Hoyt," Nathan says.

Benbow chokes on his beer and sprays foam across the table. "What? What for?"

"The agent claims he's a Communist," Nathan says. He summarizes his talk with John F. Noble. "You've known Hoyt longer than I have. Is it true?"

"Longer, yes," Benbow says. "But not better."

"Noble says he goes to all their meetings." Nathan lights a cigarette, tastes the beer, wipes foam off his mouth with the back of a hand. "Does he?"

"Don't ask me," Benbow protests. "How would I know?"

"He goes out a lot," Nathan says. "But he never tells me where. When I first moved in with him, he told me not to worry about it, not to ask. And I didn't. But now I'm worried about it."

"Why?" Benbow mocks him gently. "Are you an anticommunist?"

Nathan makes a face. "All I know is it's a system where the government is supposed to see that everybody has work and food and a roof over his head. My father says what's wrong with it"—

Nathan taps his cigarette in a sturdy glass ashtray—"is that human nature isn't like that. It's only a theory. In real life, governments grab everything for themselves." He sips his beer. "Is he right?"

Amusement twitches Benbow's mouth. "You can replace me at the university," he says, "when I take up concertizing."

Nathan feels his face turn red. "Aw, I don't know anything about it. But I don't think Hoyt is a Communist."

"But you're not a hundred percent sure," Benbow says.

Nathan stares. "You think he could be?"

Benbow shrugs. "That questing mind of his is the most exciting thing about him. Still, if I were he, I wouldn't go off evenings and leave a beautiful boy like you on your own. He doesn't know how lucky he is."

"I don't care where he goes," Nathan says, "as long as he comes back." He looks at Benbow anxiously. "What's going to happen? They can't send him to jail, can they?"

"They are the secret police. They can do whatever they like. You know that. But"—Benbow smiles a little smile and pats Nathan's hand on the tabletop—"for what it's worth, my guess is they won't." He raises his brows. "All right?"

Nathan lies awake next to sleeping Hoyt, listening to his slow, soft, easy breathing, wondering. It's a cool night but not cold. The windows are all open. Now and then a breeze rustles the tough leaves of the big old rubber tree outside. It's quiet. Cars have stopped passing on Highland Avenue. It's very late, or maybe very early. It doesn't matter. Hoyt has surprised him again. The place was full of the aroma of steamy lima beans and ham hocks when Nathan got home from Benbow's. Hoyt had taken up the cooking where Nathan left off. That was natural enough. What was surprising was that not until they were eating did Hoyt slip from a shirt pocket John F. Noble's card, reach across, lay it in front of Nathan, and ask:

"I found that on the table. Where did it come from?"

Nathan told him about Noble's visit.

"Why didn't you wait for me?"

"I never know when you're going to be here. I was worried. I didn't know what to do. So I went to Benbow's. I thought he might know."

Hoyt studied him thoughtfully for a moment, then picked up the card and tucked it back into his pocket. "And what did Benbow say?"

"He doesn't think they'll do anything to you."

"Then they won't." Hoyt filled his mouth and chewed.

"You mean he can stop the FBI?" Nathan said.

"He's got powerful friends," Hoyt said. "Remember?"

"That fat guy?" Nathan said. "The Armenian?" He had met a lot of different strangers at different times with Hoyt at Benbow's. This man had stayed in Nathan's memory. Maybe because he didn't look powerful. He looked like a grocer.

"He's chief of staff to Senator Skipworth," Hoyt said, "and he's married to Benbow's sister." He smiled. "Don't worry. I'll be all right."

"Benbow said the FBI is the secret police," Nathan said. "And they can do whatever they want to you." He shivered. "That scared me."

"Benbow likes to scare people. It's one of his little games." Hoyt swabbed his bowl with a chunk of bread. "He has a lot of little games. That's one of the harmless ones. They're not all like that."

Nathan peered at him. "What do you mean?"

Chewing the bread, Hoyt gave him a long, steady look. "I mean, don't go there again unless I'm with you."

Nathan laughed. "What would he do to me?"

"Manipulate you—to see what happens," Hoyt said. "Why? You'd never understand. You don't want power."

Nathan said, "Damn it, Hoyt, are you a Communist?"

"If I wasn't, would I go to all those meetings?" Hoyt rose and took Nathan's bowl. "You want some more?"

Nathan, lying awake, staring at the silhouettes of the leaves against the faint light of the windows, concludes the answer is no answer. Hoyt wants to keep him guessing. Does he love power too? Is that why he understands Benbow? Is manipulating Nathan a game Hoyt is playing? Nathan hates the idea. To get away from it he turns sharply onto his side and shuts his eyes tight. He doesn't want to distrust Hoyt. He loves him too much.

But what does he know about him? Nothing really. He says he comes from Texas, well-off people, oil, couldn't get along with them, ran away the night he graduated from high school. He worked in the stockyards in El Paso, drove a truck in Denver, fried hamburgers in Reno, cut up chickens in Seattle, stacked lumber in Portland, taking art classes at night. In San Francisco he worked unloading crates at the wholesale produce market and took literature classes. In L.A. he audited Benbow's history of philosophy lectures, and one day wandered into T. Smollett Books and met Nathan.

Lanky, loose-limbed, no hint of girl about him, he was handsome as hell, and a wonderful talker. When Nathan got off work, they ate goulash at a Hungarian place on Vine Street, walked over here, climbed the stairs, and went to bed together. The next Friday Nathan gave up his seven-dollar-a-week room on Yucca Street and moved in with Hoyt. He scowls. It was too fast, wasn't it? He wanted, he wanted. He didn't use his mind at all. He might as well not have had a mind.

But he was happy. The happiest he'd ever been in his life. For eight or ten weeks, even his dismal job was tolerable. Then Eva Schaffer died, and Hoyt went mute and grieving on him, and Nathan had to know why, and now? For a moment into his vision drifts Steve Schaffer's face with its soft, shining eyes. He is saying something, pleading, but Nathan can't make out the words. Then it's George Lafleur, lying on the couch naked, grinning, beckoning him, his huge cock stiff. A puppet capers, like those Lucille Bekker made years ago in Fair Oaks, nursery rhyme characters. The puppet turns around. It's Hoyt. And the puller of its strings is not fat little Mrs. Bekker but Benbow Harsch. *To strengthen my fingers*, he says, *my wrists*. Frank tells ten-year-old Nathan, *Practice, practice.* Nathan sleeps.

Hoyt says, "Wait. What's the last thing you put on before you go to work?" He sits at the kitchen table with a mug of coffee and a book—*Lafcadio's Adventures*. Nathan has just come naked out of the bathroom. He says, "My necktie. Why?"

Hoyt gets up. "Why always do things the same?" He takes Nathan's arm. They go to the bedroom together. Hoyt opens the wardrobe. "Why not do it the other way around for a change?" He tosses a necktie to Nathan, who catches it awkwardly. "You're crazy," he says.

"How many do you usually wear?" Hoyt says.

Laughing, Nathan says, "One."

"Just my point." Hoyt takes out all Nathan's ties. This doesn't make a lot. Only five. He comes to Nathan, ties the first one around his neck. "No, no. Stand still."

"Hoyt, I have to get to work."

"This won't take any time at all," Hoyt says.

"What are you doing?"

Hoyt ties a tie around Nathan's upper arm. He makes a bow, the ends hang down. He ties a tie around Nathan's other arm, the same way. Then he kneels and ties a tie around each leg, just below the knee. He jumps up, stands back, studies the effect. He nods. "Very pretty," he says.

Nathan is laughing. "You idiot, I'm going to be late." He unties the ties, dropping them onto the bed. He bends to undo the ties around his legs, and when he straightens up he sees tears running down Hoyt's face. "What's wrong?"

"I'm going to miss you," Hoyt says.

"What are you talking about? I get off at five."

"I can't let you live with me anymore," Hoyt says.

"What?" Nathan yelps. "Why? What did I do?"

"Nothing. It's what I did—" He shuts his mouth on that. "Nathan, I'm bad news. What do you think—the FBI just casually visits everybody?"

"No, and I don't think you're any Communist, either." Nathan yanks open a drawer, takes out briefs, puts them on, pulls on a shirt. "Hoyt, I won't pry, I promise, I won't—"

Hoyt puts a hand over his mouth. "You have a right to know what's going on," he says, "but I can't tell you, and that's no way for people who love each other to live."

Nathan pulls away from him, sits on the edge of the bed to put on socks. "I never minded. Did I complain? You went to—wherever you went, and I never asked. You said not to ask and I didn't ask, did I?"

"I could be in serious trouble," Hoyt says.

"But you said Benbow could—"

"Yes, well—Benbow could also let me fall. And if I fall, I don't want you dragged down with me."

Nathan laughs uneasily. "Isn't this a little stagy?"

"No." Hoyt squats in front of Nathan, hands on the boy's knees. "You can be a great writer. I can't let you fuck up your whole future for—"

Nathan grabs his shoulders and kisses him hard. "I love you, Hoyt. You're everything to me. What happens to you happens to me. That's how I want it." He stands, ruffles Hoyt's hair. "We're not part of the world, Hoyt. If we were, we'd be in uniform." He kicks into his trousers. "Stop worrying. Nothing's going to happen. Not to us."

And nothing does. Evidently Benbow's Armenian friend called off John F. Noble, because Hoyt resumes going his lonely way at nights. Nathan drudges cheerlessly away at the bookstore and with dimming hope piles up pages beside the typewriter. Days stretch into weeks.

Then something does happen. It's a day when Nathan is slated to work till nine at night, so he has the morning off.

"Did you ever see *Flesh and the Devil?*" Hoyt says.

They sit on a tattered beach towel on the steep hillside behind the house, in swim trunks, soaking up sun. They are eating watermelon, letting the juice run down their chests, and spitting out the seeds. Maybe some of the seeds will take root, and vines will grow back here, and they'll have their own melons next summer.

Hoyt says, "It's an old Garbo movie."

"I don't go to movies to look at women," Nathan says.

Hoyt has a cowboy hat stuck on the back of his head. He looks at Nathan with wide open eyes. "Women? Garbo? Garbo is a drag queen. Don't you know anything?"

Nathan laughs. "What I don't know, you'll tell me. What's this movie about—deviled what?"

"*Flesh and the Devil,*" Hoyt says. "It's about John Gilbert and Lars Hanson. Two beautiful young men who fell in love when they were just kids. And Garbo tries to move in on them, split them up, but their love is too strong, and she falls through the ice and drowns. In a mink coat."

"I didn't know they made movies like that," Nathan says.

"Ask me anything," Hoyt says.

Nathan stands up. "Maybe the mail's come." He scrambles down the bank, rounds the house, pokes into the rusty green mailbox fixed to the green shingle siding. He and Hoyt don't get much mail. He hears from Frank, now and then. And from a school friend, Dan Munroe, serving in the Coast Guard in Astoria, Oregon, and bored to death. Hoyt gets that monthly check from Amarillo. That's about it. But there's an envelope in the box today. Nathan snatches it out. Sure enough, it's from Craven & Hyde in New York. The publishers. It's been so long coming he feels dizzy. The shade of the rubber tree turns his sweat cold and he shivers.

He calls, "Hoyt," but his voice is weak. Now he starts back to Hoyt at a run. "Hoyt." He leaps at the cutbank, falls back on his butt, scrambles up on hands and knees, then is standing over Hoyt on shaky legs and holding out the envelope. "Look. They finally goddamn wrote to me."

Hoyt squints against the sun. "What do they say?"

"I don't know." Nathan sits down beside him. "I haven't opened it. I'm too scared."

Hoyt regards the envelope. "Why? They didn't send back your chapters. It's not big enough for that."

"I guess not." Nathan nods.

Hoyt waits, watches. "Well? Open it."

"I can't," Nathan says. "I'm going to throw up."

"Nathan, it's good news. Oh, hell, give it to me." Hoyt snatches it and rips it open, and Nathan crawls away and vomits. "Come on," Hoyt says. "Stop that." There's a pause while Nathan heaves sour pink sweetness into the dry weeds, and Hoyt reads. Then Hoyt says, "They like it. 'Original, alive on every page, droll and wise and craftily written. If it lives up to the promise of these first chapters, we will be proud to publish it.' Look. An option contract."

On his knees, wiping his mouth on a corner of the towel, Nathan looks up. "Contract?" He reaches for the pages. His eyes are wet. He rubs them. He peers. "Hey. They're going to send me five hundred dollars."

"Now," Hoyt says and allows himself a rare smile, "didn't I say there was nothing to worry about? You're the best. I told you that."

Nathan sits, stares at the contract. And reality won't let him be happy. "It's a win by default, Hoyt," he says. "Every other young writer is in the service."

"Jesus," Hoyt says. "You feeling guilty again? You want to go? The Armenian can probably fix it up for you."

Nathan shakes his head. "I want to stay with you."

The man the world knows as James Hawker, but who is spoken of as Gentleman Jim in Hollywood, waits on the corner by the supermarket, every morning, for a ride out Cahuenga Pass to the movie studio where these days he writes scripts. According to Angus MacKenzie, the driver of the car that picks him up is a famous novelist too. But he's not so famous as Gentleman Jim. Only Hemingway is as famous as Gentleman Jim. It awes Nathan that Hawker is his neighbor. He is. He lives only two doors south of Hoyt and Nathan's place, in a hotel that climbs the hill in a zigzag of white stucco boxes. Nathan has seen him come out of there, a beaky little gray-haired man in ratty tweeds, cross the street, stand waiting for his ride. Arms folded. Pipe between his teeth. Now and then, out early for milk or cereal or cigarettes, Nathan has found him there, and hurried past, eyes lowered, sheepish.

Hoyt: "Why don't you speak to him? Tell him you read his books. Tell him you like them."

Nathan: "What would he care?"

"Tell him you're a writer too."

Nathan, gloomily: "I'm not. Not yet."

But this morning he is. At least a publisher is betting money that he is. He was numb from shock and didn't have any trouble keeping his good news to himself yesterday at work. He meant to quit the bookshop, but he couldn't quite believe his luck, and he wanted to wait till the publisher sent that check. By evening he had become so excited and happy it was a good thing there were lots of customers, and Mr. MacKenzie, in a cloud of cigarette smoke, was busy at his desk. Otherwise Nathan would have blurted out the news.

After dragging down the big front door and switching off the lights and locking up, he ran all the way home. And when he got there, he was too keyed up to sleep. He didn't give Hoyt much chance to sleep, either. Nathan kept waking him up for sex. Hoyt is dead to the world now, but Nathan isn't tired. Hell, he never felt better. He is smiling all over his face. He laughs aloud in the claw-footed bathtub, laughs aloud as he shaves. He stands smelling of Ivory soap and Barbasol in the kitchen and decides a real writer deserves a real breakfast—not oatmeal.

He prowls the rooms, probing for coins in the chairs, picking up stray dimes, nickels, quarters from the floor. He blows the dust off them and counts them. Not enough. He puts on his jeans and pokes in their pockets. A dime and a penny. He looks into his wallet. Nothing. In yesterday's shirt pocket? A forgotten dollar, maybe? No luck. He picks up Hoyt's jeans. Two nickels, three pennies. Hoyt's wallet? But it's the last week of the month. Hoyt's check from home isn't due till the first. Hoyt's wallet is empty.

What the hell. He has almost enough. The only clean shirt he can find has buttons missing, but he doesn't care. With the shirt flapping open, he runs across to the market. Looking hangdog, he takes bacon, eggs, and jam to the checkout counter and gives gawky, horse-toothed Ethel a bleak hello. He tallies the coins on the counter, anxious, a little orphan beggar boy from the snowy streets. He comes up twelve cents short—as he knew he would.

Ethel is touched. "Never mind, Nathan honey. You can give it to me later." She detaches stamps from his ration book, drops the book in with the groceries, and hands him the bag. "If you took my advice and got yourself a screen test, you'd be rich. You are the handsomest thing."

"Until the night of the full moon," Nathan says darkly. "Then I sprout fangs and claws and jump on girls."

"I'll be out there," Ethel says, "just waiting."

Nathan leaves the market merrily with the makings of his real writer's breakfast, and here stands Gentleman Jim Hawker, waiting for his ride to work. Nathan takes a deep breath and says, "Good morning, Mr. Hawker."

Hawker's eyes look frightened. "I don't believe we've met." His voice is soft and the words come slow and sweet as sorghum. He looks desperately down the street.

"I'm Nathan Reed. We're neighbors." He points. "I live right over there."

Hawker glances across at the green-shingled house behind the old sycamore tree, and nods. "I've seen you. How do you do." He extends a hand and Nathan shakes it. Hawker's hand is small and its clasp is gentle and brief. He withdraws the hand and takes his pipe from between his teeth. He tilts his head. He hasn't smiled yet. His eyes are still wary. "What was it you wished to say to me?"

Nathan's face grows hot. "Only—only that I admire your books. I've—seen you standing here and I've wanted to tell you for a long time, but—" He dries up.

Hawker blinks. "Yes?"

"But you must hear it from everybody. I wanted to wait until—until—" A horn toots. The dark blue De Soto that picks Hawker up every morning rolls to a halt at the curb beyond a bulky green U.S. Mail box. Hawker looks relieved, says, "Thank you, sir; good morning to you," and starts to move off, the man at the wheel of the car leaning across and opening the passenger door for him.

Nathan follows Hawker. "—until I was a writer myself."

Hawker raises tufty eyebrows. "And has that day come?"

"Craven & Hyde just optioned my novel."

"Your first, I take it?" Hawker gets into the car.

Nathan laughs. "I'm only twenty."

Hawker nods again. "Congratulations." He shuts the car door. "I wish you great success." The car drives off.

"Why do you suppose he lives there?" Hoyt frowns at Nathan. He holds two slim, long-handled brushes crossways in his teeth, a third in his fingers. The air reeks of turpentine and linseed oil. He is painting Nathan's picture. He has bought satin ribbon, red, yellow, green. As he did with the neckties, he has tied the ribbons—in sets of three, each a different color—around Nathan's neck and arms and legs, making big droopy bows and letting the ends trail down. "He must get good money. He's a big name."

"Stanley Page says he has a family down in Savannah," Nathan says. "A sick wife. Maybe children, I'm not sure. Other relatives. He pays a lot of people's bills. So he lives as cheaply as he can and sends the rest back home."

"Families," Hoyt grunts.

"Yours is good to you," Nathan says.

Hoyt lays on a brush stroke. "As long as I stay away."

It's a hot Sunday, so though he's a little embarrassed, Nathan is not really sorry to be wearing only the ribbons. Hoyt has stripped to ragged Jockey shorts. But now there's a thump of feet on the stairs outside, and Benbow Harsch calls, "Hello, the house of poets." Nathan bolts. There's no privacy; the bedroom door is half glass. But, ignoring the leg ribbons, he manages to kick into jeans before Benbow puts his head in from the hall. "What's going on?"

"Men at work," Hoyt says. "Didn't you see the sign?"

"No, nor 'Wet Paint,' either." In wilted seersucker, Benbow comes inside. Damp strands of hair stick to his domed skull. He studies the canvas on the easel, and points. "May I suggest one more site for ribbons?"

"And spoil the best part?" Hoyt lays down his brush and peers at him. "You sick or something?"

"As angels cover their faces—it would show respect for human frailty." Benbow sits. "I was thinking how talented you are and how poor and with what unremitting perversity you make it impossible for any gallery to show your work."

"Luckily for you," Hoyt says. It's a cryptic remark. Shedding his arm and neck ribbons, Nathan wonders what it means. Hoyt loads a fat brush and scumbles rose gray in an upper corner of the canvas, asking Benbow, "Beer?"

Benbow raises his brows. "Ah—you've located some dissolute connoisseur, and you're in funds," he says. "You rarely offer anything but water."

"It will be champagne," Hoyt says, "when the publishers send Nathan his check."

"The publishers?" Benbow has picked up a book and opened it. Arthur Waley. Translations from the Chinese. He lays it down and cocks his head. "What are you saying?"

Having finally got the nine ribbons off him, Nathan comes in. "Craven & Hyde have optioned my novel." He breezes barefoot to the kitchen, takes a big, dewy brown bottle out of the refrigerator, and looks for glasses. None is clean. At the sink he rinses three, each from a different jelly maker. Benbow comes, leans in the doorway, studies him. Drying the glasses, Nathan notices the philosophy teacher is frowning. "Something wrong?"

"You take it for granted, don't you?" Benbow says.

"Jesus, do I?" Nathan sets a glass down, picks up another. "What do you mean?"

"Having your book accepted. It's a miracle, Nathan, don't you understand that? You're still a child. Most writers struggle half their lives to get published. Some of them never manage it. Yet you're not even surprised, let alone grateful, let alone humbled."

"I'm happy." Nathan hangs up the damp dish towel. "Will that do?"

Benbow laughs hopelessly and goes back into the living room. "What do you think," he asks Hoyt, "of Lafcadio?"

"Gide lays the irony on too thick," Hoyt says.

Benbow sits again. "What about the acte gratuit?"

Nathan comes in, sets the bottle on a table, hands a glass to Benbow, tries to hand one to Hoyt, but Hoyt is cleaning his hands on a rag soaked in turpentine and waves him off. Hoyt answers Benbow:

"He never gives the acte gratuit a chance. The kid thinks he's throwing a total stranger off the train, committing a murder that can't be traced to him because he had no motive—he did it just for the hell of it. Then it turns out the victim was involved with nearly everybody else in the book. He's in trouble up to his ass."

"You haven't finished it," Benbow says.

"How can you be sure?"

"Because of what you just said." Benbow holds up his glass and watches as Nathan fills it. "Gide's in no hurry. At first Lafcadio reacts like Raskolnikov, won't touch the money, is disgusted with himself. But something much more interesting happens later. The old queen is foxier than you give him credit for."

"All right, I'll finish it. But it's not a novel." Hoyt accepts a glass from Nathan, and Nathan pours beer into it. "It's a joke."

Nathan says, "You liked the part about the man traveling to Rome to save the Pope—the idiot who's never been outside his little town before. The bedbugs, the whorehouse, the phony priest? The part you read to Steve Schaffer and me."

Benbow sits straight. "Schaffer?"

"Eva's son," Hoyt says. "He came to L.A. for the memorial service. From overseas. Only the Army snafued. He arrived too late. He spent the afternoon here with us."

Nathan is startled and he asks Benbow, "Did you know Eva Schaffer?"

"Hoyt told me about her. Her brilliance dazzled him."

Benbow frowns at Hoyt. "I thought she was alone in the world." He seems upset, even angry, and he laughs to cover it. "She wasn't a Madonna. She was Liberty manning the barricades. It's impossible to imagine her with children."

Hoyt sits cross-legged on the rug. "Probably a youthful slip." He lights a cigarette. "Anyway, he's no child now."

"After his father died, his grandmother raised him." Nathan sits on the floor too, pours beer for himself, and lights himself a cigarette. "Eva was hardly ever around."

Benbow is restless. He gets up, stares out the open windows into the rubber tree, turns back. "No brothers or sisters?"

"An only child," Nathan says. "Like me."

Hoyt says, "Nathan thinks he's going to be killed."

Benbow raises his brows at Nathan. "And from what does this grim prophecy arise, young Tiresias—hope or fear?"

Before Nathan can answer, Hoyt says, "Fear."

Nathan sulks. These two together always make him feel stupid. Liberty manning the barricades? Raskolnikov? Tiresias? Hoyt was right. He should move out.

"What's the matter, Nathan?" Benbow says. "I thought you were happy. You don't act it."

"Tell him a limerick," Hoyt says.

"Ah, excellent suggestion," Benbow says.

"Benbow knows hundreds of limericks," Hoyt says.

"I had a friend like that, a teacher," Nathan says, bitterly. "The saddest man alive. He blew his own brains out. I discovered his body. I don't like limericks."

"Then this shall be for Hoyt," Benbow says. "It's about a painter. 'Whilst Titian was mixing red madder, His model climbed up on a ladder. Her position to Titian Suggested coition, So he upped on the ladder and had 'er.' "

Remembering poor Stone dead up in that rainy early-morning canyon, Nathan sits with bowed head, staring at the floor. But he feels Hoyt looking at him, and at last he has to look at Hoyt. Hoyt says primly:

"That could never happen here, could it?"

And Nathan can't help playing along with him. He looks wide-eyed and wistful. "You mean I should give up hope?"

Benbow laughs. "Not until you've tried a ladder."

On the cloudy morning eight dreary months ago when Nathan asked for a job at T. Smollett Books, and Angus MacKenzie seated him beside his littered desk to talk to him, he asked, "You plan to make bookselling your career?"

"Well, no, not really," Nathan said.

MacKenzie looked at the letter Nathan had brought him. "Your last employer says you have a talent for it."

"I'm going to be a writer," Nathan said.

"Oh, no," MacKenzie moaned, "not another one."

"But I have to have a job till publishers take me on," Nathan said. "And I'm a hard worker. You'll see."

And MacKenzie, after offering wages as short as he dared, did see. Nathan had done more than was asked of him for Frank and Alma at home, cleaning the house, washing the clothes, and then for Joe Ridpath at the nursery—and he did the same here. In school, Donald Donald had sneered that he had "a slave mentality." Awful as that sounded, maybe it was true. But time dragged miserably if he wasn't busy. So at T. Smollett Books, he didn't wait to be told. A secondhand-book store invited dust and disorder. He cleaned, sorted the thousands of titles on the shelves, painted the grubby washroom, replaced burned-out light bulbs, lettered new shelf signs, changed the window display every week.

More importantly, he had a knack. Once he'd handled a book, he remembered it, its title, its author, and exactly where it stood gathering dust on the shelves. With new books he remembered publisher and price too. It was a gift. He had been born with several useless gifts—like being able to play any instrument he picked up. He'd got that one from his father. Where this one had come from he didn't know. Maybe from his mother, who never forgot an astrological chart or any planetary aspect on it. Angus MacKenzie marveled at Nathan's knack—Mr. Constance passed the word along. But MacKenzie was careful not to praise the boy to his face, afraid Nathan would ask for a raise.

Now it's a Monday, and Nathan after push-brooming the shop floor and the sidewalk, unpacking the newly arrived books in the back room, and bundling books up to mail to customers, washes his hands, rolls down his shirt-sleeves, buttons his collar and

JOSEPH HANSEN

straightens his tie, puts on his jacket, and walks out into the cavernous shop, where Angus MacKenzie hunches over the order forms and publishers' catalogues that bestrew his desk.

"Excuse me," Nathan says. "May I show you something?" MacKenzie straightens and blinks at him through smoke. A cigarette burns short at a corner of his mouth. He sees the letter Nathan is holding out to him. The store owner takes it, unfolds it, and a check falls out and flutters to the floor. Nathan picks it up and hands it to him. He studies it, and his head jerks up. "Five hundred dollars?"

"Read the letter," Nathan says.

MacKenzie looks at the check again, closely, then reads the letter. It's not a long letter. It's not full of cordiality like the one that came after he'd sent back his thanks to the editor, along with the signed contracts. It's from some accountant. Very stiff. But it states the essential facts clearly enough.

"Well." Snuffing out the cigarette in a heaped ashtray, MacKenzie gets to his feet and smiles and holds out his hand. "Congratulations, Nathan."

"You thought I was dreaming," Nathan says. "You didn't think I could do it."

"I thought it would take longer," MacKenzie says.

Nathan smiles. "I was in a hurry. To get away from here."

MacKenzie's face falls. "You can't."

"I couldn't. I had to eat." Nathan picks up the letter and the check. "But now I can. And I'm going to."

"Five hundred dollars won't last forever."

"It doesn't have to. Only a few months."

"Nathan, don't do this to me." MacKenzie looks stricken. "How can I replace you? You know how long I've been trying to find a shipping clerk."

"Not very hard," Nathan says. "Not while you had me. Two jobs for the price of one."

"Nathan, everybody's in uniform. Be fair."

40

"Was eighteen dollars a week fair?" Nathan asks.

"I'll give you twenty-five," MacKenzie says. "Starting today. As of nine o'clock this morning."

"I'm sorry." Nathan shakes his head. He looks extra grave because he's fighting not to laugh. "But I can't spare the time. The book's not finished. I have to write the rest of it." Now it's he who holds out his hand. MacKenzie shakes it, looking as if he's about to weep. Nathan says, "Goodbye, Mr. MacKenzie," and, tucking check and letter into his jacket, strolls jauntily toward the sunlit front door.

It's noon, so Mr. Constance comes in the door to begin his shift. "Off to lunch?" he says.

"I won't be back," Nathan says. "I've sold my book."

"Really?" Constance is surprised as hell, and not pleased. "To whom? Do they know you're only twenty?"

"Craven & Hyde. Why should they care?"

"Because you can't know what you're doing," Constance says. "People twenty years old do not write novels."

"Oh?" Nathan says. "What do they write?"

"Dirty words in washrooms," Constance says.

Reggie Poole these days is tossing salads and waiting tables for Drossie, a tiny woman who looks like Punch, and whom Reggie met in New York long ago, where she ran a succession of cafes, mostly in Greenwich Village. When she came to Los Angeles recently, Reggie gave a welcoming party for her. Drossie talks little above a whisper, and there were loud voices at that party, but Nathan learned that she used to feed a good many artists and writers and actors—often on tick. She was forever having to move on because she couldn't pay her bills. Now she's got a basement place in L.A., and Reggie brings home his earnings in the form of coins, which he keeps in mason jars in his kitchen. He also brings home after hours the odd good-looking young male customer. Hoyt and Nathan know this, though they rarely meet them. They sometimes hear two pairs of feet climb the stairs late at night. And in the mornings now and then unfamiliar voices yelp when they try to get into the bathroom.

But today, when Nathan comes home after depositing the publisher's check—the first time he's ever put money into a bank in his life—the door to Reggie's rooms stands open, and Reggie calls to him from there. Since the publishers signed for Nathan's book, Reggie has treated him with more regard than before. Nathan steps in and sees nobody. Reggie pokes his head in from his bedroom. He is grinning all over his face. "Nathan, come and meet someone," he says.

The someone is a muscular young man whom Reggie has clothed in his favorite garment, an enormous black kimono, and has bundled into his bed. The young man has curly golden hair, blue eyes, long lashes, big ears, and a terrible cold. He reeks of menthol, and the bed is strewn with crumpled Kleenex. His nose is running, he has a gruesome cough, but as he holds out his hand to shake Nathan's hand he smiles. It's a terrific smile. Almost like a physical blow. He has glorious large straight teeth. And dimples. Reggie's bed surely once belonged to a queen, or at least a countess, and it takes up most of the room, so there's no place to sit down, or Nathan would do that. Lucky Hoyt has the foot of the bed to lean on, and Nathan notes that he is gripping it hard to keep from falling down. It's plain he is as stunned as Nathan by this improbable invalid.

"Mike Voynich," Reggie says, "Nathan Reed."

Voynich wheezes, "How are ya?"

"Nice to meet you," Nathan says.

Five minutes later Voynich, full of aspirin and cough syrup with ether in it, has been left to sleep, and Reggie sits with Hoyt and Nathan in their kitchen, drinking coffee, eating crackers and peanut butter. Reggie's eyes sparkle.

"Who does he remind you of?"

"The angels that visited Lot in Sodom?" Hoyt says.

"Where are your powers of observation?" Reggie says indignantly. "Think. He's in the Air Force now. Not on the silver screen."

Hoyt looks blank. He likes to tease Reggie.

"Clark Gable," Reggie says. "Those dimples, those ears, that smile. Even his voice."

"How can you tell with that cold?"

"The cold came on after we met," Reggie says. "When I saw him walk in, I said, 'My God, it's the next great star.' It's a wonder Drossie has any crockery left. My hands were shaking so, I dropped everything."

"And look what you picked up," Hoyt says.

Reggie's nostrils flare. He sits straight and looks haughty. "I don't care for your implications. He's alone in the world. His family lives in Pittsburgh. He's ill. He needs care. Someone has to nurse him back to health."

"How does anybody get a cold in weather like this?"

"By being drenched by studio fire hoses," Reggie says. "They're filming *The Corn Is Green* at Warners. The Welsh village boys are waiting for John Dall to come home from Oxford after his entrance examinations, waiting in the rain. They shot the scene over and over again, all day long from six A.M. The wonder is he hasn't got double pneumonia."

Nathan says, "Reggie, isn't he kind of small?"

"What do you mean? Alan Ladd is practically a dwarf."

"But he's part of a matched pair," Nathan says. "This one hasn't got Veronica Lake."

"If he's working in pictures," Hoyt says, "he has an agent. Why hasn't the agent made him a star?"

Reggie rolls his eyes, takes a deep breath, explains patiently, as to a child. "He needs coaching. He comes from a poor, working-class background. The steel mills. He has no manners. He doesn't even know how to hold a fork. His diction is appalling. His grammar simply doesn't exist."

"And you're going to correct all that?" Hoyt says.

Nathan quotes Leslie Howard as Professor Higgins. " 'I shall make a duchess of this draggletailed guttersnipe.' "

"And why not?" Reggie glares.

And later that afternoon, when they lie naked in bed together, unable to think of anything half as pleasant to do with Nathan's newfound freedom, he and Hoyt hear drifting on the warm air the cocky tunes of William Walton's *Façade*. These accompany elegant, clipped recitations by Edith Sitwell of her own nonsense verses. "When. Don. Pas. Quito arrives at the sea side, where vanilla-colored ladies ride . . ." It's Reggie's favorite record album. " 'See me dance the polka,' / Said Mr. Wagg-like a bear, . . ." But it's tricky. "In a room of the palace / Black Mrs. Behemoth / Gave way to wrath / And the wildest malice . . ." Nathan's heard it often, but he still doesn't understand all of it, and privately he bets Reggie doesn't, either.

In a dapple of leaf shadow, Nathan lays his head on Hoyt's flat, sun-warmed belly and laughs. "I'd love to see the poor dummy's face right now."

"What he needs is 'The Little Red Hen,' " Hoyt says. "And Reggie plays him *Façade*. It will put him to sleep faster than—" Hoyt's lanky frame jerks. "Hey, what are you doing?" He grabs Nathan's hair, sucks in air through his teeth. "Jesus. Are you crazy? No, no—don't stop."

Frank writes:

> *Your mother and I are proud of your success. We're even more proud that you stuck to your writing, and didn't give up just because those freaky friends of yours at that little theatre set you up and knocked you down the way they did. I never did think much of them, as you will remember. I tried to warn you.*
>
> *You know how much I love a steady job, so I'd be the last to criticize you for quitting at that bookstore. The pay was*

disgraceful. You ought to stop letting people walk all over you when it comes to money. Joe Ridpath did the same. You're young, but you work hard, always did. And you ought to make people pay you accordingly.

But maybe working for other people is a thing of the past for you now. I hope so. I hope the publishers love your book when it's finished and everybody in the country buys it and reads it (except your mother, of course), and you never have to worry about money for the rest of your life. Not that I worried about it half as much as I ought to. I know that, and I regret it. I should have done better for your mother and you. Anyway, stretch that five hundred as far as you can. Eschew blondes and fancy automobiles.

More silly women than ever seem to want their fortunes told these days, so your mother is able to put money aside for winter, when the organ loft at St. Barnabas gets frigid and my bad leg seizes up so I can't work the bass pedals. I have to dig out the old cane then, which can be treacherous on icy sidewalks. Still, Minneapolis is a hell of a lot better than California, and I can't help hoping you'll get fed up with it too eventually and come home here.

Your mother worries you're not eating right, and she says to tell you to bundle up when you go to bed. I agree. Wear sweaters and socks. You know how easily you catch cold, and what that can turn into! I still get nightmares about how sick you were after that hike up the canyon with Stone. In my dreams you always die. And you damn near did. So please take care of yourself. And congratulations again. I hope your good luck never stops. Your aunt Marie sends love. She's pretty frail these days, but she still won't let anybody else do the dishes.

They sit in a bar called the Circle. It's late. They have been drinking highballs, smoking cigarettes, and listening to Herb Jeffries and Ivie Anderson. Jeffries is a tall, rich-voiced Negro, handsome as a god. Anderson is small and impish and can break your heart without trying. They used to sing with Duke Ellington's band. With Frank, Nathan saw the show a couple of years ago in one of those vast, crumbling theaters on Broadway in downtown L.A. Now the two singers wind up "Brownskin Gal in a Calico Gown" and leave the little platform. The backup trio plays—piano, bass, drums. Hoyt slides off his stool, edges through the smoky gloom, the laughter and jingling ice, to buy cigarettes from the machine at the back. He sits on the stool again, unwraps the pack. "What's the matter with your father's leg?" He taps the pack on the heel of his hand and cigarettes jut out and he holds the pack out to Nathan.

"He got shot." Nathan takes a cigarette. "The friend I mentioned the other day, Stone, the teacher who killed himself?" He bends his head to get a light from Hoyt's paper match. "He shot Frank—it was an accident. The trouble was, Stone thought he'd killed him."

Hoyt lights his own cigarette, shakes out the match. "And that's why he shot himself?"

"Partly." Nathan tells the whole long story, and it leaves him sad all over again, and angry with himself for not getting to Stone in time to tell him Frank was going to be all right. His drink is only a tepid inch of water at the bottom of his glass. He pushes it away. "Let's go."

On the empty one A.M. boulevard outside, Hoyt says, "Moon's sounds like a place I'd take to."

"It's closed now." Nathan turns up his jacket collar and heads into the wind, hands in pockets, making for Highland Avenue. "Moon died. She wasn't old, but she drank a lot. Last time I drove Joe Ridpath's truck by there, the chairs were upside down on the tables. The windows were dirty. There was a For Sale sign on it."

They trudge on in silence. Then Hoyt says, "Even if she was alive and it was still open, it would be closed. That's how it is with those places. You can't go back."

Nathan grins at him. "I never heard you so profound."

"*In vino veritas*," Hoyt says.

Nathan stops at a sidewalk sign outside the entrance to an upstairs bar called Montmartre. "Look." There's a photo of a mild-looking, gray-haired Negro dressed in a tuxedo and holding a clarinet. "Jimmy Noone."

"You know a lot of obscure musicians," Hoyt says.

"After you hear him," Nathan says, and walks on, "he'll play on inside your head forever. There's something very pure about his music. It's the truth. Nothing added."

They turn up Highland and Hoyt says, "What if I don't want to hear him?"

"I'm trying to broaden you culturally," Nathan says. "You gave me Stendhal, I'm giving you jazz. Tomorrow Jimmy Noone, then Jack Teagarden and Ray Baduc at the Suzie-Q."

Hoyt says, "Texans get restive around Negroes."

"Teagarden is an Oklahoma Indian, Baduc's a New Orleans Frenchman. You have to hear Teagarden sing. He doesn't know how. It's perfect. Come on, Hoyt, keep your mind open."

"Just one favor," Hoyt says. "Don't buy a horn."

"If Ah didn't admiah you so much," Rick Ames says, "and place you above the ordinary run of mortals, Ah would be angry with you."

"Why is that?" Nathan says.

They have met in the market, where they always meet. Ames, in his baggy red sweatshirt, baggy corduroys, grubby tennis shoes, carries the usual heavy shopping bags that clink when moved. Nathan wears the shirt without buttons, and Ames can't stop staring at his torso with those bleary blue eyes of his. Nathan has wheedled steaks and a chicken out of the butch butcher. He stands among the vegetables now—frowning. After Pearl Harbor, the government locked up all the Japanese farmers in camps, leaving nobody to grow vegetables in California. The market's zinc bins hold little but grit and withered leaves.

Ames says, "You promised to tell me when you sold your book. But if Ah hadn't stopped in yesterday at T. Smollett Books, Ah still wouldn't know."

Nathan picks up a sorry stalk of celery. "I don't know what to do here."

"What meat are you cooking?"

Nathan tells him.

"Get rice, add chopped chives, and cook it in a can of chicken broth. With the steak, heat canned artichoke hearts and melted butter. Delicious."

They pay for their groceries, and leave the check stand, and Nathan starts off, when Ames says, "Please wait," and yaws toward the liquor counter. Nathan waits outside. Ames comes into the sunshine saying, "Craven & Hyde is a nice little house. They've done very well with the Rosamond Lehmann novel. Weeks on the best-seller lists. They ought to have plenty of money to pay you."

"They're keeping most of it," Nathan says.

"See?" Ames holds up a bottle. Nathan reads the label. It's champagne. "We are going to celebrate your wonderful news."

"Now?" Nathan says.

"Why not?" Ames glances across the street. "Go get your friend. Ah'll wait. Then we'll all walk over to my place togethah. Ah've been meaning to invite you for the longest tahm."

Hoyt isn't home. The other morning, out looking to buy a big mirror, rummaging through a jumble shop on Selma Street, Nathan glanced out the shop window and got a surprise. Hoyt was coming downstairs from an office across the way, arms loaded with rubber-banded stacks of envelopes. Lettered on the door he had closed behind him was HOLLYWOOD PROGRESSIVE COMMITTEE FOR THE ARTS. Nathan ducked behind a counter of tarnished jewelry. He wasn't following Hoyt, and Hoyt mustn't think he was. But he was too upset after that to search anymore for the mirror. He kept imagining John F. Noble must be lurking nearby, maybe in that very mothball-smelly shop, watching from behind the racks of droopy used dresses and tired tweed suits—and he went home. But Hoyt seems to have forgotten all about Noble, so he's probably stuffing envelopes for the progressives again this morning. Nathan stows the chicken and steaks in the icebox, steps into the workroom, picks up the pages he wrote yesterday, frowns, bends, begins crossing out words with a pencil. He itches to sit down at the typewriter, but knows that if he does, in a few minutes he'll have forgotten Rick Ames, so he turns over a page, scribbles on the back a note to himself about Alma's hat, and reluctantly leaves.

The house hulks up behind a tall, spreading monkey puzzle tree, on the north side of Franklin, a big old gray stucco place with bulging windows, deep porches, a porte cochere. Half a dozen houses as large stand along here, grand mansions once, probably built with movie money, now rooming houses. Staunchly, the puffing Ames climbs cracked cement stairs, leads the way to the front porch and up more cement stairs. The shadow of the porch holds coolness. A heavy house door stands open on a dim, gaping hallway with a carved staircase. A narrow passage runs back to the left of the stairs, past closed doors with metal number tags.

Ames leans his shopping bags against a papered wall and fumblingly unlocks a chipped white enameled door numbered 2. As he does this, Nathan hears a creak behind him, and glances back. Across the hall an eye shows at the crack of a pair of sliding doors. "Would you believe it?" says a woman's voice. "He's already dragged home another one." And the doors close.

"Pay no attention," Ames says, as he opens his own door and picks up the bags. "Ah am spied on constantly." He walks inside, waits for Nathan to pass him, and bangs the door to. It's a sunny, L-shaped room, with many books, and stepping into the main part of it, Nathan gets another surprise. A naked young man stares at him from a rumpled bed. He halts. Ames bumps into him, says "Oof!," then yelps, "You promised you'd be gone when Ah got back."

"Yeah, sorry. I fell asleep." The young man gets off the bed and begins to dress, snatching up Army underwear and socks. His uniform lies over a chair. "I'll go. I'll go." He is pale-skinned, with a lot of body hair, a squatty build, and in need of a shave. His eyes are bloodshot, and putting on his clothes his hands shake. "Jesus, you got a drink? I'm in bad shape." Seated on the edge of the bed, he puts his hands to his head. "Christ, what a hangover."

Ames looks at Nathan. "Ah don't know how to apologize to you for this contretemps. What can Ah say?"

Nathan turns for the door. "I'll come some other time."

"No, wait, please." Ames bends, groping in his shopping bag. "Don't go. Your book, our celebration, the champagne."

But now fists pound loudly on the door. Nathan jumps back. Outside the door, a voice shouts, "Open up. Military police. You got a Private Robert Ernest Delmar in there?"

Ames puts a finger to his lips. His blurry blue eyes plead with Nathan for silence. The boy from the bed comes into view, tucking in shirttails, and stares over Ames's shoulder at the door. He looks scared—and trapped.

"We know you're in there, Delmar. Open the door. The Army wants you back. It's just no fun without you."

Ames points to a broad, sunny window, gives the boy a push toward it, calls to the door, "He's not here. He was here, but he left." The boy struggles to raise the window sash. It is stuck. He hits the frame with the heel of his hand. The window won't budge. Desperate, he hits the frame with the heels of both hands, and one goes through the pane. There is a hail of broken glass. The soldier stares for a second at the blood spurting from his forearm, then crumples to the floor. He looks dead.

"Oh, my God." Ames claps both hands to his mouth.

Nathan twists the spring lock and opens the door. Two very

clean-shaven young men in uniform and steel helmets stand there, hung all over with guns, clubs, handcuffs. "You better come in," Nathan says. "He's hurt himself." They lumber in past him, and Nathan sees an immense, heavily rouged, middle-aged woman in a flowered muumuu standing in the open doorway across the hall, and beside her a young woman, tall, blond, beautiful—a Michelangelo sibyl. Barefoot. Ames lunges past Nathan and slams the door shut.

"She called them." He leans back against the door, panting. "Evil, grasping old witch. She'd do anything to get me out of here. So she can subdivide this beautiful room and rent it to some convict on the run. She's done it everyplace in the house. Why, some of the rooms she collects rent for are no bigger than closets. Some of them don't even have windas, which is, of course, illegal. Because we are the oldest tenants here—Ah mean, we have been here the longest, years and years—Ah have dismissed the notion that we could be vulnerable. Until this moment. We were friends. We had an unduhstanding. But now Ah see there is no depth to which she would not stoop—"

"Excuse me, sir," one of the MPs calls. Both have been kneeling beside Delmar, who doesn't stir, doesn't open his eyes. They have ripped off the sleeve of his shirt and used it and a billy club for a tourniquet on the arm with the slashed artery. The speaker stands up. "We gotta get an ambulance here. Where's your phone?"

"He's wrong," the MP says. "She never called us. Nobody called us." He stands with Nathan at the top of the steps that lead down to the sidewalk. They are waiting for the ambulance. The other MP is inside with the still-unconscious Delmar. Ames was last seen lugging his shopping bags down the hallway, urgent to get his groceries into the refrigerator. "We check out the bars. It's routine. We show the bartenders photos. We lucked out today. Pansy bar called Slim Gaylord's on the Boulevard. They know Ames there. They seen Delmar walk out with him last night."

"And you found Ames in the phone book?" Nathan says.

The MP twitches a brief smile. He has stubby little teeth. "Nothin' to it." He eyes Nathan curiously. "How come you know Ames?"

"He's a writer," Nathan says, "I'm a writer."

"That's all?" the MP says.

"We're neighbors, and we sometimes meet at the market. Today, he'd heard I'd found a publisher for the novel I'm writing, and he bought a bottle of champagne, and asked me over to celebrate my good luck."

"He's a pervert," the MP says. "You want to look out for them. This town is crawling with them."

"They walk upright," Nathan says, "just like you."

"That's why you gotta be so careful," the MP says. "You want to show me your draft card?"

Nathan digs it out and shows it to him.

He hands it back. "What's wrong with you?"

"Lungs," Nathan says, putting the card away.

The MP says, "What does that mean, a novel?"

"A book," Nathan says, "a story."

The MP wrinkles his brow. "A story about what?"

"My father and mother and me when I was a kid."

"Yeah? And they pay you for that?"

Nathan shrugs. "That's what they say."

"Jesus." The MP wags his head. "I mean, everybody was a kid once, everybody had a father and mother. I mean, I don't get it. Why would they want to print that? Who'd want to read a book like that?"

Nathan is stuck for an answer, but he doesn't need one, because here comes the ambulance, and the MP clunks down the steps and into the street to wave at it.

"It was, of course, a thrill," Rick Ames says, "getting a letter from Whit Burnett, a letter not just praising my piece, but saying *Story* magazine was going to print it." He's slumped in an easy chair with a slender champagne glass in his paw and the sun slanting into his eyes through the shattered window. Near him on a table the champagne bottle stands empty, glinting green. "But of cawse nothin' like the thrill the day the magazine hit the newsstands with mah name on the covah."

His accent has got much thicker with the wine. Nathan doesn't understand the accent. Richard Sheridan Ames's real name is Emil Bilharz, and he hails from Iowa, sturdy German immigrant stock. He borrowed his first two names from the Irish playwright, and his last from the town where he went to college. He has told Nathan a lot about himself this afternoon, but never once said he ever lived in the South. Nathan doesn't plan to ask him. His head is muzzy. There's still champagne in his own glass, but he doesn't mean to drink it. He means to leave. He's already stayed too long.

Ames was hopeless at it, so Nathan scrubbed Private Delmar's blood out of the carpet, then took bucket and brush and rag to a set tub on the far back porch to rinse them out. After that, he would leave. The tall, barefoot girl was at the kitchen table drinking Coca-Cola. She gave him an arch smile as he passed, then came and watched him, leaning hipshot in the doorway, sucking in her cheeks, cocking her eyebrow, twisting a lock of blond hair around a finger. She asked him his name.

"Nathan," he said, sloshing bloody water down the drain. "What's yours?"

"Linnet," she said. "It's a little brown bird."

Turning off the tap, wringing out the rag, he threw her a grin. "You're not."

"Did Ricky bring you home for sex?" she said.

He blinked. "No. How old are you?"

"Sixteen," she said, "but I'm married. To Percy Hinkley. He owns this house."

"The older lady I saw you with"—Nathan laid the rag open over the side of the set tub to dry—"I thought she was the owner."

"She's my mother," Linnet said. "Flora Belle Short. She's the manager."

"I see." Nathan laid the scrub brush on a shelf under the tub. He stepped to the doorway, but she didn't move. "Excuse me, please."

"You're so good-looking," she said, and ran a hand down his arm. "You shouldn't associate with fairies. It will spoil your reputation."

Nathan said, "You want to let me pass, please?"

"There's more Cokes." She moved out of the doorway. "Why don't we take some and go to the beach in Perc's pickup? You can drive, can't you? There's plenty of gas. I want to get to know you. I'll tell you about my trip to Mexico. Perc never gets enough traveling. He's a ship's radio operator, always out at sea, but the minute he gets back, we have to take off for someplace. Do you like Mexico?"

"I've never been there," Nathan said.

"Perc loves it. He wants me to learn Mexican, but I can't. He bought me books, but I just can't."

"Maybe you need a teacher," Nathan said.

She took two Cokes from the icebox. "I hate school."

"My friend Hoyt's from Texas. He used to go to Mexico a lot. He speaks Spanish. Maybe he could help you."

"Oh, good. Would you ask him for me? I have to learn at least some of it. Before Perc gets back."

Ames appeared in the kitchen. "Ah, there you are." He glared at Linnet and took Nathan's arm. "Ah was afraid Ah'd lost you. It's so hard to keep anything to oneself in this house." He led Nathan away, raising his voice to be sure Linnet heard him. "Groceries one buys and pays for and stores in the refrigerator, for example. Certain individuals simply cannot understand the concept of 'yours' and 'mine.' "

"I have to go," Nathan said.

"But we haven't had our festive champagne," Ames said.

And here he is, hours later. Ames wanted to talk, didn't he? He wouldn't let Nathan leave. And now it's late.

"You'll see when your book comes out." Ames nods, squinting at him against the sun. "There is no thrill like holding your printed work in your hand for the first time. It makes a pusson feel like a conqueruh. You remembuh that wonduhful moment in Thomas Wolfe where George Weber goes up on top of a tall building in Manhattan and looks down on the city, the night his novel—?" Now he registers that Nathan has set down his glass and stood up. "You're not going?" He struggles out of his chair. "But I've been talking about nothing but myself. I want to hear about you."

"You're more interesting," Nathan says. "Thank you." He goes to the door. "The champagne was very nice. And we'll visit again." He opens the door and bumps into a mountainous man in coveralls with GOOD HUMOR lettered across the front. He says, "Excuse me," and over Nathan's head calls in a desperate voice, "Rick?"

"Tony?" Ames comes at an eager waddle. "Ah, youah home. May I present Nathan Reed. He writes, you know. He's sold his book. We've been celebrating with champagne."

"Rick, I have to sit down." Tony falls toward Ames, who supports him, limping, to the chair where Nathan has been sitting. They go like a pair of wounded elephants. Tony drops onto the chair, eyes closed, obviously in pain. He gropes out with a great hand, blindly. "Drink. Drink."

Ames gets bourbon from a cabinet, pours a tumbler full, and puts it into the desperate hand. "Oh, mah poor darlin'. It's bad, today, isn't it?"

"Worse than ever," Tony says in an exhausted voice, tilts back his head, empties the glass down his throat. His chin then rests on his chest while he holds the glass out for a refill. "I don't know how much longer I can stand it."

Nathan should leave. He can't. It's like a dream.

While Tony moans softly to himself, Ames fetches him another glass of whiskey, then looks at Nathan. "He works in a walk-in freezer, lifting huge cartons of ice cream bars all day. It's his legs." He crouches and yanks up one leg of the dirty white coveralls. The leg inside is in a plaster cast, and from cracks in the cast blood has seeped and dried. Ames begins taking off Tony's high-top shoes. "Varicose veins. Abscesses. The longer he works, the worse they get."

"Rick—don't bother the boy with our troubles." Now Tony has downed the second glass, and he slowly opens his eyes. They are large, dark eyes. There's an ancient Greek painting of a young boy with eyes like Tony's.

Nathan says, "Why don't you quit that job?"

Tony is unbuttoning the coverall. Under it are layers of sweaters. "I'd lose my pension."

"But it's making you a cripple," Nathan says.

Tony forces a smile. "I'll be all right." Ames helps him to his feet. The coveralls are shucked. The two of them pull the sweaters off over Tony's head. Standing there massive in long johns and the ponderous leg casts, Tony says to Nathan, "Congratulations. It's wonderful about your book." Ames has carried off the coveralls and sweaters to a closet. Now he brings back a gigantic white terry-cloth robe and wraps Tony in it. Motherly tenderness is in his every move. Tony knots the sash of the robe and drops onto the chair again. Under his weight its frame gives an ominous crack. He says to Nathan, "When Rick told me about you, he was sure it would sell." He gazes up at his fat, slack, red-faced friend. It's a look of total adoration. "Rick knows these things. He can sense talent. It's uncanny." He looks at Nathan again. "He's a wonderful writer himself, you know. I work so he can write."

"Tony was a dancer when we met," Ames says dreamily. "One night at the Hollywood Bowl. Slender. Beautiful. Such *entrechats*. How Ah wish you could have seen him."

The apartment where Stanley Page lives is above a garage back of a rough gray stucco duplex on the south side of Franklin just east of Highland. The floor is bare. There are two wicker barrel chairs, two upended orange crates of books. Dime-store lamps stand on top of the crates. Manuscripts in colored paper covers are heaped loosely in a corner. Beyond a counter is a tiny kitchenette. A door to the left stands slightly open on a bedroom. The morning is hot, so the windows are up, but there's no breeze, and the air has the sweetish-sour-milk smell of baby. In the kitchenette Page takes groceries from the sack he's brought and puts them away. A refrigerator door sucks open, thumps shut. He comes into the living room, loosening his tie. He tosses his hat into the bedroom. A woman's voice speaks, but he doesn't answer. He lays his jacket over the counter, rolls up his shirt cuffs two turns, sits in one of the creaky chairs. He lights a cigarette. "Sit down. Let me see that contract."

Nathan hands him the contract and sits down.

Slouched in the chair, Page flips the pages over, frowning, grunting to himself. "You should have shown this to me before you signed it."

Nathan is alarmed. "What's wrong with it?"

"They'll get your second book for the same advance as the first," Page says in his tough, gravelly voice. "You have to watch them. They're not crooked, exactly. But they always try to get the best deal for themselves. If they were buying from anybody but writers, they'd expect the seller to do the same. But writers are lousy businessmen. That's why there have to be agents."

"What agent would want me?" Nathan says. "I never sold a piece of writing in my life till now."

"Now is what counts," Page says, and passes back the contract. "You want me to be your agent? Fine. I'll get you a better deal on your second book than what you signed for there. Besides, there's serial rights, reprint rights, movies, radio, and overseas translations." He eyes Nathan. "You think you can handle all that?"

"I don't know anything about it," Nathan says. But he is looking at the naked apartment and wondering how much Page knows. It hasn't made him rich, has it? "But what I'm writing is a quiet story about simple people. It will never make the best-seller lists."

"You can't be sure," Page says. "That's why it doesn't take any brains to be a publisher. Just luck. Anybody's a liar who claims he can predict which book is going to make it. Look at *The Human Comedy*. Talk about simple."

"Did you sell that?" Nathan says.

"Saroyan's my client. I thought you knew that. I also sold it to the studios. That's where the real money is. Don't let this place fool you. When I came out of Q, I still owed money on the store, but I found a good bookie. I'll be in the clear, soon. Then we'll buy furniture, and a car."

"And a castle in Spain." This comes from a slight, olive-skinned woman in a housecoat who steps out of the bedroom. She looks tired. "Hello. I'm Maud, the lady of the house. I see Mr. Hospitality has extended himself as usual." Pushing at her tousled hair, she goes to the kitchenette. "Would you like some iced tea?"

"Thank you," Nathan says. "I'm all right."

The refrigerator opens. "Stanley?" she says.

"You know I can't stand that slop," Page snarls.

And in the bedroom, baby Bill starts to cry.

The picture of Nathan naked with ribbon bows leans against the green-shingled wall. It's tall, almost life-size. When it was new, the colors were bright. Then Hoyt went to work on it with a rag, turpentine, and something black. The flesh tones are almost gone. Only glints of the ribbons' vivid colors show in the murk. It might almost be a drawing in ink wash. Benbow studies it, standing, head cocked, a glass of beer in his hand. "It's a dream, or a memory," he says. "And ineffably *triste*."

"But not sentimental," says skinny little George Lafleur. He sits on the floor, turning over pages of one of Hoyt's art books. " 'Cast a cold eye,' " he says.

Benbow adds, " 'On life, on death . . .' "

Nathan comes from the kitchen with a wax-paper bag of potato chips. " 'Horseman,' " he says, " 'pass by.' "

"Inscription on Yeats's tombstone," Hoyt says, and tears open the potato-chip bag.

"In Drumcliff churchyard, County Sligo," Benbow says. He sits on the buttsprung couch. "I see you took my advice and added another set of ribbons."

"Not where you wanted," Hoyt says. The extra ribbons he painted bind Nathan's brow, the bows and ends trailing over one ear. Hoyt holds the bag out to Benbow, who takes a handful, and says:

"No, not sentimental. Sentimentality is what rushes in to fill the vacuum where there is no real emotion."

"There's real emotion," George says, turning over another page of the art book, studying the picture there. "When I said 'a cold eye,' I didn't mean a cold heart." Now he looks up at Nathan. "How does it make you feel? Do you think it's you?"

"Lonely." Nathan shivers. "I don't like the idea of hanging in some gallery in the dark night after night."

"It's not you." Hoyt kisses him. "It's only paint."

Nathan sits on the floor beside George. "A cold eye?"

"The difference between a great painter like Manet"—George shows him a picture, turns pages, shows him another—"and a second-rater like Renoir." Benbow has left the couch and come to stand over Nathan. George turns the page back. "They're essentially the same crowd of young poets and painters and composers and their girlfriends—dressed up, enjoying themselves. But Manet's people, you know some of them have syphilis." He flops the pages back again. "Renoir's people are made of marzipan."

Nathan looks up at Benbow. "Your friend is smart."

Benbow says, "He's reached the 'I' volume, hasn't he? In the *Britannica*? 'Impressionism'?"

"Shut up," George says. "Don't listen to him, Nathan. He preferred me ignorant."

Nathan is wearing the suit, the one he and Hoyt share, the one Hoyt wore to Eva Schaffer's funeral. This is only Nathan's second time wearing it. He sits in the backseat of a taxicab with Stanley Page and Maud, who are quiet, their faces stiff, as if they'd just had a fight. Page wears a tuxedo and a homburg, and Maud an evening gown and a yellow hibiscus flower in her newly marcelled hair. Nathan doesn't know much about such things, but he has a hunch both tuxedo and evening gown are borrowed. They are going to a party. The Pages have been invited. But not Nathan. He is only going because Stanley kept at him:

"In this town you're nobody till everybody knows you. If you want to get anyplace, you gotta get out there and meet people. Picture people."

"I'm not in the picture business," Nathan said.

"You're a writer. That's the only money there is in writing. What do you want to do—starve all your life?"

"The book's not done," Nathan said. "It's too soon."

"You're not going to get any better looking. Christ, they'll love your looks."

"Excuse me, but what's that got to do with my novel?"

"In Hollywood, it's got to do with everything."

"I think I better wait till the book comes out."

"Fuck it. To them a book in the head is the same as a book in the shops. They can't read, anyway. Junk men and pants pressers. Ignorant Hebes."

"I better not," Nathan said.

"Wear a dark suit," Page said.

And here they are, climbing out of the taxi in front of long broad steps leading up to a vast house, windows all ablaze with light, orchestra music drifting over the high tile roofs from some place back of the house, laughter, voices raised in talk, voices raised above the voices raised, female voices shrill, male voices roaring.

Well-dressed people—many of the men in dress uniform, blue, white, khaki—stand in groups on the terrace, move in couples around the terrace, move past the windows indoors, most with drinks in hand, cigarettes. Sorry he came, Nathan follows Stanley and Maud up the stairs. On the terrace, Nathan sees famous faces, but the one who catches his eye is tall Alex Morgan, a girl he went to school with. She smiles at him in a blank way that says she's become a movie star, all right. It's warm inside the house, though the beautifully molded ceilings are high, and the windows are open.

Now people begin to notice Stanley, speak his name, stop him to shake his hand and to meet Maud. And Nathan. He shakes a lot of hands. Squat men, desiccated men, gray men, florid men, men who yammer at him in staccato bursts and call him "kid" and give him advice as Stanley does. Studio executives, producers, agents, God knows what. He gets congratulated on his book, over and over again. All of the men say they want to see his book. He has to explain over and over again that it's not finished yet. A heavy, bald man with glowering brows, seated on a couch with attentive men all around him, waves a thick hand, croaks:

"I don't need the book. Send me two pages. A story you can't tell in two pages audiences can't follow, anyway." He glances around at his troops, hard black eyes sly, expectant. "Nobody ever lost money betting on the stupidity of the American people—right, boys?"

They laugh and nod. "Right, Mr. Dryrot."

His name is not Dryrot but it's near enough.

"We'll send you the two pages," Page promises him. He takes Nathan's arm and leads him onto a rear terrace. Below, a large swimming pool glows blue in the night. Chinese paper lanterns— not Japanese, not with the war on—hang from oaks in a vast backyard. Here is where the orchestra plays. A dance floor has been laid down and couples are dancing. It's a scene from a movie. Page says, "We've gotta dream up a new title. The Jewboys all think it's a western."

They go down the stairs. There are tables with food and drink and Filipinos in white coats to serve. Page heads for the tables and Nathan follows. And the next thing he knows, he is shaking hands with the great Charles Laidlaw. It seems Laidlaw was a customer of the Stanley Page bookshop before it came to grief. "I miss it sorely," he says in his glorious voice. "I miss you, Stanley." But his piggy eyes are fixed on Nathan. He marvels, "So young—and already a published novelist?"

"Not yet," Nathan says. "A publisher's paid me a little money to finish it, that's all."

"Your honesty is refreshing." Laidlaw's blubbery face twitches exactly as it does on the screen. He blinks and blinks. "So very young. How—old are you, exactly, Nathan?"

"Twenty," Nathan says.

"Imagine!" Laidlaw turns to the men standing near him— what's it called, an entourage? All homosexuals, aren't they? Laidlaw drapes a bulky arm over Nathan's shoulders. "Gentlemen, I give you Nathan Reed. At twenty years of age, already a master novelist. Raise your glasses."

And they do, leering, laughing. Nathan wants to run. He looks around for Stanley Page, but the agent has disappeared. Laidlaw's hand is crawling slowly down Nathan's back. The million-dollar voice is murmuring in Nathan's ear, "I have a mountain hideaway." His breath smells of gin and onions. "Suppose I send a car for you next Saturday morning. We'll have a restful weekend, high up among the pines beside a quiet lake." The hand reaches Nathan's ass, where it gently squeezes. "Just the two of us. You can read me your novel."

Nathan can't get his breath. "Well, Mr. Laidlaw, I—"

"I'm in earnest. I think you and I would—hit it off. Speaking of hitting"—he gives a little tug to Nathan's belt—"be sure to wear this when you come. Hmm?"

"My belt?" Nathan pulls away and stares at him.

"Yes—in case I get out of line." The twitching and blinking are very rapid by now. Nathan can't tell whether he's trying not to laugh or not to cry. "I do sometimes. I do get out of line. Then I have to be chastised. Severely." He glances at his group, most of whom aren't watching now, are loading plates with slices of ham and roast beef and turkey and salads, or getting drinks or ice for their drinks. "I have this loathsome, dirty, detestable schoolboy side of me which simply must be punished. It's no secret from my friends. And"—he moves to embrace Nathan again, but Nathan dodges—"we are going to be friends, aren't we?"

Nathan backs away. "Stanley's calling me," he says.

Stanley isn't calling him. Stanley is drinking. And laughing. With a bunch of tough-looking men in evening dress—gangsters, gamblers, what?—in the rosy glow of the Chinese paper lanterns under one of the big oaks. Nathan heads for him, and sees Maud heading for him from the other direction. She gets to him first. Her voice sounds angry, though he can't make out the words. The orchestra is too loud. But people near them on the lawn turn and stare. Nathan pushes through them. He sees Maud strike at Page's hand. His drink goes flying, glass, ice, and liquor arching shiny in the soft light.

Page's face is blank with surprise. "What the hell?"

"You promised me," Maud cries. "The day your son was born. Gave me your solemn word. You promised me to live, Stanley Page. You promised to live to see him grow up. No more alcohol. Never again."

Page doesn't seem to know who she is. "What?"

Some of the mobsters or whatever they are stay and watch and grin. Some stroll away.

Maud says, "You know what the doctor said. If you start drinking again, you'll be dead in a year. I love you, you rotten egg. I'm not going to let you do this to yourself."

Now Page wakens to where they are, who she is, what's happening. His face turns red. "Not now, Maud, not here."

"Your liver is the size of an orange," she says, articulating carefully. "It's got cleats all over it, like the sole of a football shoe. It won't take any more."

"My liver is my business," Page says and pushes her.

She stumbles backward. Nathan keeps her from falling. Page walks away—straight toward the drinks table. She runs after him, clutches him. "It's my business too. It's Bill's business." He pushes her off, and this time she falls. He breaks for the drinks table again, where he picks up a glass, snatches a bottle from the surprised Filipino, and tilts it straight up over the glass. Nathan helps Maud to her feet. "No, Stanley, stop!" She runs toward him, stumbling because her high heels dig into the turf. "If you do this, I warn you, I'll take Bill and leave. And I won't come back." Vodka, gin, rum, whatever it is, cascades into the glass, over the rim of the glass, over Page's shaking hand, onto the table, onto the grass. Maud doesn't go any nearer. She cries in a broken voice, "I mean it, Stanley." She stands staring, aghast at what he's doing, tears on her face, little fists clenched helpless in front of her. "This time I really do mean it."

He turns to her, sneers, lifts the glass, tilts the contents down his throat in one, long drink. He lowers his head, laughs at her, then throws the glass. He means for it to hit her, but it misses. Still, it's too much for her. She turns, almost falls again on account of the heels, kicks off the shoes, and runs through the gawking, gossiping crowd, up the long slope of lawn toward the glowing house. Page stops where he is, wavering on his feet, watching her go, a crooked smile on his face—half triumph, half despair.

"Run like a rabbit, you son of a bitch!" he calls.

Nathan picks up the little shoes.

Where beer has spilled, the sand on the floor sticks to the soles of the feet. The only light in the bar comes boring in hard through

the open front door. It's light mirrored off the ocean. But that
hasn't cooled it. Stand in it and sweat streams off you. It's late
September, and ninety degrees in Hollywood, too hot to stay upstairs in their place and write and paint. Or do sex. Or even listen
to records. They have come to Venice Beach.

They have passed the morning on the sand among thousands
of women, toddlers, dogs—no school-age kids, because school has
started, hardly a man in sight because of the war—wading in the
surf, swimming, but mostly lying on their ragged towel, reading
Eliot's *Four Quartets* aloud to each other, dozing, and soaking up
sun. Nathan's back and shoulders throb. Hoyt's skin is fiery red.
They have eaten hot dogs. Now they are drinking beer. And gawking around. Because this is a gay bar. That's what Hoyt said, and
was the reason they passed up half a dozen taverns that surely must
have been better kept than this one where nobody sweeps, nobody
swabs off the bar or collects glasses from the little black shiny
tables, and where surely many more bodies are crowded together
than the law allows.

The jukebox plays "Right in Der Führer's Face," "The
White Cliffs of Dover," "Coming In on a Wing and a Prayer"—
there's a din of talk, shrieks of laughter, shrieks without
laughter. The jukebox plays "The Last Time I Saw Paris," and
in a rear corner, where the sunlight doesn't reach, it looks to
Nathan as if boys are dancing with each other. There aren't
many mature men here; almost everyone's young. And most of
them slim. Some of these are in uniform, soldiers, sailors, marines,
but at least half are as near naked as they dare get. Hoyt goes off
to piss.

Right away somebody takes his stool. Nathan hears its tired
metal legs complain. He smells cologne. "You've got a very severe
sunburn," the somebody says. "I've got just the thing for it. Glyc-
erin and rose water. In my car." Nathan looks into two brown eyes.
The kid is a cupid from an eighteenth-century French painting. A
tumble of chestnut curls. Dimples. Cherry lips. Teeth with ugly

brown spots. "Come with me. I'll rub it on for you. So-o-o cooling. You won't believe how good it'll make you feel."

"What happened to your teeth?" Nathan says.

"What happened to your nose?" the boy says.

Nathan shrugs. "Back in high school. A bunch of kids jumped me in the dark. They thought I was somebody else."

"I was raised on a backwoods farm in Maine where there weren't enough minerals in the water, or too many, or something." The smooth blond shoulders lift and fall. "It's the luck of the draw. Your nose makes you look rugged. I'm pretty if I keep my mouth shut."

"You certainly are," Nathan says. "But I'm taken, and so is that stool, by my sleeping partner. He'll be back in a minute, and he's a rawhide Texas cowboy, very jealous."

"I can understand that," Amour says. "You're too beautiful to trust." And he slides off the stool and into the crowd.

When Hoyt comes back, he seems angry. Or is he laughing? He hikes onto the torn black oilcloth cushion of the stool, finishes off his beer, lights a cigarette.

"Guess who I ran into?" he says. "I mean 'whom.' "

"Whom?" Nathan says.

"Your old pal from the bookstore, Mr. Constance. In a Hawaiian shirt and white ducks."

Nathan looks around. "Here? You're kidding."

"In the men's room." Hoyt stands on the rungs of his stool and leans far over the bar to wave his empty glass and shout for a refill. "It's got three urinals." A lissom and leathery not-so-young man behind the bar swishes past and plucks Hoyt's glass. Hoyt sits down. "And Constance is at the middle one. I stepped up beside him, shoved down my trunks—well, you have to, it's the only way—and right away he reached over, and guess what."

"It couldn't have been him," Nathan said. " 'He.' "

"It was. I knew him—" The bartender sets a beer in front of Hoyt, slides dimes from the coins Hoyt has strewn on the wet counter, and pirouettes away, with the dimes held high above his head, bony wrist drooping. There is a scattering of applause. He curtseys deeply. Hoyt says, "But he didn't know me. See, he hadn't even looked at my face. He had his eye on just one thing."

"And his hand," Nathan says. "So what happened?"

"I said, 'Connie, you surprise me.' Then he looked at me, all right. Shit, you should have seen his expression. He was out of there like a jackrabbit."

It's past three in the afternoon. Bored with drawing and reading, Hoyt is asleep in the next room. Nathan has been no company for him. He has been writing steadily since breakfast, but the voices keep speaking to each other inside his head—Frank's, Alma's, Aunt Marie's, his own piping ten-year-old voice—which means he has to keep on. To stop now would be bad strategy. He gropes in the box and there's no more paper. He gets stiffly off the hard chair, stretches to work the ache out of his shoulders, rubs his numb backside, then crosses the hall and knocks on Reggie Poole's door. He thinks he heard Reggie leave, but he doesn't register much that happens in the real world while he's in Minneapolis and it's 1933, so he's not sure. But Reggie doesn't answer. He steps inside, goes straight to Reggie's desk, starts opening drawers. And then hears a chair move in the kitchen.

"Reggie? May I borrow some typing paper?"

He looks up, and Mike Voynich, he of the ears and the radiant smile, stands in the doorway, wrapped in Reggie's huge black kimono. A playing card is in his hand. He looks troubled. "He's gone to Drossie's. Can I talk to you?"

Nathan is of a mind to say no, but he says yes.

"Look here." Voynich steps into the kitchen and points to cards laid out on the table. "That's my fortune." He sits down. "Reg told it for me at lunch."

Nathan takes the card from his hand. "And this is you?" he says. It's the king of hearts.

"It belongs right there." Voynich taps the table.

"I know." Nathan lays the card in the vacant space.

"He says it means I'll be the King," Voynich says. "Like Clark Gable. But my name's against me. I gotta change it. He wants it to be Regent—that means king."

"Pro tem." Nathan hides a smile. Regent is Reggie's brand of cigarettes. They come in a flat white box with red trim. And they will knock you on your ass. "Michael Regent?" he says, consideringly. "It's got a nice ring to it." He leans over Voynich's shoulder and touches the circle of cards. "He's right—it's a very promising layout."

Voynich blinks up at him, forehead wrinkled. "You know all this stuff too? Jesus, I'm ignorant."

Nathan sits down. "It's how my mother makes her living—fortune-telling." He gathers up the cards and puts them in their box. "You're only ignorant if you believe it."

Voynich objects. "Reg believes it. And he went to Yale."

"He also believes Mary Baker Eddy discovered the atom."

"Yeah?" Voynich peers. "Didn't she?"

Nathan shakes his head. "It was the ancient Greeks."

"No shit?" Voynich is impressed. "What's the atom?"

"Atoms are the invisible particles of which all matter is made up," Nathan says. "Touch the table. It feels solid to you, doesn't it? But it's not. It's atoms, moving all the time. Whirling around like little solar systems."

"Oh, Christ," Voynich moans. "What's a solar system?"

"The earth and the other planets," Nathan says, "revolving around the sun. Sol. The solar system. See?"

Voynich squints. "How the fuck old are you?"

"Twenty," Nathan says.

"And what college did you go to?"

"None. You don't have to go to college to learn things like that. You just have to want to know things enough to open books and look inside them."

"Yeah? That's what Reg says." He sighs and shakes his head in disgust. "Three books is all it takes." He gets up, goes away, comes back with the tattered dictionary from Reggie's desk, and another book, and plunks them down on the table. He says, "Here's his instructions: 'Open that and start reading at page one, and any word you don't understand, open this and find out what it means. If it's a person, place, or thing, use the encyclopedia—it's in the closet.' "

Nathan picks up the book and turns it over in his hands. "*The Letters of Madame de Sévigné*," he says. "Who the hell is that?"

"Most brilliant woman who ever lived." Voynich takes the book back glumly. "That's what Reg says. French. Seventeenth century." He lays it on the dictionary. "Hell—I don't know what the old broad's talking about."

Nathan privately thinks Reggie, first, is hopeless as a teacher and, second, is backing a loser here, but he says to Voynich cheerfully, "Keep reading. You'll pick it up. That's what Reggie means. He thinks you can master it. He respects you." Nathan claps him on the shoulder. "Don't let him down. Give it a try." He stands up and revisits Reggie's desk to get the paper. "I have to go now. I'm working."

"I oughta be." Voynich comes out of the kitchen. "If my old man knew what I'm doing, he'd die of shame."

"Sleeping with Reggie, you mean?" Nathan says.

Voynich reddens. "A hoor, that's what he'd call me."

"You think he'd be right?" Nathan says.

"He's old country. He don't understand a lot of stuff."

"You're not hurting anybody, are you?" Nathan says. "And you're making Reggie happy."

Voynich looks glum. "You think he can make me a star in pictures, like he says?"

"I think he's trying." Nathan gives him a pro forma smile, steps into the hall, reaches to close the door behind him, but Voynich has hold of it. He says:

"You and Hoyt—you do it because you like it, right? You're queers. Like Reggie."

Nathan stops and looks at him but doesn't answer.

"Well, I don't like it," Voynich says. "I like girls. I've had girls. Back home in Pittsburgh. Lots of girls. I want you to know that. I'm not queer."

"Then your old man would be right," Nathan says, "wouldn't he?"

Voynich glowers. "Reg doesn't give me money."

"Only because he hasn't got it to give," Nathan says. "But I'll bet other men have, haven't they? You know your way around. Handsome young would-be actors don't drop into Drossie's at dinner time looking for girls."

Voynich thrusts out his jaw. "I wasn't looking for no rich old queen."

"And you didn't find one, did you? Treat him kindly, Mike. He's had a lot of bad breaks lately. And he wants the best for you, he really does."

The day after the party in Beverly Hills, he typed up a two-page synopsis of the novel and, though it seemed lame to him, took the pages across to Franklin Street, and down the driveway, and up the stairs to Stanley Page's apartment over the garage, and knocked and pushed the bell button, but no one came to the door, so he folded the pages and put them into the mailbox. Days have passed. Stanley hasn't turned up at the market, and Nathan would like to know what's happening. He crosses Highland again, and starts along Franklin, and halts on the sidewalk, startled. Trash cans from the gray stucco apartments have been set out for collection, and he sees colored paper pushing up out of them, the gaudy covers of scripts he last saw stacked in the Pages' living room. He lifts out the scripts and finds his contract with Craven & Hyde in its blue backing. And here is the manila envelope that holds the carbon copy of his novel—the finished pages. And here are the two pages Stanley promised Mr. Dryrot at the party. Nathan opens the envelope and pushes contract and synopsis inside and closes the flap of the envelope with its little tin brads. Frowning, he walks down the driveway, climbs the stairs, knocks at the door, waits, rings the bell, waits. He steps along the gallery and, putting his face close to the glass, using his hands as blinkers, peers in at a window. The two orange crates stand all alone in the main room. He goes along and peers in the bedroom window. No bed, no chest of drawers, no mirror. No nothing. An open closet door. An open door to a bathroom. He pushes up the window and steps inside. The air is warm from being trapped upstairs. But there's no smell of baby now. No smell of anything at all. The phone sits on the bare floor, disconnected from the wall, its cord wrapped around it. In the kitchen, the refrigerator door stands open, but its little light isn't on, and it doesn't hum. Inside, a withered lettuce leaf lies on a wire shelf. He steps out the window and closes it. Wanting to ask where Stanley and Maud and baby Bill have gone, he tries both doors of the duplex, but no one's home.

Benbow's mother looks like Benbow in a dress. She sounds like Benbow, only her voice is deeper, and she is folksy, which Benbow rarely is. She is also a lot more physical. One night she took exception to George Lafleur having a marine in his room and stormed upstairs to tell him so. He opened the door, stark naked, grabbed the door frame, swung both feet at her, and toppled her backward down the stairs. She scrambled back up there, knocked George out with a single blow to the jaw, and threw the startled marine down the stairs. Tonight she seems in a better mood. She has fixed dinner and with a jovial shout of "Come and get it!" banged a big platter of fragrant pot roast down on the table.

Besides her, George, Hoyt, Nathan, and Benbow—who keeps dropping his fork, spilling wine, rubbing his fingers as if they were numb—there's another diner, a little, fat, old-maidish bald man, with skin like a schoolgirl's—the blushes come and go prettily:

Dr. Marriott, one of Benbow's professors. Busy as he keeps his fork, he finds time to flatter Mrs. Harsch on her cooking and to flirt with Nathan, twinkling his blue eyes, and making moues with his rosebud mouth.

Later, when Nathan—the only volunteer—has finished helping Mrs. Harsch clear the table and wash and put away the dishes, he finds the men in the room with Benbow's tough piano, drinking, smoking, and listening to Benbow's latest favorite recording, *Belshazzar's Feast*. William Walton again. The light is dim, but when Nathan comes in, Marriott hops boyishly up out of his wing chair, twinkling and blushing. "There you are," he flutes over the bombast of the music. "I thought we'd lost you." He takes Nathan's arm and steers him into a shadowy corner where a daybed sags under a faded blue slipcover. "I was about to sew a black band on my sleeve."

"I'm too wicked to die young," Nathan says.

"I do hope so," Marriott says. "Sit down. Let me get you a drink. We must talk."

He bustles off on little-girl feet. Nathan is full of pot roast and homemade peach pie and doesn't want a drink, definitely not the gin and tonic Marriott fetches—the war has put an end to Scotch. But he accepts it and sits holding it while Marriott, a hand on Nathan's thigh, chatters away.

"You know, I'm quite smitten with you," he says. "Have been from the moment weeks ago when Benbow introduced us."

Jesus. Nathan doesn't even remember. But he did get very drunk at Benbow's the second or third time Hoyt brought him here. That must have been the night Marriott means.

"I've never seen anyone in my life so desirable. I can't get you out of my thoughts. I can't get you out of my dreams. Oh, dear, that sounds like a cheap song lyric, doesn't it? Sorry." He sips nervously from his own drink. It glows blue in the semidarkness. "But, of course, I know there's no hope for me." He scowls at Hoyt, who is stretched out on his back on the floor, an arm across his eyes, listening to the music. Marriott play-acts jealous rage. "You are soppy over that handsome hillbilly." He heaves a melodramatic sigh. "How little judgment the young have. Maturity of mind and spirit mean nothing to them. Physical beauty is all."

"It's not a matter of judgment," Nathan says. "It's animal instinct, Darwin and all that—it's about making the best possible babies."

"Not you two," Marriott says.

"We keep trying," Nathan says.

"No doubt," Marriott says, suddenly bleak. "How I wish there were fewer taboos. Imagine a society in which it was perfectly proper for you to invite someone like me to watch. Simply good manners."

"Margaret Mead hasn't written that one up," Nathan says.

"Alas," Marriott says almost tearfully. And then he's bright and bouncy again. He clutches Nathan's arm. "But there's a ray of hope. Benbow tells me your Lone Star friend—what's his rustic name?"

"Hoyt Stubblefield."

Marriott nods. "That he is a gifted artist. And he has painted you—" His voice develops a squeak. Nathan glances at him. His lips quiver. He moistens his lips. He stammers, "—in the—in the—uh—"

"Buck naked," Nathan says. "Yes. It's a good picture."

"I want it," Marriott blurts. "I simply must have it."

"Hoyt made it," Nathan says. "You'll have to ask him."

"He said it's up to you," Marriott says. "Please? Say yes? I'll pay any price. Within reason."

Nathan has no problem with the question. The answer is no. But he doesn't say it. After all, Hoyt did the work and Hoyt can use the money. So instead of answering, Nathan drinks some of the gin and tonic and, aware of Marriott watching him aquiver with anxiety, lights a cigarette, blows out the match, and says with a little smile, "I'll think about it."

Linnet Hinkley, the tall, barefoot teen-age daughter of the landlady at the rooming house where Rick Ames lives, twists up her sibylline face with doubt. "Well, gosh, I don't know." Clutching her Coca-Cola, she gets up from the kitchen table, pads stealthily across the linoleum, opens the door cautiously, and pokes her head into the hallway. She draws it back and whispers, "Today it won't be easy."

"It has to be today," Nathan says.

"But Flora Belle is home today all day." Linnet shuts the door and stands with her back against it. "It'd be easy as pie if she was out."

"Where does she keep the key?" Nathan says.

"In her shoulder bag, with all the other keys." Linnet drops her big, handsome frame onto the kitchen chair again. Loosely. She is a slouchy girl. She leans an elbow on the table, rests her head on her hand. She drinks from the Coke bottle, sets it down, sits back, pushes pins into her hair that are threatening to fall out and let it all come down like a mismanaged haystack. "Except when she goes out and they've got to be here in case of emergency, they're in that bag, a great big old Mexican leather thing. And mostly she sits on that. It's never out of her sight."

"Is there a room for rent?" Nathan says.

"Sure. But you won't like it. It's in the attic, hot as the hinges, and when he's home, Perc plays his records up there—real loud. *Paris, the Song of a Great City.*" She makes a face. "In the tower room. Or he runs his ham radio into the wee small hours—you know, bringing in static from all over the world? And when he does get a voice, ten to one it's speaking Albanian or something."

"I don't have to like the room," Nathan says. "I've already got a place to live. I'll just be taking her away with me so you can—borrow that key."

"Well . . ." Linnet tilts her head at him and gives him a smile. "All right. I guess I want to go riding with you as much as you want to go with me. Let's do it." She opens the door and starts down the hall. "Mama?"

Nathan follows her. "Is there gas in the truck?"

"Of course. Nobody's used it since Perc sailed. Mama?" She gives the sliding doors a rap with her knuckles and parts them. The room is gaudy with serapes and painted tin trays, black backgrounds, flaming flowers. Linnet's enormous mother is heaped in an easy chair, reading the newspaper, sections of it strewn around her feet. A mug of coffee is at her elbow. "This is Nathan Reed, and he's looking for a room."

Flora Belle Short peers at Nathan over her reading glasses. "Haven't I seen you before?"

Nathan swallows. "I—don't think so."

"It's away up at the top of the house." She lays the glasses aside under a table lamp made of a Mexican jug and heaves to her feet. Nathan is six feet tall. She is taller. "I hope you're serious." She pulls a heavy leather bag out of the chair, and Nathan realizes his plan isn't going to work. She says, "I hate climbing stairs."

"Rooms are very hard to find," he says, and nudges Linnet's ankle with his sandal. She looks at him, startled, and he frowns and nods at the bag, and she sees what he means, and holds out her hand.

"Give me the keys and I'll show him. Save your feet."

She digs out the keys but doesn't pass them to Linnet. She says to Nathan, "Have you got a steady job?"

He nods. "T. Smollett Books."

She hands Linnet the keys. "All right. You show him. But don't you talk. You bring him back down here, and he and I will talk." She gives Nathan a wolfish smile.

"What if he doesn't like it?" Linnet says.

"Why wouldn't he like it?" Flora Belle says. "It's all freshly painted."

"I know." Linnet leads Nathan into the hallway. "I painted it, didn't I?"

"Don't forget winter's coming, Mr. Reed," Flora Belle says. "Heat rises, and that makes it very snug in winter."

They climb the stairs.

Flora Belle calls after them, "You'll love the view."

The truck is noisy to begin with, and Nathan makes it worse by mishandling the unfamiliar shift lever and grinding the gears. Backing as fast as he can down the driveway under the porte cochere, he is afraid Flora Belle will come lumbering out and stop them. She looks big enough to do that by just grabbing hold—like Powerful Katrinka in the comic strips. But it doesn't happen. They get away cleanly and roar eastward along Franklin.

"Whee!" Linnet laughs, and hands Nathan a cold bottle of Coke. "I just love riding around free. I get so sick of being shut up in that house sometimes I could scream." She tilts up her Coke bottle and her beautiful throat pumps. She wipes her mouth with the back of her hand and leans forward to look into his face. "It's hot. After we do this errand of yours, could we go to the beach? I wanta ride the roller coaster."

"After you get through riding with me"—Nathan skids to a halt at Cahuenga—"maybe you won't need that."

She laughs. "You're funny. Is it true, what Ricky told me—you're writing a book?"

He has stalled the rattly engine. He shifts into neutral, waggles the lever, toes the starter button. The cylinders don't spark. "I'm trying," he says.

"You should write for Jack Benny," she says.

For a minute, he panics. What if the truck won't start again? Flora Belle could have him arrested for stealing Percy Hinkley's truck. And kidnapping his child bride. He sweats, pushes the starter again, pumps the gas pedal.

"Leave it," Linnet says. "You'll flood it."

She's right. He can smell fumes. He forces himself to sit back, take a swallow of the cold sweet drink, light a cigarette, and smoke it down. He tosses the butt out the window, gulps some more

Coke, draws a deep breath, and tries starting the truck again. It catches, and he swings onto broad, empty Cahuenga, heading south. He asks her:

"Did you really paint that room?"

She laughs again, but there's no joy in it. "That one and all the rest. Paint, wallpaper, electric wiring, plumbing, carpentry, window glass—you just ask. I do it all. Flora Belle's too old for it, so she trained me, then she peddled me to Perc. He'd never have married me if I couldn't keep the place up for him."

Nathan halts for a stoplight at Hollywood Boulevard and glances at her. "I expect he thinks you're beautiful. Is he beautiful? Why did you marry him?"

"Because that's what the two of them wanted," Linnet says. "Nobody asked what I wanted."

The light changes to green, and the pickup clatters across Hollywood Boulevard.

"I don't blame Flora Belle," Linnet says. "She never had a real job. She just managed apartments and like that. So she can't get Social Security. If Percy should turn her out, what would happen to her? I'm her ticket to a safe old age, a roof over her head, a bed to sleep in, food on the table."

"I shouldn't have made you do this today," Nathan says. "It's putting her at risk. I didn't know."

"Even if she finds out, and threatens to tell Perc when he gets home, she won't do it." Linnet drinks off more of her Coke. "If he notices the gas level is down or something, she'll back up whatever lies I tell him. She's not going to let Perc think he got a bad bargain in me. If he ever divorced me, it would be doomsday for her."

"Here's the place," Nathan says, and makes a U-turn.

He has stood it in a corner of the room, a full-length oval pier glass. Hoyt stares at it, walks over to it, touches it, gazes at his shirtless self in it, then turns his eyes to look at Nathan's reflection, who stands behind him. Nathan grins. Hoyt says, "How much did it cost?"

"The price tag said ten dollars," Nathan says, "and I'm so dumb I would have paid it. But Linnet stepped in and argued the old guy down to seven. She's an expert at buying used furniture—learned it at her mother's knee."

"And she helped you carry it up here?"

"It's too heavy for one person, too clumsy."

"This must be some girl," Hoyt says.

"She's got shoulders like Johnny Weissmuller," Nathan says. "She wants you to teach her Spanish."

Hoyt makes a face. "Maybe—if she really was Johnny Weissmuller." He tilts the pier glass, frowning, backs away, squinting at it, crouching, leaning to this side, that side. He goes back and readjusts the tilt.

"Will it be okay?" Nathan says.

"It's perfect." Hoyt kisses him. "You're something strange and wonderful, did you know that?"

"I'm selfish," Nathan says. "I want a painting of you naked in your cowboy hat."

"You mean you don't want Dr. Marriott staring at you naked all alone." Hoyt begins unbuttoning Nathan's shirt. "You want me hanging there beside you on his creepy bedroom wall. Dividing up the chagrin."

"If it comes to that. I'd rather keep both pictures, but you're an artist. You should be paid for your work."

Hoyt licks Nathan's chest. "We're not starving."

"I'm going broke." Nathan unbuttons Hoyt's Levi's.

"Soon as the book's finished, they'll pay you again."

"Maybe." Nathan kneels. "But I'm worried. In the play, people could hear the music." He tugs the Levi's down. "The story's not the same without the music."

John F. Noble wears a tweed jacket today, a sweater, wool trousers, but his brush haircut and steely eyes are the same, and his tough, fatherly air. And these are out of place among the scruffy, jeans-clad customers in the art supply store where Nathan has gone with Hoyt to pick up the canvas the store has stretched for him, and to buy tubes of paint. Hoyt is in a back room talking with a clerk now. Nathan has been wandering around the vast, bright shop, looking at everything, filing it in his memory, in case he wants to describe such a place in a novel someday. He touches the long, clean, yellowish handles of pig bristle brushes laid out in graduated widths side by side. And John F. Noble is standing next to him, saying:

"Maybe I was wrong, and Stubblefield isn't a Communist."

Nathan stares at him. "I never thought he was."

"I only said 'maybe,' " Noble says. "Because his friend George Lafleur sure as hell is—or was till they canned him. Lafleur comes to Stubblefield's place, Stubblefield goes to his. In Silverlake. Often. I know."

"How?" Nathan's skin crawls. He looks to the back of the shop for Hoyt, but there's no sign of him. "It's been months since you came around. I thought you'd given up."

"Senator Skipworth phoned Director Hoover, and orders came down for me to forget Stubblefield, but I can't stop worrying about you. You're a nice, clean-cut kid, but you're still wet behind the ears, and since the Army isn't doing it, somebody's got to keep you out of trouble. Why don't you go home to your parents, Nathan?"

"Because I'm not a child. Leave me alone."

"I have sons, and if you were one of them," Noble says, "I'd be sick about the friends you've fallen in with."

Nathan scowls. "At least I chose them."

"Did you?" Noble says. "Wasn't it the other way around? They chose you, didn't they? Did you ever ask yourself why?"

"I wish you'd get away from me," Nathan says.

Noble nods. "In a minute. But first let me tell you the reason the CPUSA stripped George Lafleur of his party card and threw him out in disgrace at an open meeting."

Nathan turns away. "I don't want to hear it."

Noble grips his arm. "Because he's a homosexual. Do you know what that is? Yes? Well, even the Communists don't want them. And yet Stubblefield is his friend. And you associate with both of them. Nathan, take my advice before it's too late. Get away from those people."

"Nathan?" It's Hoyt calling. Nathan turns to look. Hoyt stands at the faraway door to the back room, a canvas as tall as he is leaning beside him. He wears his leather jacket and waves a fringed arm. Nathan turns to speak to Noble, but Noble has vanished. Nathan goes to help Hoyt.

The news about Noble wants to jump out of Nathan's mouth, but he keeps it back. Once they have walked the clumsy canvas home, he helps Hoyt haul the biggest easel into the living room and brace the canvas on it, and move the pier glass three or four times until it's right, and brings a chair from the kitchen for Hoyt to sit on, because Nathan wants the painting to be of Hoyt sitting on just that kind of chair. Naked. In his cowboy hat. Nathan arranges the pose the way he has seen it in his mind, and Hoyt suggests this alternative and that, until they are both satisfied.

They take beer and glasses into the bedroom and strip and lie down in the heat of the afternoon and drink the beer and do what comes to them to do with each other. And lie smoking and finishing off the beer, which has grown a little warm meantime. And Nathan doesn't mention Noble. He is afraid Hoyt this time will really make him go away—for his own protection.

He sits on the floor, watching Hoyt draw himself in charcoal on the canvas, and swear, and wipe the drawing out with a chamois, and draw it again, and wipe it out, until it's as he wants it. By that time, it is even better than Nathan has been seeing it in his mind's eye. It is because of how this happens, of how so often they think alike, see alike, anticipate each other's thoughts, feelings, desires, that he can't make himself mention Noble.

He is wrong and selfish in this, isn't he? He has no ethical choice but to warn Hoyt, so he can defend himself, hide, run away, send Nathan away, whatever he is moved to do. Nathan is sick with guilt by the time they wander out to the Chinese place down Highland for supper. In the stiff green-painted booth, idly stirring hot mustard and ketchup with a fried shrimp, he says:

"We don't have to stay here."

Hoyt blinks. "But we've got our food."

Nathan shakes his head. "I mean in L.A. We could live in the desert or the mountains. A shack on some beach. Away from everyone. Let's go, Hoyt. Tomorrow."

Chewing chow mein, Hoyt studies Nathan's face till Nathan lowers his gaze. He has no appetite, but for something to do he starts on his egg fu yung. Hoyt pours from a dented metal pot into thick little teacups and says:

"Who was that you were talking to at the art store?"

"Nobody. It was about brushes. Nothing."

"He didn't look like a painter," Hoyt says.

"He said he has sons. Maybe they're art students."

"I can't leave," Hoyt says. "Not now."

"Why not?" Nathan says. "Forget your Communists, Hoyt."

Hoyt says, "I can't. But it isn't that. You're not thinking. Dr. Marriott is waiting for his pictures."

It's very late at night. Screams wake him. And Hoyt. They sit up together. The screams are loud and come from outdoors. Up the hill behind the house. They are hoarse, deeply felt screams. Someone is in awful pain or awful fright. Not a woman. A man. They fall over each other scrambling naked out of bed, finding their jeans in the dark, kicking into them. They run through the turpentine-smelling living room and into the hall, where Reggie Poole's door jerks open. Reggie is flapping into his monster kimono.

"What's the matter? Are you all right?"

"Sounds like somebody's being murdered." The door to the outside stands open. Hoyt bolts out and down the stairs. The shrieking goes on. Nathan runs after Hoyt, and Reggie follows. Hoyt stands under the rubber tree, staring up the steep, brushy slope. Far above, the windows of the top unit of the Highland Hotel are lighted up. And on the balcony, running around, batting at the air, cringing, covering his head with his arms, is Gentleman Jim Hawker. Nathan has known for some time this is Hawker's apartment. He has seen him out there on weekends in shorts and a straw hat, typing.

"My God," Reggie says. "Do you realize who that is?"

"Yes, but what's the matter with him?" Nathan says.

"Looks like delirium tremens," Hoyt says. "He thinks snakes are after him, alligators, the Union army."

"Shouldn't somebody do something?" Nathan says.

"What's going on?" Voynich comes down the stairs in torn boxer shorts, groggy, hair mussed from sleep.

"Doesn't anyone in the hotel hear it?" Nathan says.

Reggie tells him, "Run wake up the manager."

But it's too late. Shrieking and gibbering, Hawker clambers frantically onto the wall of the balcony, stands there, teetering, kicking with one foot at unseen attackers, loses his balance, and falls. They hear the thud of his body hitting the slope. They hear the crackle of brush as he rolls down the slope. There is no more screaming. Nathan claws his way up the cutbank to the level place where he and Hoyt sometimes sunburn themselves, and begins climbing the hillside in the dark. He hears Hoyt behind him. And Voynich, who says, "Reggie's getting a flashlight."

"You go left," Hoyt says. "Nathan, you go right."

They call out to one another. But none of them finds Hawker.

Then Reggie arrives. Not by climbing the cutbank; he has used the rickety footbridge that crosses from Hoyt and Nathan's kitchen. Reggie comes tramping through the chaparral in heavy wooden shower clogs. "What do you think you're doing?" he says crossly. "Here he is, right here." And sure enough, Hawker lies on his face at Reggie's feet. The flashlight shows his shirt and trousers are torn by the brush. The boys crowd around. Reggie bends and rolls the small, ragged figure over. Hawker's eyes are closed. He is scratched and bleeding. And he looks terribly pale.

"Jesus." Voynich crosses himself. "Is he dead?"

"I've told you"—Reggie kneels—"there is no death." He is a devout Christian Scientist. He once trained to be a practitioner, but never worked at it. He hands the flashlight to Hoyt. "Hold that steady, please."

"Nathan, go call an ambulance," Hoyt says. He means at the pay telephone across the street beside the market.

"No, no," Reggie says sharply. In the flashlight's glow, he is carefully checking out Hawker's unconscious form. "Don't you realize this is a very famous man? One of the greatest writers in the English language?"

"Is that the reason he can't have an ambulance?"

"I'll explain later. Please be quiet." Reggie continues his examination. He straightens, blowing out a deep breath of relief. "Nothing is broken. Breathing and heartbeat are normal. No evidence of internal bleeding. No concussion." He pushes heavily to his feet. "He'll be all right when he's slept for a while." He takes the flashlight from Hoyt. "You have a couch. Just put him on it and cover him with a blanket. Don't stare like an idiot. I tell you, he's perfectly all right."

Hoyt looks up at the balcony. "It's a long fall, Reg."

"When you're as drunk as he is," Reg says, "things that would kill a sober man have no effect at all." He turns away. "Come along, pick him up and carry him gently."

Hoyt and Voynich do this. Nathan trails after them. Reggie

holds the flashlight behind him so they can see their footing. Hoyt asks, "You were going to explain."

"Ambulances draw reporters. Picture tomorrow's headlines. 'World-renowned Author James Hawker Hospitalized in Fall. Pulitzer Prize Winner Disgusting, Self-Destructive Sot.' Do you want to ruin him?"

"Okay, okay," Hoyt says. "I see your point."

"Then again," Nathan says, "what if he dies?"

Reggie steps onto the creaky bridge. He plays the circle of yellow from the flashlight on the splintery planks. "Didn't you hear me?" he says. "There is no death. Now, come along. We all need coffee."

He brews it in Hoyt and Nathan's kitchen and they sit around the table drinking it, smoking, and talking softly while Gentleman Jim Hawker snores in the living room. Later, the snoring stops, and Nathan gets up to go look at him, sure he'll find him dead. There's no light, so he bends close, and Hawker startles him by opening his eyes. "Young Reed? Is that you? Unforgivably drunk. I do apologize. Your place, is it? I am deeply grateful." His eyes close. Nathan turns away. Hawker plucks his sleeve. "One more favor—please don't tell Jack Warner." He begins to snore again.

Once a month Hoyt uses the typewriter—to write home to Amarillo, thanking his family for the check. The check came yesterday. And when Nathan sits down this morning to work on his novel, here lies a letter beside the machine—the letter that must have come with the check. He doesn't read other people's mail. Frank and Alma didn't raise him that way. He picks up the letter to take it to Hoyt, who is painting in the living room. But he pauses. The letter is on cheap ruled pulp paper, at a guess from an Indian Chief tablet, price five cents. It's in pencil, and the handwriting is childlike. Hoyt's people are well off. Oil. Cattle. Big showy house. Mexican servants. He frowns and without meaning to reads the first words of the letter.

*Dear Son Dwayne, Thank you for the money. You are such a
good boy. I don't know what would happen to us without you
sent them two hundred dollars ever month—*

Nathan feels dizzy, and sits down again. He looks at the end of
the letter. It is signed *Mama.* Hoyt has been lying to him. He
doesn't get money from home. He sends money home. But what
money? Where does he get it? Nathan folds the letter, steps into
the bedroom, tucks the letter into the drawer where Hoyt keeps
his underwear.

Hoyt calls, "You're very quiet. Everything okay?"

"I don't know," Nathan says, "probably not."

Benbow's hands are thickly bandaged. "I tore the finger ligaments,"
he shouts. He has to shout because the Black Cat is a noisy place.
The jukebox plays, and the crowd of men at the bar, at the tables,
standing against the walls, laughs and shouts and whoops and
whinnies without ceasing. Benbow has a table in a corner with a
willowy, light-skinned Negro youth and a stocky, pug-nosed sailor
in whites. They all have glasses of beer. Benbow tells Nathan, "It
was a mistake about the piano. I'm having the action changed back
to normal—if you'll forgive the expression."

"Good—now maybe I can play it sometimes," Nathan says.

"As often as you wish," Benbow says. "The nerve damage
looks irreversible. The doctors doubt I'll ever play again."

Nathan is appalled. "You're not serious."

"I ought to have checked with a teacher before I did it,"
Benbow says. "A coach, an expert. I ought to have stopped prac-
ticing when the pain began. Instead, I worked even harder. Pushed
it from four to six hours a day." Made clumsy by the bandages, he
carefully picks up the glass and swallows some beer. "I have only
myself to blame."

The willowy Negro pouts. "If you're going to talk as if I wasn't
even here, I guess I'll go someplace I'm wanted." He stands up.

Benbow catches his wrist, says something to him Nathan can't hear because of the racket. The Negro laughs, but he walks off anyway. Lurches off. One leg is shorter than the other. He vanishes into the crowd.

The sailor says, "I thought they all loved music."

"You haven't got a beer," Benbow says to Nathan. "Let me get you a beer." And he goes to do that, joking his way through the crowd, waving his bandaged hands in a flurry of mock agitation, like Alice's White Rabbit.

"Everybody seems to know him," the sailor says.

"He lives near here," Nathan says.

"Do you? I'd like to go to your place. This place"—he looks around—"is too fucking noisy."

"I live in Hollywood," Nathan says.

"An actor," the sailor says. "I figured that. Did I ever see you in anything?"

"I'm a writer," Nathan says. "Nobody ever sees them."

"I been at sea a long time," the sailor says. "I'm really horny. Could we go to your place now?"

Before Nathan has to answer, Benbow comes back clutching three glasses of beer to his chest with his forearms. "Help me with these," he says, and they do, and he sits down.

"Thank you," Nathan says, lifts his glass to Benbow, and drinks some of the beer. Hoyt made chili for supper; Nathan is thirsty, and the beer tastes good.

Benbow returns his salute and quaffs some of his own beer. "What brings you here alone?"

"Hoyt's at a meeting," Nathan says. "I have to talk to you about something." He glances at the sailor, but a bony man with stringy hennaed hair has stopped behind the sailor's chair and is whispering in the sailor's ear. Nathan says to Benbow, "I'm sorry. You're here for a good time. But I need advice."

"Not to the lovelorn, I hope," Benbow says.

Nathan shakes his head. "It's about money. And lies."

Benbow smiles. "How often they go together." He drinks off his beer, sets down the glass, and stands. "Shall we amble slowly homeward?"

"You sure you don't mind?"

With a hurried wave of the hand, the sailor goes off with the hennaed man. Benbow glances around the place. "It's too early anyway. At this hour nobody's ready to get serious. But George is off with half a dozen large servicemen in a tiny automobile, bound for parts unknown—private, no doubt—so I thought I'd look in here for a minute, just in case. And unless you plan to spend the night locked naked in my arms, I'll come back at the witching hour."

"I won't keep you late," Nathan says. "The last streetcar's at ten-forty."

They climb the steep street slowly. The uproar from the bar fades. The sound of passing cars on Sunset turns to a low, steady hum. From the yards of the houses they pass, crickets chirp. The night is cooler than Nathan expected. He shivers in his thin shirt. And tells Benbow about the letter. And why it perplexes him.

"Where does he get the three hundred dollars?"

"Nathan, how would I know?" In a circle of yellow cast by a street lamp, Benbow turns to blink at the boy. "Why don't you ask him?"

Nathan shakes his head. "If he wanted me to know, he'd have told me—he wouldn't have lied."

"This isn't the first time he's lied to you." Benbow halts for a minute and studies Nathan. "Maybe he doesn't deserve your love."

"Maybe not." Nathan moves on. "But he's got it. He tried to send me away when Noble came around—the FBI man. He said Hoyt was bad news. And Hoyt agreed, but I didn't go. He's everything to me, Benbow. I'd die without him. I don't know how you and George can be so—can go with other people. Hell, if Hoyt did that to me, I'd kill myself."

"Not him?" Benbow grins. "Nathan, you'll look back on this someday and seriously question your sanity."

Nathan says, "Could be. But I don't know how to change what I feel." He kicks a dry twig off the walk. "Did I tell you Noble turned up again? They took him off Hoyt's case, but he's been following me." Benbow is a step behind him. Nathan looks back. "He worries about me, wants me to go home to my parents. As if I were ten years old."

"There's less difference than you think between ten and twenty," Benbow says. "Let's go up here and sit." He nods at a yard with a walk that leads only to front steps and a foundation—the house is gone. The yard is weedy, brushy, with a couple of shaggy trees. They go sit on the steps. Benbow's hands rest on his knees, the bandages very white in the darkness. He says, "The best advice doesn't always come from our friends, Nathan."

"I think it will tonight," Nathan says. "You stopped Noble chasing Hoyt. Your brother-in-law did."

"If you say so," Benbow says.

"Noble said so," Nathan says.

Benbow shrugs. "You came to me for help—I helped."

"You knew what Hoyt was doing that got the FBI after him," Nathan says. "They had it wrong, didn't they? And you straightened them out. What is he doing, Benbow? What's he getting paid three hundred dollars a month for?"

Benbow says, "I've stopped smoking, but I'd like to smoke now. Aren't those cigarettes in your breast pocket?"

Nathan takes out the pack and they light up. The smoke blows away on the cool night breeze.

"Take Noble's advice," Benbow says, "and go home."

"Clear to Minneapolis?" Nathan says.

"Clear to Papeete, if possible," Benbow says.

"Who is Hoyt working for?" Nathan says.

Benbow sits silent for a moment, then draws a deep breath

and says, "First, let's be clear on this—I do not know. But since what he is doing means telling no one, not even you, and worrying that staying with him is putting you in jeopardy, my guess is it's both important and dangerous." Nathan only stares at him. Benbow sighs impatiently. "All right. Answer me this: what reason did Hoyt give you for not being in the armed services?"

"I never asked him. It's none of my business. What is the reason, Benbow?"

"If he wouldn't tell you, would he tell me?" Benbow says. "But I've often asked myself—why isn't he stationed at some dusty fort in Texas, drawing military maps, or designing camouflage nets, or humbly painting barracks?"

"What is he doing, Benbow? You suggesting it's the Army that's paying him three hundred a month, the Navy, Marines, Coast Guard, Air Force? To do what?"

"I admit it sounds farfetched," Benbow says, "but since he is of sound mind and body, and somehow Uncle Sam hasn't scooped him up, and the Communists are the enemy within—"

"Oh, shit," Nathan says, and throws away his cigarette. "Do you expect me to believe Hoyt Stubblefield of all people is a—a—spy? Come on, Benbow."

"Did you read that book of Gide's I lent him?" Benbow tosses away his cigarette, gets to his feet, brushes the seat of his trousers with his bandaged hands. *"Lafcadio's Adventures?"*

"No." Nathan rises too. The cement step is cold and has left his butt cold. He's cold all over. He was stupid not to have worn a sweater. He was stupid to have come at all. Benbow is playing with him, just as Hoyt warned him he would. He asks grumpily, "Should I?"

"I think so." Benbow starts down the broken strip of cement that leads to the street. "At least one sentence will appeal to you: 'The simplest course for the simpleminded is to draw the line at the things they know.' "

"Maybe, but it sounds dangerous," Nathan says.

Benbow stops on the walk, turns sharply back, and says gravely, "Oh, it is, Nathan. It is."

Nathan slices up a brown paper grocery sack with a butcher knife, flattens it out, lays on it the pages of his novel written since he got the contract, folds the paper around them neatly, licks the glue on the curly brown tape he's swiped from Reggie's desk, and tapes the package shut. He's typed a gummed label, and he licks this now and sticks it on. To get rid of the glue taste, he drinks a mug of coffee and smokes a couple of cigarettes with Hoyt, then sets off in his sandals for the post office down Highland, across from the Chinese restaurant. The morning is gloomy; there's a cold, fitful wind, black clouds sit low to the south. Three or four people wait in line, and by the time the gray little man with the green celluloid eyeshade at the barred window has weighed Nathan's parcel, and Nathan has shelled out for the stamps, raindrops are pattering against the post-office plate glass. He pulls the heavy glass door, steps out into the rain, and here comes Rick Ames in an old mackintosh, splay feet in shredded tennis shoes slapping puddles on the sidewalk. He is carrying three manila envelopes.

"Ah am told," he says, "that you have struck up a romance with the barefoot babe."

"Babe?" Nathan says.

"That's what Percy calls her," Ames says.

"It's not a romance," Nathan laughs. "She has a truck, and I happened to need a truck." He explains why.

"She told me all about it," Ames says, "and I respect the urgencies of art—but I can tell you without fear of contradiction that she has fallen in lust with you, and if you value my advice, from now on you will avoid that concupiscent child at any cost."

"And her truck?" Nathan says. "I was planning—"

"Percy Hinkley's truck," Ames says. "He'll be furious if he

finds out she let a good-looking young man use it once, let alone twice."

"Is he big?" Nathan asks. "Is he tough?"

"He is tall, skeletal, and asthmatic," Ames says. "But he is likely to do cruel things to Flora Belle Short in order to punish Linnet for consorting with you."

"She wants Hoyt to teach her Spanish," Nathan says.

Ames blanches. "Don't you let her near him—not unless you want to see your relationship in fragments at your feet."

Nathan smiles. "She's just a lonesome sixteen-year-old girl with too much time on her hands." Ames's envelopes are growing very damp. Nathan touches them. "You mailing off some manuscripts?"

"Ah have simply got to get some money somehow."

"Stories?" Nathan says.

"Articles," Ames says. "On Thornton Wilder, Somerset Maugham, Graham Greene." He rolls the envelopes and pushes them into a pocket. "Ah once wrote for them all, *Scribners, The Atlantic, Harper's*. It's been years. Ah want them to remember me now."

A champagne-sodden Rick told him about these articles that crazy day they celebrated the optioning of Nathan's book at his place. The articles were written long ago, and rejected. He probably tried all those magazines with them then. But Nathan only says, "I'm sure they will. How's Tony?"

Ames looks bleak. "That's what I need money for. Those legs of his. Those abscessed varicose veins. There's no keeping up with them, not as long as he's on his feet all day every day. Now he's begun developing infections."

"I'm sorry," Nathan says. "Can't he get time off?"

"He's used his sick leave up for the year," Ames says. "They'll let him rest on his own money, of course. But he hasn't anything saved. How could he? It all goes to those quacks that do nothing for him but cluck over how much more grisly his legs look this week than last week, and bandage them up again."

The rain has flattened Nathan's hair. He paws it off his forehead, out of his eyes. "I'm sorry. I hope the editors buy those articles."

"It's horrible"—Ames paddles off—"what life can do to a pusson." He pushes into the post office, and Nathan heads at a jog for home.

In the Suzie-Q, Erroll Garner is playing a big piano on a drum-shaped platform striped with iridescent glitter. It is late, and, rain or no rain, the narrow room is packed. Nathan and Hoyt's table is right up against the platform. Garner sits directly above them. He works hard at his art, sweats like a prizefighter, flings his grinning head back while he plays, bows it over the keys, wags it from side to side, and Nathan and Hoyt get showers of sweat. Garner has big hands and big ideas and does his astonishing best to turn the piano into a symphony orchestra. He is pumping up an Ellington number, "Satin Doll," and grunting with delight as the music crashes out of the Steinway and ricochets off the walls. Nathan and Hoyt have hardly any money, but they have come here to celebrate. Hoyt has finished his picture.

At first, Nathan sometimes abandoned his typewriter for days at a stretch to sit on the floor, lie on the floor, lean against the wall, sit on the windowsill, and watch Hoyt work. But then one day Hoyt looked at him as if he were a bug and said, "Nathan, go away."

"Why? I'm being quiet. I'm not bothering you."

"If you see every move I make, where's the magic? Time it's finished, I won't have any secrets left—"

Nathan had to laugh at that. Hoyt didn't notice.

"—and you'll be bored. Anyway, you've got your own work to do. It's more important than this."

"I don't think so. What makes you say that?"

"I haven't sold a painting. You've sold a book. Aren't they waiting for it in New York?"

Nathan gave a skeptical laugh. "I doubt it. It's been two weeks now since I sent them those middle chapters, and they haven't written. They don't know what to say, do they? Nobody likes to admit making a lousy bet."

"Come on," Hoyt said. "It's wonderful. It's funny and sad and very grammatical."

"You say the sweetest things," Nathan said.

"Well, it is," Hoyt said. And grinned. And kissed him.

After that, when he wasn't working on it, Hoyt kept the picture covered with an old bedsheet, and Nathan worked on his book, drudged at it without joy—waiting for the letter, angry at the editor for not writing, and fearful every time he checked the mailbox that the letter would be there. And then, this cold, gloomy, rainy afternoon when Nathan was ready to throw out every word he'd written so far, Hoyt, smoking a cigarette the way you smoke to reward yourself after working hard, a black smudge across his forehead as a badge of working hard, came in his painty old, raveled old sweater, leaned in the workroom doorway, and said:

"All right. You can see it now."

Erroll Garner is staging a one-man riot with "Blues in the Night." He plays as if he had four hands.

Nathan got up numbly from the typewriter and followed Hoyt into the living room. And there the picture was. Finished. Hoyt had done to it what he'd done to Nathan's picture: streaked it with lamp black so you had to stare for a minute before the image and the colors came through to you. But they were the image and colors Nathan had hoped for.

"It's better than the one of me," he said.

"I learned things, doing that one," Hoyt said.

Nathan stood silent. The picture flooded him with love for Hoyt. And pity. The painted Hoyt, sitting on that lean hard chair, with his lean hard legs innocently spread, paintbrush in his hand, cowboy hat on the back of his head, lean hard body straining a little forward, studying his model, was terribly real in his concentration, and terribly lonely. His model was of course himself in the oval pier glass. But if the two pictures were hung together, the viewer would believe Hoyt had painted himself in the act of painting Nathan. Not lonely. An act of love.

Hoyt wiped tears from Nathan's face. His fingers smelled of turpentine. "What's wrong?"

"It's very personal. I don't want Dr. Marriott to have it. I want it. I want to sit and jack off in front of it for the rest of my life. To hell with writing."

"The sooner we get it out of here," Hoyt said, "the better. Tell what's-her-name we need that truck tomorrow."

Erroll Garner whomps the keyboard above their heads. "Caravan" turns into a locomotive. Hoyt and Nathan's glasses are empty, and so are their pockets. They stand, throw smiles and salutes up to Garner, and push out of the Suzie-Q into the rain.

On the deserted Boulevard, Hoyt pauses and turns his face up to the rain. "Wash off the nigger sweat," he says.

"It's the same as anybody else's," Nathan says.

Hoyt takes his arm to walk on. "I only like yours."

"They're naked," Linnet Hinkley gasps. Nathan didn't intend for her to come with him, but she climbed into the truck without being invited, and now stands openmouthed, Coke bottle in hand, gaping at the pictures. Hoyt hasn't had time yet to cover them. He's only laid sections of newspaper out on the floor and taped these together. Now, in a state of shock, he tries to rush covering the pictures, and the floppy, cumbersome sheets keep slithering out of his grip. She says to Nathan, "I mean, you can see everything." Her handsome cheekbones flush. She turns to Hoyt in amazement. "Can you do that?"

Hoyt shrugs. "I did it, didn't I?"

"But I mean," she says, "isn't it against the law?"

"Probably. There's a law against just about everything enjoyable." He smiles. "Haven't you noticed that?"

"Not if you're married," she says.

Hoyt laughs, and manages to get a scrap of tape fastened to the stretcher of the picture at the top and thus hide shocking Nathan in his ribbon bows from view. He bends and rips lengths of tape off a roll and fastens sides and bottom, then jerks his head at Nathan, who goes and takes the picture and moves it out into the hall, and down the stairs, where he slides it carefully into the bed of the truck.

"*Cómo esta usted?*" Hoyt is saying, while he covers his own image with a patchwork of newspapers. He looks at Linnet with raised brows.

"*Muy bien, gracias,*" she says.

"See how simple it is?" Hoyt says.

"I'm going to enjoy learning it from you," she says. "I'll help you carry that down." She steps across the room and takes one side of the stretcher. "Nathan says somebody's going to pay you for these. Who?" She and Hoyt carry the picture out. "Some fat old pervert like Ricky Ames?"

"You want them?" Hoyt says. "You can have them."

"You're kidding." She turns and starts down the stairs. "Perc would kill me." Nathan follows them, watches them lay the canvas in on top of the other one. The breeze is cold. He looks up. The sky is darkening. It's going to rain again. They'd better hurry. He climbs into the truck, wondering in despair if Linnet means to go to Dr. Marriott's with them. What will she do with her mouth when she meets him? But she doesn't try to get in. She goes around to Hoyt's side and smiles up at him as he slams the door.

"They're very good pictures," she says. "I mean, I can't draw a straight line. But—you painted them for money, didn't you? You didn't paint them for you and Nathan?"

"How could I?" Hoyt grins at her and starts the engine. "We're not married."

The street in Westwood near the university is curved and tree-lined. Benbow stands on a corner, holding a briefcase above his head to keep off the drizzle. With a hand not bandaged anymore but gloved, he waves at the truck. Hoyt stops. Benbow hustles into the street. Nathan rolls down his window. Benbow says, "Go back."

"What's wrong?" Nathan says.

"There's been a change of plans. You really should get a phone. I rang the woman downstairs at your house, but she refused to take the message."

"She got sore at me," Hoyt says, "when Nathan moved in. She figures now she'll never get me into bed."

"We can't go back, Benbow," Nathan says. "It's too hard to borrow this truck."

"It's now or never," Hoyt says, and guns the engine. "Get in out of the rain. Place should be in this block."

"It's in this block." Benbow opens the door, Nathan slides over, Benbow gets in and slams the door. "That's not the point. The point is, Dr. Marriott has a house guest."

"Who hates art?" Hoyt rolls the truck along slowly.

"He'd probably love it, but Marriott's afraid having nude portraits of you two hanging up will queer his pitch."

Hoyt barks a laugh. "You mean he's got a new nephew?"

Benbow nods and sighs. "And he's infatuated, as always. And the nephew is very much present this morning."

Hoyt stops in the middle of the empty street and peers through the rain at Marriott's white stucco house behind its iron-gated patio. "We can truck them up the driveway and right into the garage. You go in and get the garage key, and tell Marriott to keep the kid's face in a pillow for five minutes. We'll stand the pictures in the garage and clear off. And later, when the kid gets tired of the nephew game and leaves, Marriott can drag them in and hang them up."

Nathan feels a spark of hope. "Or doesn't he want them anymore?"

"He's dying for them." Benbow digs into his briefcase and pulls out an envelope. "Here's his check. But he wanted you to keep them till he sends for them."

Hoyt shakes his head. "They're too stimulating for young Nathan. He'll never get any writing done."

"I haven't seen the one of you," Benbow says.

"It's glorious," Nathan says. The envelope is in his hands, but he doesn't want to open it. "I wouldn't part with it, not for any money, only we're broke."

Hoyt says, "Benbow, are you going?"

"Well"—Benbow pushes the creaky latch of the truck door —"if you insist." He climbs down. "But it seems plotty to me." He slams the door. "What if something goes wrong?"

"I kind of hope it does," Hoyt says. "We could use a laugh on a day like this."

Frank writes:

A man called John F. Noble has sent me a letter from your neck of the woods. He doesn't explain what business it is of his, but he advises me to bring you home here. He says you are keeping bad company and could get into serious trouble. The letter is on FBI stationery, and he styles himself an "agent," so I am naturally a little bit curious. People in his game have never struck me as high types—nosing into other people's business seems a shady way to earn your board and keep. On the other hand, I can't help wondering what brought you to his attention. Just who are these friends you've taken up with? I know you're older now, but back there in Fair Oaks you ran with some types I didn't esteem. I hope you're not going to make a habit of it.

I know you're more intelligent than most people, and finding anybody stimulating to associate with is harder for you than for us ordinary mortals, but keep a level head and don't mistake off-kilter for interesting. Write and explain about Noble, will you please? I'm uneasy. I haven't told your mother. She is fine, and clients are plentiful, as fools always will be. She pretends she doesn't, but I know she misses you. However, she still wants an apology about that seance you wrecked. Work yourself up to it, will you? I'd love having you back here. If you want to come, just say so. I'll play a few extra funerals and buy you a train ticket. Hope the writing goes well. Your aunt Marie sends love.

Hoyt reads the letter over his bowl of curried lentils. And laughs, blowing soda cracker crumbs around. He hands the letter back to Nathan, shaking his head. "Isn't this the man who kept an attic full of old musical instruments and used to go up there and fool around with them all day when he was supposed to be out looking for a job?"

"That's Frank." Nathan tucks the letter away.

"And your mother? The fortune-teller?"

Nathan frowns. "They're all right, Hoyt. Don't make fun of them. They love me, I love them."

"And that's fine, Nathan, but they're not exactly Mr. and Mrs. Normal from Everyday, Iowa, are they?"

Nathan's mouth is full. He shakes his head, swallows. "For one thing—they read too many books."

"Yet here he is warning you against unconventional friends. What kind of friends did he expect you'd pick?"

"Yeah. I see what you mean." Nathan gulps some milk and gives a rueful smile. "It is funny."

"People are not too self-aware," Hoyt says. "Especially when they're handing out advice."

"How do I answer him? It's bad enough letting him think I'm straight. I don't want to lie to him about everything."

"Tell him about that fancy Beverly Hills party and all the important movie people you met. Charles Laidlaw. That'll impress him." Hoyt shovels down some more of his supper. "He's a reader. Tell him James Hawker is your neighbor. Dropped in just the other night."

Nathan laughs, then turns glum. "Same as lying."

"Well, what's the matter with Benbow? Associate professor of philosophy at UCLA—what could be more respectable than that? You don't have to mention George."

"I won't, but Noble might." Nathan takes a scared breath and tells Hoyt of his encounter with Noble in the art shop. "He could write to Frank next time that my friends are worse than Communists—they're homosexuals."

Hoyt shakes his head. "It's the last thing he'll mention." Nathan looks bewildered, and Hoyt says, "Don't you see—mooning around after you, all big-brotherly concern, whispering warnings in your ear." Hoyt snorts derision, shakes his head. "He's trying to get you into bed, Nathan."

"I don't believe it. Noble?"

"Even FBI agents have sex lives." Hoyt makes a clatter with his spoon, scraping the last traces of curried lentils out of his bowl. "On vacations, J. Edgar rents a whole floor of the old Hotel Del Coronado down the coast, beautiful boys running in and out day and night. It's common gossip."

Nathan rinses the bowls at the sink, lays them in the rack to dry, comes back to the table. Hoyt is smoking. Nathan takes the cigarette pack, lights up, looks hard at Hoyt. "And Noble never thought you were a Communist? He just told me that, hoping I'd run scared into his arms?"

"It adds up," Hoyt says.

"Not with writing to my father to order me home. Hoyt, you

agreed with what he said—you're dangerous to me. Hell, you tried to get me to leave you that day. Have you forgotten? I haven't. Hoyt, why do you lie to me so much?"

"I told you—to keep you out of trouble, if I can."

"But about your family. They're not rich, they're poor. You said they send you money every month. They don't. You send them money."

Hoyt stares. "Who told you that?"

"No one, but it's true, isn't it?"

"My old man can't work. He's got cancer."

"But why not tell me so?"

Hoyt says, "Halloween's coming. There's going to be a costume ball at the Black Cat. Benbow got us invitations."

"I can't dance," Nathan says. "I never learned how."

"That's because it involved girls. At the Black Cat there won't be any girls. You'll learn to dance in no time."

"Where does the three hundred a month come from, Hoyt?"

"The reason I made up a lie was to keep you from asking that. You don't want to know." Hoyt puts out his cigarette. "What do you think you'll wear?"

"To the Black Cat?" Nathan says. "A diving suit."

" 'Is this a dagger that I see before me?' " Mike Voynich stands in a tense half-crouch in the middle of Reggie Poole's lamplit living room and holds up a square, workman's hand as if to fend off the vision. " 'The handle to my hand. Come' "—he lunges—" 'let me clutch thee' "—he grabs for the dagger of Macbeth's sick imagining, and misses. He gapes at his empty hand, astonished. " 'I have thee not' "—he pops his eyes at the empty air—" 'and yet I see thee still.' " He narrows his eyes, scowls. " 'And on thy blade and dudgeon gouts of' "—he gulps, and hoarsely breathes the word—" 'blood, which was not so before. . . .' " It's a corny reading, but at least he doesn't sound like a steelworker delivering it. He doesn't sound like Maurice Evans either, but Reggie has dragged him a step in that direction. After it's over, and Voynich stands breathing heavily for a minute, golden head drooping, fists clenched at his sides, Nathan and Hoyt applaud and shout "Bravo!" Then the four of them sit around drinking Reggie's thirty-nine-cent tokay and eating Oreo cookies, and Reggie tells them his exciting plan. Judith Anderson is doing a play in Santa Barbara. Reggie knows her, worked on dialog on the set of some RKO thriller she was in—and next week he's going to buy two bus tickets north, and after the performance take Voynich backstage and have him recite for her. He beams at Voynich. " 'And the rest is history.' "

In their dark bed, Nathan murmurs in Hoyt's ear, "I thought that quotation was 'The rest is silence.' "

"If it wasn't," Hoyt says, "it will be."

"Okay, the glue is dry." It's nine at night. Hoyt comes out of the bathroom, waving a pair of jock straps, one glittering with gold sequins, the other with silver. "Time to get ready. Benbow will be here at ten. And there's a lot to do. Go on, baby—put it on."

Mutely Nathan undresses and, shivering in the night chill, puts on the gold one. "It's stiff. It'll rub me raw."

"Here. Stuff in some Kleenex."

Hoyt has cut stencils, and now he uses these to paint gold and silver stars and planets all over Nathan—face, neck, shoulders, arms, chest, belly, back, legs. Saturn on his navel. And the moon on one buttock and the sun on the other. He paints faces on the sun and the moon. Looking over his shoulder at the pier glass, even in the murky lamplight, Nathan can see the sun and moon winking lasciviously.

"Okay, my turn," Hoyt says, and drops his clothes.

There is a diversion, but finally Nathan takes the stencils and, carefully following Hoyt's instructions, with shaky fingers paints large and small stars and planets all over Hoyt. He does a passable job even with the tricky faces of the sun and the moon. Hoyt has cut helmets out of cardboard and gilded them. Each has a star on top. They put these on and stand together in front of the pier glass admiring themselves and each other, but it's cold.

"We'll freeze to death," Nathan says.

"Wait," Hoyt says, and goes away, and comes back with a silver domino and a gold domino. He puts the gold one on Nathan and the silver one on himself and they stand looking at each other again in the glass, side by side. "No one will be able to tell us apart. Do you know which one is you and which one is me? I don't."

Nathan says, "The one that's me is getting a hard-on. Hoyt, it's too sexy. We'll be raped."

"Not by anybody that knows mythology. Castor and Pollux were prizefighters, champions." Hoyt snaps his fingers. "The slippers. I almost forgot the slippers." He goes off and comes back with them, flimsy satin things, gold, silver. He crouches and puts Nathan's on for him. He balances on this leg, that leg, and puts his own on. "Those are magic." He kisses Nathan lightly. "In case you don't want to fight, they'll fly you away like the wind." Peering down, he touches his stars and planets. "Good. They're dry."

"We can't go on the street like this," Nathan says.

"After our Spanish lesson, I imposed on Linnet for a loan." Hoyt goes away again and comes back carrying a raincoat and a wool topcoat. "Property of Percy Hinkley. Away at sea." Hoyt drapes the warmer coat over Nathan's shoulders. "What he doesn't know can't hurt him."

"I hope Flora Belle didn't see you," Nathan says.

"She sees all." Hoyt flaps into the raincoat. "But she'll never be able to tell old Perc the best part of the story." He buttons up the coat, extinguishing the stars. "She won't be at the Black Cat."

"Too bad." Nathan shrugs into his coat and buttons it up. The sleeves are too long. "She'd fit right in."

Hoyt shakes his head. "Mother and daughter are going to a horror movie."

"Sweets to the sweet," Nathan says.

And outside, Benbow honks his horn.

About fifteen minutes out Sunset, it starts to rain again. Benbow, in the shining breastplate of a centurion, reaches a muscular arm to switch on the windshield wiper.

"Our helmets will melt," Hoyt says.

"I'll let you out at the door," Benbow says, "before I park the car. If there's any place to park the car."

"Nothing you're wearing will melt," Nathan says.

"My cuirass could rust," Benbow says. He glances at them again in the rearview mirror. "The Heavenly Twins. One was mortal, did you know that? Castor. He was killed in a fight, and Pollux mourned him so, he asked his father, Zeus, to let him die too."

"They were lovers," Hoyt says.

"But"—Benbow fakes shock—"that would be incest."

"Not with twins. They're the same person. Worst you could call it is masturbation. I'm serious. It happens all the time with twins. Read your Krafft-Ebing."

"Did Pollux get his wish?" Nathan asks.

"No." Benbow rolls the car to a cautious stop on the wet paving for a red light. "Instead, Zeus arranged for him to spend alternate days with the gods in heaven and with his brother in hell." The light turns green. Benbow drives across the intersection. "Which of you is the immortal?"

Nathan says, "We can't tell each other apart."

"Except for your voices," Benbow says, "neither can I. No matter. Eventually Pollux grew bored with commuting and asked Zeus to turn him and his brother into stars. So they both ended up immortal—the morning and evening stars. That's why you chose gold and silver, gold for the sun, silver for the moon—*n'est-ce pas?*"

"Boy howdy"—Hoyt dusts off his Texas drawl—"ain't it awe-inspiring to spend tam with educated people?"

"I think I'd get tired of being immortal," Nathan says.

"You may be spared," Benbow says. "Most of us are."

The Black Cat is crowded, noisy, smoky, dark. All present are busy dancing, drinking, smoking, gossiping, joking, prowling, showing off their costumes. But there is a pause, a gasp, a buzz of comment, a nervous giggle, an "ooh" and an "ah" when Nathan and Hoyt— they have left Percy Hinkley's coats in Benbow's car—push open the door and enter on a gust of damp wind. They smile and bow, and in a minute, the noise level is back up to unbearable, and only a few celebrants are still staring with their mouths hanging open.

Hoyt takes Nathan's elbow and they push into the crowd. Swags of black and orange crepe paper hang from the ceiling. Jack-o'-lanterns leer from the back bar. Sheaves of dry corn stalks lean in alcoves. Skeletons. The walls are painted with toppling gravestones, twisted trees that claw out with scraggly branches, dismal ghosts, drooling ghouls. Bats swarm from the steeple of a deserted country church. A witch on a broomstick flies across a bloated orange moon.

"They keep celebrating Christmas earlier and earlier," Nathan says.

"Capitalist greed run amok," Hoyt says. "I'll get us beers."

Someone takes Nathan's arm and says in his ear, "My God, you're a bold one. You're practically naked."

This seems to be a giant rat, ears and whiskers twitching.

"I come from a poor family," Nathan says. "We can't afford clothes."

"Dance?" the giant rat says.

"You'll have to teach me," Nathan says.

"Nothing to it," the rat says, takes Nathan's starry body firmly in his arms, and, counting instructively into Nathan's ear, teaches him. By the end of "Moonlight Cocktail" Nathan knows how to dance. "You're a quick learner. I thought you would be. What's your name?"

"Castor," Nathan says. "The morning star."

"A brawler, a cattle thief," the giant rat says. "A rapist and kidnapper of helpless Greek girls."

Nathan shakes his head. "You've got me mixed up with somebody else." He sees the star on Hoyt's helmet and goes toward it in his gold satin slippers, calling over his shoulder, "Thanks for the dance lesson."

"And a happy Walpurgisnacht to you," calls the rat.

As Nathan passes Marie Antoinette, she says in a husky baritone, "Always face life with your back turned, darling. Your ass is gorgeous." A white-gloved hand caresses it.

"Careful. You'll smear the paint." Nathan walks on.

Hoyt hands him a glass of beer, and Nathan says, "You were right. I learned to dance. A rat taught me."

Hoyt looks around. "We must offer him some cheese."

A clown takes his hand. He doesn't know who this is. The makeup is very good, professional. The checkered costume has a big ruff collar and is blowsy. Not until the clown puts an arm around him does Nathan realize the man in the costume is fat. Then he speaks, and Nathan knows who he is.

"Abou Bekker," Nathan says. "What are you doing here?"

"My kind of place," Abou says. "Didn't you know?"

"I knew, but you were always—"

"Circumspect?" They bump into a moth-eaten gorilla dancing with the Sugar Plum Fairy, and Abou apologizes to them. "I was always counseling you to be circumspect. And see what good it did. Look at you. Stark naked."

Nathan grins. "Are you sorry?"

Abou laughs. "What do you think? You were tempting enough clothed. My God—if I'd seen you like this—"

"I wasn't ready," Nathan says.

"No. You went and played hermit at Joe Ridpath's. I saw you a few times, driving past in that rickety produce truck of his. Sunburned, ragged. I hardly knew you."

"The truck had an old train bell," Nathan said. "I always rang it, passing your house, just for old time's sake. I thought you were in Hollywood. Swallowed up by that movie studio. Why didn't you come out and buy some tomatoes?"

"I was ashamed of how I'd treated you," Abou says. "We did live in Hollywood for six months. But then came Pearl Harbor, and they canceled that program I was on—you know, to give theater students from the schools working experience at the studios? They had to cut expenses, though God knows I didn't cost them much. So we moved back to Fair Oaks." He winces. "You really ought to learn to dance."

"Sorry," Nathan says. "So what are you doing now?"

"For a while I scraped along, directing amateur theater in places like Tustin and Orange." The clown face turns mournful. "But the city wouldn't hire Mother back. And puppets are all she knows. We were starving. I signed on at Lockheed. So much for my life in art. What about you?"

Nathan tells him.

"It's the same as the play? And they've bought it?"

"Probably thanks to you. You showed me how to fix it, how to make it work." Nathan broods. "You promised to direct it. And then you just up and left town without even saying goodbye. Do you know how that hurt?"

"Nathan, I've said I'm sorry." Abou dances in silence. At last he says, "The boy you came with—he's your lover?"

"An artist. He's good. Really. Just sold two big paintings. Come meet him. You'll like him."

"I've seen him," Abou says bleakly. "That will do."

"And why are you at the Black Cat?" Nathan says.

"I've lost someone. I thought I might find him here."

George Lafleur shows up as Pinocchio, cocky Tyrolean hat, long papier-mâché nose sprouting twigs and leaves at its end—Pinocchio the liar. Benbow leads Hoyt and Nathan to a table where George sits guarding four glasses of beer, and they sit with him to drink the beers and watch the costumes. Benbow is magnificent in his gold-plated Roman armor and a helmet crested with a splendid black horsehair brush. From his natty little Pinocchio jacket, George produces Luckies. Nathan smokes his gratefully. There was no place in their galactic getups for him and Hoyt to carry cigarettes.

"Coffin nails," George says, and tucks the pack away. "The very thing for this particular night."

Benbow leans toward Hoyt. "I wasn't going to mention it. But I hate remorse of conscience. Anyway, alcohol has loosened my tongue. A man of scandalous morals has seen Dr. Marriott's paintings, and he wants to commission you to do another—with both of you in it. Engaged in"—the helmet gleams in the jack-o'-lantern light as Benbow looks this way and that, as if he could be overheard in the shrieking racket—"si-mul-ta-ne-ous fel-la-tio. Shall I spell it?"

"Can you?" Hoyt says. "You weren't going to tell me?"

"He'll pay you a thousand dollars," Benbow says. "But take my advice, don't do it. You'll get a reputation as a pornographer. No one will ever take your work seriously."

Hoyt snorts. "I suspect your motives, Benbow, but don't worry, I won't do it."

"I told you not to sell them," Nathan says.

Hoyt grins. "I suspected your motives too."

George has been nervously squinting around the dark, teeming room. Now he looks at Benbow through the cigarette smoke. His voice is anxious. "No sign of the skeleton?"

Benbow frowns at him and shakes his head in a warning.

Nathan wonders what George meant, and glances at Hoyt. But Hoyt's eyes look out untroubled from the silver domino. He says, "Skeletons? I counted three—one near the entry, one over yonder, one beside the men's room door."

"Not quite enough for the Apocalypse," Benbow says.

"And no horses," Hoyt says. "Show us your sword."

"Short but sturdy." Benbow draws it, waves it around. "I'd have brought my spear"—after two misses he manages to slide the sword back into its scabbard—"but as you can see, anyone might turn up tonight. I feared running into Jesus. One wouldn't want to open old wounds."

"Ho-ho," George says.

It's late. Nathan is tired and would like to quit dancing, but someone is always taking him out of someone else's arms. He feels shopworn. His stars and planets are fading. Since everyone strokes his butt, the sun and moon went first. Now a thin young woman in top hat and tails and a cape with a crimson lining relinquishes him to a skeleton. The suit is black; the bones are painted on it in luminous white. A papier-mâché skull covers the whole head. He dances badly, and it comes to Nathan that this is because he doesn't want to dance with a boy, yet he clutches Nathan urgently against him. He is just tall enough to speak into Nathan's ear. And he says in a hoarse whisper:

"You're wasting your time. You've been looking in all the wrong places. You want to know who killed Eva Schaffer? I can tell you."

Nathan says, "No, no. It's not me you want. It's my twin, the silver one—Pollux."

But something is wrong with the skeleton. It groans. The body inside the black coverall goes limp and drops to its knees. The room is dark and smoky as ever. The crowd is even more tightly packed. Dancers stumble over the black bundle under their feet. They exclaim. That's all Nathan has time to take in. Then Benbow has him by the arm.

"Time to go," he says, and steers Nathan in panic haste toward the door. Benbow has hold of Hoyt with his other hand. He lets Nathan go a moment, yanks open the door, pushes both boys outside into shocking cold. Rain still sifts down. The Black Cat's door slams behind them, cutting off the music, the laughter. It's silent out here.

Benbow hurries the boys up the tilted street as fast as he can make his sturdy legs in their brassy shin guards go. He pushes them into the car, flings his helmet after them, gets behind the wheel, starts the engine, and careens away before he's even turned on the headlights.

"Benbow," Hoyt says, fighting his way into Percy Hinkley's raincoat, "what the fuck?"

"People were growing rowdy," Benbow says primly. "Starting fights, shedding their clothes, passing out from drink right on the dance floor. It was time to leave."

"But the prize for the best costume," Hoyt says. "Nathan and I would have won. Everybody said so. I put a lot of time and thought into our costumes."

"I dread to think how skimpy they'd have been if you'd thought any longer," Benbow says. He glares into the rearview mirror at Hoyt. "And I haven't forgotten, even if you have, that Nathan is underage. Suppose the police had arrived. It's been known to happen."

Hoyt slouches in a corner of the seat, clutching the coat around him. "You gave him an invitation."

"And I hope he enjoyed himself," Benbow says.

"I'll never forget it," Nathan says from the depths of Percy Hinkley's overcoat. "But I'd have liked the prize."

"Well, I'm not taking you back," Benbow says. "Anyway, it's too late now. Your helmets have melted."

Hoyt goes to piss. Nathan goes into the dark bedroom and peels off the jock strap, which has lost half its sequins. His ass wasn't the only thing people were always putting their hands on. It's cold.

The rain patters on the roof. He could crawl into bed, and the blankets would warm him, but he feels a strong need to be clothed, and finds jeans and a sweater, and hurries into them, then sits on the bed, bent forward, head hanging, weary—and frightened. The toilet flushes; Hoyt's heels in their silver satin slippers thump across the living room. Hoyt stands in the doorway, lamplight at his back. "What's the matter?"

Nathan tells him. "And then Benbow was rushing me out." He looks up at Hoyt. "You never told me she was murdered. You never told me you were looking for who killed her."

"She didn't fall under that streetcar—she was pushed," Hoyt says. "Yes, I'm trying to find out who killed her. At the Chinese place when you asked me to forget my Communists, and I said I can't—that's the reason."

"Hoyt, it's a job for the police."

Hoyt scoffs. "The motorman's their only witness. And he didn't see it. He heard her fall and felt the streetcar bump her, and slammed on the brakes, but that's all. He doesn't know how it happened. But nobody in the Party is in any doubt. They knew from the first it was murder."

"They didn't say so at her memorial service."

"No, but they knew. And one of them knows it better than any of the others—the one who did it. Why? I don't know." Hoyt pulls a sweater on over his head. "But Eva was a leader, and she was on her way to the top. That put her in danger. It's a tightly structured organization, the CPUSA, rigid, controlled." He gets into jeans. "If you were very ambitious, it'd be easy to get frustrated, and maybe decide the only way to get ahead is to kill whoever's in your way." There's a pause. Hoyt sits down beside Nathan on the edge of the bed. "You weren't at the memorial service."

"Yes, I was. I followed you. I had to know why you'd been feeling so miserable. I was worried about you."

"Now who's been keeping secrets?" Hoyt says.

"I was afraid to tell you," Nathan says. "I was afraid you'd throw me out. And I can't live without you."

"I couldn't throw you out." Hoyt kisses him, smooths his hair back with his fingers. "What was this man like?"

"Like? I told you. He wore a fake skull over his head. Benbow said he passed out from drink. But he didn't smell of drink." Nathan reaches cigarettes from the chest of drawers. They light up. "Maybe five feet ten. Not fat, not thin. Middle-aged, I think. He sounded middle-aged."

"George asked Benbow about a skeleton," Hoyt says.

"And Benbow shut him up. That's why I kept quiet in the car. They must have known who the skeleton was. And didn't want you and me to find out. And we'd have found out, wouldn't we, if I tried to help the poor bastard, and pulled his mask off? That's why Benbow rushed us out of there."

Hoyt shakes his head. "There's more to it than that. He's up to something." He smokes in brooding silence for a minute. Then he gives Nathan a shadowy smile. "You know what I think—I think you ruined his whole night by not telling him what the skeleton said to you."

"The message was for you, not him," Nathan says, and then is angry at himself. "I didn't give him time to finish. I interrupted him to say I wasn't the one he should be talking to. And then he dropped that way." Nathan shivers. "He went so limp, Hoyt. It was like he was dead."

"Don't you believe it." Hoyt jumps up, walks excitedly into the living room, walks back. "It was a hoax, Nathan." He laughs, a short, harsh laugh. "The whole damn thing. A practical joke. That's Benbow. Typical. Idle. No piano to beat up on all day, so he sits around and concocts this asshole charade to make a fool out of me. He was jealous of Eva when she was alive. She was brighter than he'll ever be. He knew it—but worse, he knew I knew it."

"If I know you," Nathan says, "you told him so."

"We were pretty well strangers then," Hoyt says. "I didn't know how vain he is. He keeps yapping how he's a seeker after truth, but he doesn't want to hear the truth about himself. And it rankles him that I won't forget Eva, that I keep looking for her killer. He says I'm crazy."

"And he staged all this tonight to bring you to your senses?" Nathan says.

"Ask yourself. If this informant is real, why didn't he come to me long ago? Eva's been dead for months. Why wait for Halloween—a costume ball?"

"Because at a costume ball, everybody hides who he is, and no one thinks twice about it."

"Right. But not exactly an original device. Except that everybody there was queer, it was one cliché after another. Dim lights, mystery, melodrama, masks. Hints dropped like anvils about a sinister somebody dressed as a skeleton. Then, right on cue, in he comes, the Grim Reaper himself, whispers half a horrible secret into the shell-like ear of the beautiful ingenue, and drops dead in her arms. Did you ever hear anything so corny in your life? Lon Chaney would have gagged."

"I hope you're right." Nathan keens and reaches down. "Jesus, my feet hurt."

"I'm not surprised. You danced with everybody."

Nathan would like to be able to explain that. It had something to do with the bedazzlement of finding everyone wanting him. But he didn't want them, did he? All he wants is Hoyt. So he says only, "It was my last chance. Tomorrow I go into a nunnery." Wincing, he pries off the slippers. They are sticky wet inside. Not from rain; from broken blisters. "Shit. Look at that. Blood."

Hoyt crouches, examines Nathan's feet, then hauls him across his shoulders in a fireman's carry, and stands. "Come on. We've got to do something about this."

"Hey." To be borne along in this sudden, crazy way, helpless, upside down, is wonderful. Nathan has never felt so loved, so happy to be loved. He scolds, "Have you lost your mind?" but he wishes it would go on for miles. "Put me down, you screwball."

Hoyt sets him on the edge of the tub, bathes his feet in shallow lukewarm water, dries them tenderly, snips away the dead skin, swabs the raw places with Merthiolate, wraps the feet in gauze and adhesive tape. Nathan grips his shoulders and pleads, piteously, in a thick Russian accent, "Doctor, will I ever dance Odette again?"

"At conservatory always are needed teachers," Hoyt says.

"The public will forget me," Nathan wails. "No more ovations, no more bouquets tossed at my feet, no more late-night champagne and caviar by candlelight."

"But you will not starve," Hoyt says. "In glorious workers' paradise of Soviet Union, no one starves," and he picks Nathan up and carries him to bed.

It's not the next morning, it's the morning after; and when they've got their coffee, their spoons go into the sugar bowl and scrape around and come up empty. Hoyt picks up the bowl and goes across the hall to borrow sugar from Reggie Poole. He is gone longer than seems right. And when he comes back it is with mail in his hand. And he looks pale.

"Where's the sugar?"

In the act of laying a letter down in front of Nathan, Hoyt stares at him. "What?"

"You went to borrow sugar from Reggie."

"Oh, yeah, right." Hoyt stands as if he has forgotten how to move.

"Are you all right?" Nathan says. "You look sick."

"I—have to go home," Hoyt says. And leaves the kitchen by the door that takes him through the room where he keeps his art stuff and where Nathan writes, and goes into the bedroom. Nathan goes the other way, through the living room, and finds Hoyt dusting off his battered cowhide suitcase with a dirty T-shirt. He tosses the T-shirt aside and unfastens the straps of the suitcase and sees Nathan.

"I got a letter." He opens his drawer of the chest and takes out underwear and lays it in the suitcase. "My old man is dying."

"I'm sorry," Nathan says. "Oh, Hoyt, I'm sorry."

"Don't be too sorry. You love your old man. I never even come close to likin' mine. He sure as hell never liked me." He folds shirts and lays them in the suitcase. "Reggie didn't have no sugar. Run acrost and git some, will you, honey? I'll want coffee 'fore I go." His Texas accent is back. It must be the thought of landing up in Amarillo, where he has always sworn he will never go again. "Git cigarettes, too, will ye? Wait. You got money?"

"I got money," Nathan mumbles, and goes.

When he gets back with the sugar and cigarettes, the old valise leans at the top of the stairs. It's a bright day. Like yesterday, which they spent in bed, enjoying hell out of each other. The leathery leaves of the rubber tree shine with the dust washed off them. Yet it's as warm and dry as if it had never rained and would never rain again. Hoyt is getting into clean clothes and his hair is wet and combed down flat. He has had a bath. Nathan can smell the soap on his skin. He comes into the kitchen wearing his cowboy hat, sits down as if he's in a hurry, drinks his coffee and smokes his cigarette the same way.

"The bus or the train?" Nathan says.

"Bus. It's cheaper. Nathan, I'm taking most of Marriott's money." Dr. Marriott's check had been for five hundred dollars. "I know, we agreed on a fifty-fifty split—"

Nathan shakes his head. "I only agreed because I didn't want you to beat me up. You did the work, Hoyt."

"I haven't got time to argue," Hoyt says. "I know them— they'll be behind in doctor bills at home, there'll be the hospital to pay for, medicine, funeral, God knows what else. I'm leaving you a hundred. Don't know how long I'll be gone. I hope it's enough."

"Take it," Nathan says. "Mr. MacKenzie will give me my job back at T. Smollett. It's all right."

"You stay home and write your book," Hoyt says. "No reason my dumb family's dumb luck should stop that."

"Maybe he won't die," Nathan says.

"Mama knows better than to trick me back there," Hoyt says grimly. "She knows I'd sooner visit hell." Wiping his mouth with the back of his hand, he gets up, bends to Nathan, kisses him hard and for a long, yearning time, then mutters "Bye" and runs out of the place.

"Wait." Nathan jumps up and runs after him. "I'll come see you off."

At the foot of the stairs, suitcase in hand, Hoyt pauses for a moment, looks up with tears in his eyes, and says, "Stay the fuck where you are, Nathan. It's going to be hard enough this way. You want to kill me?" And then he's gone, at a trot, his feet crunching the gravel.

Nathan stands feeling hollow for a long minute, then turns back and finds Reggie Poole framed in his doorway in the black kimono and the heavy shower clogs. His gray hair is tousled. A smear of egg is at a corner of his mouth. "Where is Hoyt rushing off to so suddenly?"

"Amarillo," Nathan says. "Home. His father is dying."

"Not dying. Passing to another plane." Reggie holds out a bowl. "He said you needed sugar. Then I showed him the newspaper, and he forgot all about it." Nathan stares. Reggie asks, "Something wrong?"

"What newspaper?" Nathan takes the bowl numbly. "What do you mean?"

"I'll show you." Reggie turns back into his rooms. "It's bad manners to crow, to say I told you so. But perhaps you'll listen to an older and wiser head next time."

Nathan follows him into the kitchen, where Mike Voynich, in yet another pair of torn undershorts, is washing dishes at the little sink. "Morning, Mike," he says, and Voynich nods and says dismally, "Yeah." Reggie picks up from the book-cluttered table a copy of the *Daily News* and holds it out, pointing at an item with a finger like the one that wrote on the wall at Belshazzar's feast. "I warned you, or at least I warned Hoyt, the Black Cat was not a safe place to go."

"Not me." Nathan starts to read the item. It is only two paragraphs long. The body of an unidentified man clad only in undershorts was found in an alley in such and such a block off Sunset Boulevard. He appeared to be in his forties. He had been stabbed in the back and died from internal bleeding. Nathan's knees give, and Reggie catches him and sits him on a chair. No wonder Hoyt forgot the sugar.

"That's within a block of the Black Cat," Reggie says, taking back the paper, though Nathan hasn't finished reading the story. "The police think he may have been at that Halloween orgy."

"May have been?" Nathan says. "Is that all?"

"It was a cold, rainy night. Where were his clothes? They reason he must have worn a costume. Which the killer took away so the victim couldn't be identified."

"What's it got to do with me?" Nathan says.

"It could as easily have been you," Reggie says. "Or Hoyt. Naked as you both were. I never heard of such bad judgment. The Black Cat is a very disreputable place. The worst types of degenerates go there. I warned Hoyt—"

"Your needle's stuck," Nathan says, and gets up and walks out.

"Sugar," Reggie calls.

"I bought some, thanks." Nathan closes the door.

Stunned, Nathan pours coffee, sits down, drinks coffee, smokes cigarettes. Hoyt was wrong—it was no joke. A man died. Nathan is scared. But also puzzled. Why the hell has Hoyt run? It wasn't Hoyt the skeleton spoke to in the Black Cat. He spoke to Nathan. And his killer saw that. Close enough to stick a knife into the skeleton's back while he was in Nathan's arms, he'd have got a good

look at Nathan. So shouldn't Nathan be the one to run? He jumps
up. Percy Hinkley's coats still lie on the couch where Hoyt and he
dumped them that night. Nathan rummages in the pockets of the
overcoat. The golden domino is crumpled. He flattens its wrinkles
with his fingers as best he can, fits it over his eyes, snaps the elastic
around his head, and goes to study himself in the pier glass. Is
such a small mask really a disguise? Hoyt must have thought so,
and that Nathan would be safe here. Or maybe Hoyt just plain
didn't think. Maybe that item in the paper panicked him out of
thinking. But it didn't panic him out of lying, did it? Nathan is
getting fed up with Hoyt's lies. He rips off the domino, flings it
away, and goes to the bathroom to clean up.

He is afraid to stay here. He wasn't told who killed Eva Schaffer,
but can the man who stabbed the skeleton be sure of that? Nathan
latches the windows, snaps the lock, stiff from disuse, on the back
door, scouts up the front door key they've never used, and locks
that door as he leaves. He goes to an early double feature at the
Admiral, and doesn't know what he is watching. He eats a grilled
cheese sandwich and drinks a Coke at the lunch counter of the Owl
drugstore. He goes to another movie, and doesn't know what he is
watching. Either picture. In the newsreel, GIs on a Pacific island
shoot jets of fire into caves, and Japanese soldiers come running
out, writhing and screaming and dying in flames. Nathan wonders
what's become of Steve Schaffer.

He eats goulash at the Hungarian place on Vine where Hoyt
took him the day they met. He strays into T. Smollett Books and
browses in the new books for an hour. In charge is a woman of
forty, brassy voice, dyed frizzy yellow hair down to her shoulders.
Angus MacKenzie's wife, Annie. When it's dark outside, Nathan
walks. He was a demon walker in his teens, spent long nights
wandering all over Fair Oaks, stumbling home only at dawn, to
fall dead asleep for an hour or two before school. He didn't understand why then. He doubts he ever will. Looking for something,

maybe. Anyway, he stopped it after they lost Aunt Bessie's house on Oleander Street, and Frank and Alma moved back to Minneapolis, and Nathan went to work for Joe Ridpath and slept in a room full of rusty tools at the nursery.

Now, tonight, on his bandaged feet, he walks again, for miles, for hours. At last he limps up the stairs to the dark-paneled, leather-padded Montmartre, buys a tall, weak whiskey, and listens to Jimmy Noone, a guitarist, a bassist, and a drummer, all old black men, play a set. This time, the carefree music doesn't lift him. He is afraid to go home, but there's no place else to go. He raps Reggie Poole's door and looks in, but no one's here. And he remembers with a sinking heart that this is the date when Reggie has taken the reluctant Mike to Santa Barbara to impress Judith Anderson. Nathan is going to be all the hell alone up here tonight. He blindly scrapes the key into the lock, opens the door, steps inside, shuts the door, stands with his back against it in the midnight silence, listening to his heart beat. "Hoyt?" The name goes into the dark rooms and comes back empty.

But can he really have gone to Amarillo? Why should he? The people who pay him—why wouldn't they be hiding him from danger, right here in L.A.? He'd never tell Nathan, would he? Nathan opens the bedroom windows so the tree branches can come back in. No matter the danger, he can't sleep in a closed room. He strips and crawls into bed and begins to dream right away. On a Greyhound boring through a black desert night, Hoyt sleeps, head over against the window glass, mouth a little open, hands slack on a book forgotten in his lap. All the other riders are asleep too. Nathan tiptoes down the dim aisle, takes the seat beside Hoyt, slips the book from under his hands, and with sly fingers unbuttons Hoyt's fly.

But the dream falls apart. "Who's there?" He sits up sharply, mouth dry, heart knocking, eyes and ears straining for an intruder. When he can make himself move, he switches on the lamp. And of course there's no one. He gets up and goes to the kitchen, switches on the light there, rattles a butcher knife from the drawer, switches off the light, takes the knife back to bed, and slides it under the pillow. He hears his aunt Marie's voice—*God helps those who help themselves*. Absolutely. One good knife deserves another.

He switches off the lamp, lays his head on the pillow, shuts his eyes. But he can't sleep. What the hell does he know about fighting with a knife? He sits up again, wide-eyed, four years old, clutching his knees, imagining black shapes creeping closer, listening for ominous sounds. There's no way out of it. He must do this till daybreak. But the black shapes turn out to be shadows—of the lamp, the chest of drawers, a stack of books. And the only sounds he hears are the familiar creakings of the old house, the drowsy rustlings of leaves in the night wind.

And when he wakens at ten past ten, sunshine flooding the room, he smiles a sorry smile. He didn't keep watch. Not for ten minutes. He slept, didn't dream, didn't even move. The killer from the Black Cat could have kicked in the door and stabbed him dead twenty times for all he'd have known about it. Or maybe cared. Without Hoyt, he doesn't care about much. He totters to his feet, staggers to the bathroom, and can't help laughing. He has such a piss hard-on he practically has to stand on his head to hit the toilet.

The letter Hoyt laid in front of him on the kitchen table yesterday he's forgotten about. Now when he sits down with his coffee mug—no food, he isn't hungry—he notices it again. Reaches for it, stays his hand, frowns. It's Alma's writing. She never writes, never. Frank, yes; Alma, no. Slowly he picks the envelope up, turns it over, as if feeling it with his fingers would tell him what's inside. At last he tears it open.

I think you had better come home as your father suggests. He has been worried about you, especially after getting those letters from Mr. Noble.

Nathan's heart skips a beat. "Letters"? Plural? Damn Noble. What did the second one say? And would there be a third?—Was he at the Black Cat, too? How would Nathan have known? Christ! He lights a cigarette with shaking hands and takes Alma's pages up again.

> It reassured us both to hear from you that your friend Benjamin Bowen Harsch is a college professor, and that the young man you're sharing the rent with has had such success with his art, and about your neighbor the famous writer, but I don't like the look of your planetary transits right now. I know you think astrology is nonsense, but time will change your mind—about that as about many things. Nathan, Mars and Uranus squaring your solar return in July was no laughing matter. This is going to be a difficult year for you. Worse than that. Dangerous. You are in peril, there. You'd better take your father's advice and come home.

Not a word about her anger at him for the hurt he gave her over that seance. No demand for an apology, no mention of forgiveness. Without an apology, she never will forgive him. But she is willing to have him underfoot again. Which means she really must be scared. He snorts, folds the letter up, and stuffs it back into the envelope. She is gifted at scaring herself with eclipses and transits, malign aspects, punishing progressions, ominous occlusions, sinister solar returns. And at scaring others. Which is how she has made a living all these years. Others, but not him. Not since he was seven years old. And a good thing, too. He is scared enough without her.

In what looks like a man's skivvy shirt dyed dark blue, and a skirt run up on the sewing machine out of a pair of faded dungarees, barefoot Linnet Hinkley pushes a lawn mower under the monkey puzzle tree in front of the hulking house her husband owns, her mother manages. The smell of cut grass is heady in the air. Coats in his arms, Nathan climbs the steps from the sidewalk. Linnet stops the noisy old mower, wipes strands of blond hair back off her glorious forehead with a dirty hand.

"Where's Hoyt?" she says. "Did he forget my Spanish lesson?"

"His father's dying. He's gone home to Texas. I brought back the coats. Thank you very much."

"You're welcome, I guess. I shouldn't have done it, but that Hoyt—he could talk a person out of anything. He's got the sweetest way with him." She gazes glumly at the half-mowed lawn and abruptly turns for the house. "I'm sick of this. It always takes so long. Come on. Let's get a Coke."

Nathan follows her indoors, where she hangs the coats in a hall closet. Sequins shower out of them. Linnet doesn't notice. She heads down the hall to the looming kitchen. "Was the party fun?" She takes Cokes from the refrigerator. "Hoyt said you'd dress up like twins. Casper and somebody."

"Two Greek gods. Gods don't wear much. That's why we needed the coats." Nathan takes the bottle she hands him and sits at the table. "Thank you."

"Did you win the prize?" she says, and sits down too.

"We didn't stay that late," Nathan says.

She swigs her Coke and studies him thoughtfully. "You look like gods—maybe not Greek, but gods, anyway. I expect you would have won."

"We had to leave." Nathan smiles. "I danced too much. I wore little thin slippers and I got blisters on my feet."

"Oh, that's too bad." She frowns in absentminded sympathy. "Was it a big party, lots of people?"

"Gorillas, fairies, Bette Davis, clowns, Roman soldiers, Carmen Miranda, Pinocchio, Marie Antoinette, Dracula. Yes. It was a big party."

"Beautiful girls?"

"None as beautiful as you," Nathan says.

She gives him a slow grin. "You can be as sweet as Hoyt when you try." Her eyes lose brightness; she sighs. "We went to a twenty-five-cent picture show. *The Wolf Man* and *Frankenstein*. Old pictures, really old. We both saw them about a hundred times already."

"Maybe next year you can go to a costume party," Nathan says. "You and Percy."

She looks dreamily at a sunlit window dappled with leaf shadow. "I think I'd go as Heidi. I love that book. I think I look a little bit like her, don't you?" She reaches up, takes fistfuls of her abundant hair and pulls it back. "I always wanted to wear it in braids around my head."

"Perfect," Nathan says. "What about Percy?"

"The Scarecrow," she says. "The Scarecrow of Oz."

Toting shopping bags, Rick Ames comes along Franklin toward Nathan, red-faced, crinkly pale hair glinting. "Ah, it's you, this time. Been to Felony Manor, have you?"

"Returning those coats Hoyt borrowed," Nathan says. "Any luck with the essays you sent the magazines?"

"My hideous old mother has parted with a small loan," Ames says, setting down the bags, "so at least for the present, Ah needn't fret about the illiteracy of editors. She owns a string of hotels, you know, she's as rich as the queen of Sheba, but until Ah turn heterosexual, stop drinking, get a job, Ah am low on her list of charities." His look at Nathan turns secretive, scandalized. "Gossip has it, you and Hoyt were naked at the Black Cat ball. Caused a sensation."

"For about a minute," Nathan says.

"In the dear, dead days beyond recall," Ames says wistfully, "Tony and Ah used to go to such parties every year. But never naked, of course. Things weren't so free and easy then. Or so dangerous. Ah heah there was a murder. A man knifed right there on the dance floor."

"We left early," Nathan says.

"The police found his naked body the next morning in the alley out back." He peers from the corners of his white-lashed blue eyes at Nathan. "Ah expected to see Hoyt today—isn't it Spanish lesson time?"

Nathan tells him about Hoyt.

"So you gave the coats to Babe?"

"She's mowing the lawn. We had a Coke together."

"Did she show you Hoyt's portrait of her? Ah wouldn't put it past her. She hasn't a shred of tact."

"No." Nathan sounds surprised, and tries to hide that. "But—but of course Hoyt—Hoyt told me about it."

Ames smirks. "Ah'm certain he did. He must also have told you how they pass the time. That tutelage has long been forgot. She hasn't the brains to learn Spanish—or anything else, for that mattah. Her grades at Hollywood High were so bad as to constitute a crime. If Percy Hinkley hadn't married her, she'd have spent the rest of her life trying to graduate from high school."

" 'How they pass the time'?" Nathan feels a little sick. "What are you talking about?"

"Gin rummy." Ames picks up his shopping bags. "Endless games of gin rummy."

Nathan laughs. "What's wrong with that?"

Ames moves off. "Ah warned you to keep her away from him. You'll lose him, Nathan."

Nathan catches him up. "Rick, gin rummy's not sex."

"It's also not spending time with you, is it?" He shuffles away. "When he comes home from Texas, tell him she's canceled her Spanish lessons and moved to Alaska." His voice drifts back on the morning air. "If you give her the chance, she'll lure him from you, Nathan. She will."

Nathan goes home to the typewriter. The book isn't going to finish itself. And writing is the one sure way he knows to stop aching for Hoyt, and fearing the knifer from the Black Cat will come and kill him. He's neglected the book too long, and it's hard to get going again. But after a hopeless hour or so, his fingers begin to fly.

And by late afternoon, he's writing well, hearing clearly again the voices from the shotgun flat in wintery Minneapolis long ago. Which means he doesn't hear footsteps, doesn't know anyone has come here until a shadow falls across him from the doorway. His head jerks up, he yelps, and the typewriter keys jam.

Benbow says, "I knocked and hallooed."

"Sorry." Nathan glances backward. Can he scramble down the room and out the back door before Benbow can jump him? "I was—absorbed."

"Are you all right?" Benbow says. "You don't look it."

Nathan pushes back his chair and stands. His legs quiver. "I'm fine. What—what do you want?"

Benbow tilts his domed, balding head and studies Nathan. "Nathan, you're afraid of me. That's it. Scared to death. You are. Why?"

"Afraid?" Nathan's voice breaks like an adolescent's. "Don't be silly. Do you—want some beer?"

Benbow waves a hand. "No, there isn't time. I've come to take you with me."

"With you?" Nathan feels cold. "Where?"

"To my house. Calliope summons. But first I need to know why I'm suddenly an ogre."

Nathan says, "You're not, Benbow. Honest."

"You're endearing when you lie. So boyish. It's about the Black Cat, isn't it? Of course. The man in the skeleton outfit. It was a joke, Nathan. Hoyt would have grasped that at once, but my minion got hold of you by mistake. Forgive me. It must have been a nasty shock for you."

"Hoyt told me afterward it was a joke." Nathan backs slowly away. "But yesterday morning, when he read in the paper about the dead man in the alley, I guess he didn't think so anymore. He packed up and left town."

" 'Dead man in the alley,' " Benbow repeats. He looks stunned. "But that had nothing to do with it."

"He must have thought it did. He's scared shitless."

Benbow sits on the desk chair and tries to laugh and does a poor job of it. "You're not serious."

"Well, look around," Nathan says. "Do you see him?"

"No, but Hoyt is my friend. He knows I'd be the last person—" He frowns at Nathan. "Do you believe I could take a human life? Surely not, Nathan."

"No, no," Nathan lies, the back door in sight now across a short space of screen porch. "But Hoyt ran scared of somebody, and I don't know whether I should be here either."

"Now, now. It was all a fabrication," Benbow says soothingly. "The man in the skeleton costume whispered to you he knew who killed Eva Schaffer—isn't that right?"

"That's right. And you told him to say it?"

"But not to you—to Hoyt. He's obsessed with that Schaffer woman. Her death was an accident, but he's made up his mind there was some dark plot behind it. And it's too fine a mind—I refuse to stand by and watch it slip into madness. He has a sense of humor. I thought a joke might—"

"What was the rest of the joke?" Nathan says.

Benbow makes a face. "Don't ask. The whole thing was sophomoric. I confess that freely and abjectly. But it had nothing to do with the murder in the alley. Bizarre. Freud is wrong. There are coincidences. This one shocked me, I can tell you."

Musing, he touches the typewriter.

"I feel like an author whose plot has got away from him and run amok among real people. Where did Hoyt go?"

"Home to Amarillo," Nathan says. "That's what he said. He claimed his father was dying. Said he got a letter, but I didn't see any letter." He peers hard at Benbow. "Are you sure nothing happened to the man in the skeleton suit? The way he dropped to the floor—"

"Actors learn that early in their training."

"Was he an actor?" Nathan says.

Benbow smiles. "He still is."

Nathan hops off a streetcar and ambles up Highland, smiling. He has played Benbow's piano all evening. Stiff-jointed, making awful mistakes. But no one overheard. Benbow was chairing a seminar on German cultural history at UCLA for Army intelligence officers. There will be four of these. So Nathan will get to practice one night every week for a month. Benbow's mother was away visiting a sister in San Diego. George was out entertaining the troops in selected public men's rooms. So Nathan could blunder freely. And curse and weep aloud.

But rusty as he was, he has come away sure his old skills— "A true little Mozart," Minneapolis *Tribune*, 12 November 1931 —will come back. Why does this please him? He doesn't know. Music never repaid his father's devotion. It only kept him away from home for months at a time. And except when Frank asked Nathan to accompany him in Beethoven cello sonatas in the attic in Fair Oaks, he hasn't touched a piano since he was eleven years old. He swore then he never would again. But that was hurt and anger talking. Anyway, you can't make up your mind at eleven. And this one night of laying waste to Bach, Grieg, MacDowell has shown him, as Joe Ridpath's banjo never quite did, how much he's missed making music since Frank gave away all his junky instruments and the house fell silent.

Now ahead of him Nathan sees the big weary figure of Reggie Poole, passing in and out of the streetlights, on his way home from waiting tables at Drossie's. Nathan breaks into a run to catch him up.

"Nathan," Reggie says. "Where did you come from?"

"Where have you been?" Nathan says. "You were supposed to be back yesterday. I was worried about you."

"I was—delayed," Reggie says.

"In Santa Barbara? How did it go? Did Mike impress Judith Anderson?"

"Mike did a bunk," Reggie says. "He had terrible nerves on the bus. When we reached the station in Santa Barbara, he made a wild dash for the men's room and threw up. He kept on throwing up. We didn't have much time. I finally went ahead to pick up the tickets, he gasped greenly that he'd be along, I waited outside the theater, but he never came."

"That's a shame." They turn in at the dark driveway of the green-shingled house. "But he was scared, I knew that. Where is he now?"

"I hoped you'd be able to tell me."

"I haven't seen him." Nathan starts upstairs.

Reggie follows. "I hunted through every cheap bar and flop-house in Santa Barbara. Not a sign of him."

"I'm sorry," Nathan says. They open their opposite doors in the dark hallway. And Nathan is in the bathroom emptying his bladder when he hears a wail from Reggie. Still buttoning up, he hurries across the hall. Reggie has dropped tragically onto one of his kitchen chairs. Tears are streaming down his face. "Look," he says in a broken voice, and stretches out both hands in a theatrical gesture, "just look."

A glass jar stands on the counter beside the chipped little sink. Its lid is off, and it is empty. Another jar lies shattered on the floor, a few pennies among the glittering shards. Into these jars every night Reggie decants from his pockets his tips from the restaurant. It's the only money he makes. Drossie gives him his dinner free, but she can't pay him. It's all she can do to pay her rent.

"You've been robbed?" Nathan stoops to pick up the sharp curved pieces of broken glass and drops them into the wastebasket under the sink. "That's terrible."

Reggie blows his nose. "It's pathetic." He tucks the hand-kerchief away. "Nickels, dimes, quarters—there wasn't ten dollars in those jars."

"I thought you hid them."

"On a top shelf." Reggie points. "Behind heaps of gravy-stained cookbooks."

"Don't worry. Hoyt left me money to live on while he's gone. You're welcome to whatever you need." Nathan drops the last bits of broken glass into the wastebasket and stands up. "But it looks like you're going to have to start locking your door when you go out." He lays the pennies in Reggie's hand. "Did Hoyt give you a key?"

Reggie peers into his face, head tilted. "You are the dearest, most innocent child, aren't you?" A faint wry smile twitches his lips. "Nathan, no housebreaker did this."

"What do you mean?"

A very old sadness fills Reggie's face, and he turns away and opens a cupboard. "It was Mike, of course. While I was searching high and low for him in Santa Barbara. I'd let him hold on to the return part of his bus ticket. How intelligent of me." Reggie brings out a half-spent bottle of gin, a new bottle of tokay, and cheese glasses. "He fretted that I never gave him pocket money." He concocts his cheap-jack cocktails, and he and Nathan sit at the table and light up two of his killer cigarettes. "But how could I?" Reggie shakes out the paper match. "I was saving to buy him a suit for this audition. I managed it, too. Ungrateful wretch." He desolately drinks off his gin and tokay. "Nathan, cling close to Hoyt. Stay together always." He sighs bitterly. "Strangers are exciting, but they are not the answer." While he tilts the bottles over his empty glass again, there's silence, because Nathan doesn't know what to say. He thinks Mike Voynich is a shit, but he doubts Reggie wants to hear that. At last Reggie smiles wanly to himself. "But he did look stunning in that suit."

"Maybe he didn't do this," Nathan says. "Maybe he'll be back.

He's probably only hiding out because he's ashamed of himself for letting you down and doesn't know how to face you. But he'll get over it. You were good to him."

Reggie tosses off his second gin and tokay. "And he was good to me. I expect he thinks I got the better of the bargain—and that I owed him more than a forty-dollar suit."

"You taught him a lot," Nathan says.

Reggie grimaces. "To hope for worlds beyond his reach." He fills his glass again, half gin, half tokay. "That really wasn't kind, was it?"

"You meant it to be," Nathan says.

"You judge people too gently," Reggie says. "You must arm yourself against a lifetime of deceivers." He adds with a self-mocking laugh, "And self-deceivers." His mouth is wet. He is getting drunk. "I'm one of the latter. Which makes me one of the former. Or did in this case. Mike Voynich is an oaf. He doesn't stand a chance."

"He'll keep landing on his feet." Nathan puts out his cigarette. "As long as he's got his looks."

"May he do better next time," Reggie says bleakly, lifting his glass in a toast. "I really had nothing to give but empty promises."

"Maybe they weren't empty. He didn't stick around to find out." Nathan knocks back the rest of his awful drink. "It wasn't your fault. He just didn't have the guts." He stands up. "Reggie, I'm tired. I have to go to bed. You going to be all right?"

Reggie blinks up at him in the forty-watt light of a ceiling bulb. "All right? Oh, yes." He laughs a sorry laugh. "I've survived heartbreak a hundred times. Mike is not the first good-looking lad to leave me—or to rob me. None of it is new, Nathan." In his hands the bottles chink and chime again. "And there's something to be said for that. Surprises lose their surprise when they've surprised you too often." He sets the bottles down slowly, with studied care, since they seem to want to topple over. Then he remembers Nathan and smiles up at him. "Good night."

"Good night." Nathan leaves the kitchen.

"Oh, Nathan?" Reggie calls. "Before you go, could you bring me my *Science and Health*, please? It's the limp leather book by my chair."

Nathan knows which one it is. Sometimes, arriving home late on warm summer nights, when Reggie leaves his door open for air, Nathan and Hoyt have glimpsed the big man in his black kimono, seated in that corner chair, booze at his elbow, cigarette smoke wreathing his head, seeking consolation in Mary Baker Eddy's cock-eyed bible. Nathan picks the book up now, and takes it to him.

Tired as he is, Nathan keeps waking up in the dark, trembling, breathing quickly, scared of the killer from the Black Cat. He's locked the doors, but locks don't stop imaginary menaces. He never really sleeps until the sky begins to grow light beyond the tree branches. And when knocking at the door wakes him up, the clock's hands make the time a quarter to eleven.

"Nathan?" It's Reggie.

"Coming," Nathan says hoarsely, and puts on jeans. He is clumsy with sleep and it takes a minute for him to twist the old lock open. He pulls the door.

Reggie is dressed to go out and smells of cologne. "Oh, dear. I didn't mean to waken you. But Drossie wants me for lunch today, and while I have carfare from last night's generous gratuities, she also told me not to appear without a haircut. If you could let me have a dollar?"

Nathan points. "Top drawer of the chest." He moves groggily off toward the bathroom. "Take whatever you need." He's finished the more urgent rites and is running water into the tub when a tap comes on the door. "What is it?"

Reggie puts his head in. "Are you sure that's where Hoyt left the money? I don't find it."

"Try the other drawers," Nathan says.

"I took that liberty," Reggie says. "And while riffling through your ragged undershorts filled me with boyish nostalgia for the works of Horatio Alger, I found no money, Nathan. No money at all."

Nathan stares at him. "Oh, shit." He turns off the taps, edges past Reggie, runs into the bedroom, looks through the drawers himself. Nothing. He feels dizzy. He can't believe this. "Right here is where we kept it. He cashed the check for the paintings, five hundred dollars in twenty-dollar bills, and stowed them all right here."

"Perhaps you misunderstood, and he didn't leave any of it for you."

"He left it," Nathan says. "I saw it."

"You were out last night, as I was," Reggie says. "Was your door locked?"

Nathan numbly shakes his head. "You mean Mike—?"

"Who else?" Reggie says. "How much was there?"

"A hundred dollars," Nathan says.

"Dear God." Reggie sinks onto the edge of the rumpled bed. "What have I done to you? Oh, Nathan, I am so sorry. Can you ever forgive me?"

"Nothing to forgive." Nathan wants to kick the drawers closed, but instead he slides them to very gently. A sock hangs out of the top drawer, and he tucks it tenderly down and closes that drawer even more softly than the others. He is getting angrier by the moment. He wants to yell and smash things. "Don't miss your streetcar, Reg."

"Right." Reg, looking pale, stands up, starts out of the room, turns back, pulling an envelope from his pocket. "I almost forgot." He lays the envelope in Nathan's hand. "Hoyt dropped this letter in my kitchen the other morning."

"Thank you," Nathan says mechanically. He stands where he is until he hears the last of Reggie's footfalls on the stairs outside. Now he can yell and smash things. But he is too stunned. How long this paralysis lasts he doesn't know, but in the end he remembers the envelope and looks at it. Dully. It's an airmail envelope

with childish writing on it in pencil. That writing stirs a memory.
Heart fluttering, he reads the postmark—Amarillo. The date is
four days back. He takes out the letter and without scruple reads
it. And laughs aloud. Hoyt didn't lie. Not this time. He didn't
run off for fear of being stabbed and dumped in an alley. Long Tex
Stubblefield really is dying.

Myra Stubblefield writes:
  *The doctor says he cant last but a few days. He dont know
none of us no more. Jesus is calling him home.*

Nathan unlocks and hoists high the enormous front door of
T. Smollett Books. Rolls the table of gritty bargain books outside.
Trudges to the workroom at the rear of the cavernous shop to scoop
a dustpanful of red sweeping compound from a steel drum. Sprinkles
the sawdust along the aisles. Push-brooms the aisles. The entryway.
The front sidewalk. The sky is noncomittal gray. There's a chill in
the air, but the air is dry, and the sun may appear later to fade the
book jackets in the window, so he cranks down the awning, and
returns to the back room to put away broom and dustpan.

Books are stacked on the shipping table with address labels
and packing slips sticking out of them. He begins to wrap these
in brown corrugated board, brown paper, brown gummed tape from
a machine that keeps clogging—peering out every few seconds to
see if customers have come into the shop. None does. Angus
MacKenzie in his usual gray suit, the usual damp cigarette burning
in the corner of his mouth, arrives by the back door, grunts in
answer to Nathan's "Good morning," and goes out to count cash
into the drawer of the old register, wetting his thumb and counting
quickly through the banded stacks of ones, fives, tens, twenties
from the bank. Mr. Constance, handsome, suntanned, fair-haired,
won't stroll in till noon, which is a relief.

"Book finished yet?" he keeps asking. He is pleased as hell
that Nathan has run through the publisher's advance money and

has had to come humbly back to T. Smollett Books. Another of his lines is "Didn't I say you were too young? Writing a novel is a job for a grown man."

"Don't worry, Connie," Nathan says. "I'll finish it."

"Working all day?" Mr. Constance sniffs. "I seem to remember long tearful plaints from you that no writer ever finished a book and held a job at the same time."

"It's nearly done. I work on it nights."

"Yes, of course," Constance says. "Without your cowboy friend to roll you in the hay every ten minutes, time must weigh heavily on your hands."

Hoyt sends picture postcards of the Alamo, the Lone Star flag, cattle brands, Wild Horse Lake, a gusher with oil-blackened men capering around and tossing their hats in the air, but he doesn't write much on the back—only that he hopes Nathan is all right, that he misses him, and that his father is hanging on to life. Nathan doesn't like himself for it, but he wishes furiously the old man would die. He aches for Hoyt to come back. So Mr. Constance is right about one thing—the reason weary Nathan writes these nights is to forget Hoyt for a few hours.

"If I want a roll in the hay," Nathan says, "I can always go down to the Captain's Cabin at the beach and drop my swim trunks in the men's room, can't I?"

Constance gets red in the face and goes huffily away.

On the fourteenth day of Hoyt's absence, it starts to rain again. Nathan wishes it wouldn't. The gloom of the days, the weeping of rain on the roof all night make his loneliness worse. He has Saturday afternoon off. His shoes are soaked through by the time he's slogged up Highland to the house with green shingles. He crunches over the gravel of the driveway and mechanically lifts the lid of the mailbox. The letter he draws out is the one he's been expecting and dreading. From Craven & Hyde. He takes it upstairs, sheds his wet clothes, puts on dry ones, corduroys, two sweaters, and a moth-eaten muffler against the damp and chill—he still won't close those windows. He opens a can of soup and heats it, dumps it into a bowl, gets a spoon, sits at the table, and tears open the envelope.

We are sorry to have been so long in responding to the chapters of The Shotgun Flat *which you sent us a few weeks ago. Please forgive the delay. Vacations and illnesses have slowed us down here. But now everyone has had the chance to read this middle section of your novel, and I regret to report that we are all a little disappointed. These chapters seem to lack the sprightliness of the opening ones. At first, no one could quite understand why, but we all agreed that something vital was missing. Every editor here is in love with this book, so we were upset and perplexed. Then we realized that what accounted for the letdown was Frank's absence. With Frank away on the road playing with the dance band, the novel goes slack. Winning and winsome as he is, ten-year-old Nathan alone cannot fill in for Frank. Nor can Alma's loony lady clients, nor the ongoing conflict, handle it though you do with such whimsy (the five crates of cabbages are hilarious), between mystical Alma and down-to-earth Aunt Marie. Uncle Chester, the all-thumbs carpenter, is a comic diversion, but he's no stand-in for Frank. The story goes flat without the ironic spice of Frank's droll humor. We do hope you'll take these criticisms in the spirit in which they're offered. We are all rooting hard for your book here, and are certain you will find a way to get Frank back into these passages. We look forward to that.*

Nathan doesn't want his soup.

Reggie shakes him awake. He is in bed, curled up tight on his side, covers pulled over his head. He crawled in here yesterday afternoon. He woke at twilight to the sound of the rain, told himself to get up, didn't get up. What the hell was there to get up for?

He slept again. Sometime he crept out of bed in the dark and went shivering to the bathroom. After that he lay awake in misery for what seemed like hours but was obviously not forever. He blinks at Reggie, who has on his good suit, which means he is off to church. Of course. It's Sunday morning.

"Are you sick?" Reggie says.

"I don't think so." Nathan sits up.

"You have all your clothes on," Reggie says.

"I forgot to take them off," Nathan says.

"I came in yesterday before I left for Drossie's," Reggie says. "You were here then."

"Life makes me sick," Nathan says. "Sometimes. I was trying to sleep it off."

Reggie pats his head. "Never mind. He'll be back one of these days. Concentrate on that. How happy you'll be." He turns away, opens the top drawer of the chest, tucks something under the clothes there. "I can't manage ten this week," he says. "Rain discourages people from going out to eat. Only five. But I'm not forgetting."

"You can't survive on nothing," Nathan says.

"I've managed it for months." Reggie closes the drawer. "It was my folly that cost you that hundred dollars. I mean to pay it back. Every penny."

"Later." A pack of Sensations is squashed in Nathan's pocket. He takes it out and lights bent cigarettes for Reggie and himself. "When you sell your play."

Reggie brightens. "Dorcas Blaufisch is handling it now. Here. In Hollywood." He breezes out. "Broadway was a waste of time. She thinks it's made for the movies."

"So do I," Nathan calls. "Good luck."

"Oh, wait," Reggie says, "wait, wait, wait," and comes back into the bedroom. "Have you heard? You haven't. You never listen to the news."

"I prefer music," Nathan admits. "Highbrow stuff. André

Kostelanetz. Fred Waring. Phil Spitalny and his all-girl orchestra. What did I miss?"

"That man they found murdered in the alley behind the Black Cat?" Reggie says. "It turns out he wasn't at the costume ball." He tightens the corners of his mouth in a token of chagrin. "He was a traveling salesman from Oak Park, Illinois, married, with children—and he was robbed and murdered after picking up a prostitute. With the unlikely but patriotic name of Merry Furlo. It took all this time to identify her victim. The only records of his fingerprints were on file in Washington, D.C. After the local police got them, they located his hotel, and traced his actions on that night from there. So mea culpa. I slandered the Black Cat. Obviously, their Halloween party was totally blameless."

"I tried to tell you," Nathan says. "We sat on little red chairs in a circle and sang 'Jesus Loves Me.' "

It is a long climb, half indoors, half outdoors, to the boxy white top units of the Highland Hotel. Nathan is out of breath and damp when he knocks on Gentleman Jim Hawker's door. A muffled cry is followed by bumping and stumbling on the far side of the door. But at last it opens. The Great American Novelist's hair is uncombed. His cheeks are bristly with white whiskers. He is in filthy pajamas, and he peers at Nathan through the two-inch slot he's made between door and door frame with bleary, bloodshot eyes.

"Ah, it's young Reed," he says. "I regret that I am not prepared to receive visitors." He starts to close the door. "Please come back tomorrow."

Nathan blocks the door with his foot. "I wasn't prepared to receive visitors the other night when you dropped in, but I didn't turn you away, did I? I made you comfortable, let you sleep it off, lent you my razor in the morning, came up here and got fresh clothes for you, saw to it you got to the studio neatly dressed and in your right mind. Well, now I need your help, Mr. Hawker. Be fair."

Hawker stares at him for a moment, then sighs, his shoulders sag, and he swings back into the room. "Come in. What is troubling you?"

Nathan steps in. "The publishers don't like the middle section of my novel because it doesn't have the father in it. He's a musician. He's gone off on the road to earn money to support his family. His son hates this."

The apartment has been shut up because of the rain and the air is stale and reeks of whiskey, tobacco smoke, unwashed clothes.

"It's unreasonable, but he's only ten years old—all he knows is he misses his father, can't eat, can't sleep. He blames music. He has talent. Stokowski has called him a genius. But now he slams down the cover on the keyboard and swears off music for life."

The place has two rooms divided by a bathroom, whose door stands open, giving a glimpse of dropped towels and a sharp smell of vomit.

"It's the book's big crisis—can the split between boy and man ever be mended? Frank can't come back until the job with the band runs its course. He has no choice. It's the only work he can find. And when he finally does get home, it looks for a while as if Nathan will never forgive him."

The sitting room, in which they stand, is strewn with books and magazines. The typewriter on the desk is almost hidden by scripts, tobacco pouches, briar pipes. The wastebasket overflows. Whiskey bottles lie empty under chairs, couch, tables; drinking glasses teeter everywhere.

"The rift between them doesn't resolve itself until the end of the story. Now these assholes tell me they don't want Frank to go away. He's funny, even when he's grouchy. And they think the parts without him are boring."

Hawker has been standing in one spot, staring at him. At him? Or through him? Nathan doesn't know. Now, the man picks up one of the glasses, drinks off the inch of whiskey in it, shudders, makes a face, and says:

"Excuse me. Permit me to improve my appearance."

He disappears into the bathroom. Will he ever come out? Nathan lifts printed matter and an empty bottle out of a chair and sits down. But he's too nervous to stay seated. He gets up, crosses the room, slides open the glass doors, steps out onto the balcony. The sifting rain feels pleasant on his flushed face. He hears the shower start in the bathroom. He looks out over misty roofs, trees, hills, and is reminded bleakly of that long-ago canyon hike in the rain with Ken Stone. This view is handsome, and maybe makes up for the long climb. He leans over and looks down. Hoyt was right. It's a hell of a drop to the backyard of the house with green shingles. That Hawker didn't break his neck that night seems impossible. The shower runs on and on. At last Nathan goes to the bathroom door and taps on it.

"Mr. Hawker? Are you all right?"

No answer. Nathan tries the door. It isn't locked. The room is full of steam. Hawker lies naked in the bathtub, eyes closed, water streaming over him. Nathan turns off the hot tap, turns up the cold one. And Hawker opens his eyes. Suddenly, and very wide.

"Ah," he splutters, and struggles to sit up. "Young Reed. It's you. Ah, yes—what you must do"—with Nathan steadying him, he steps shakily out of the tub—"is go right on with your book as if no one had written to you." Nathan turns off the shower. "Simply ignore them." Hawker reaches for a towel. Nathan hands him one from a rack. He wraps himself in it and sits on the edge of the tub. "If they understood what you were doing . . ."

"That's what's so crazy," Nathan says. "I sent them an outline with the first chapters."

Hawker holds up a shaky hand for silence. "If they understood what you were doing, they wouldn't have written. They will never understand. Almost no one but the writer ever does. You must accustom yourself to that. No one will ever understand."

"But if you're writing," Nathan says, "aren't you writing to someone?"

Hawker looks up at him and blinks, and his small mouth forms a wry smile. "Of course. But from that someone you will never hear."

"So what do I do?" Nathan cries.

"Finish your book," Hawker says, "exactly as you meant to. Change nothing."

"But what if they still say the middle is no good?"

Hawker indicates he wants to rise. Nathan helps him. "Thank you," Hawker says, and strays out of the bathroom. He peers into the sitting room. "If that window remains open, I shall perish of the cold." He turns for the bedroom. His voice comes back: "Much may fairly be said against delta weather, but it is never miserable in quite this way."

Nathan shuts the glass door to the balcony. He doesn't follow Hawker, because he has seen the bedroom once and doesn't want another look. He waits, again doubtful Hawker will ever come out. But in a few minutes, the man appears in slacks and a pullover, wet hair combed back. "Ah, it's you, Reed," he says once more. "Glad you could come by. A man grows lonesome on Sundays far from home." He opens a desk drawer and takes out a full bottle of whiskey. He lifts it to Nathan. "Care for a drink?"

Nathan wouldn't, but he nods. "Thank you."

"Companionable," Hawker says, and pours a glass full and hands it to Nathan. "Sit down. You appear troubled. Is there something on your mind?"

Nathan sits down, tastes the whiskey. It is strong and sweet. He looks across at the label on the bottle. Southern Comfort. Cloying. No wonder Hawker vomits. "My book," he says hopelessly. "We've been talking about it."

"So we have. My apologies." Hawker nods and holds up a finger. "An unresolved chord." He leans forward, peering, eyebrows raised. "I take it you do know music, do know what an unresolved chord is?"

"The middle of my book?"

"Exactly." Hawker sits back with a smile and gulps down half the contents of his glass. "And of course this creates great uneasiness, as such a chord is meant to do in listeners to a musical composition. To build tension in the hearer."

"Yes." Nathan braves another small swallow of his drink. "And when the book is finished, when the chord is resolved, they'll stop worrying about the middle—is that what you mean?"

"Nor will they ever know why," Hawker says.

"But one reason I sent them those middle chapters was I hoped they'd advance me a little more money to keep me going till I can finish it."

"Money?" Hawker laughs without mirth. "No, no. Disabuse yourself of that illusion. Publishers are not there to send you money. They are there to keep you hungry, to keep you writing. They are there to keep money from you."

"Five hundred dollars?" Nathan says.

"For that sum, the publisher can dine with a lady friend at '21,' " Hawker says. "And will." Then, gently, "Money and writing have nothing in common, my young friend. Learn that now, and spare yourself bitterness down the years. We write because we have no choice; they know it, and take advantage of it. If you dwell on how meagerly you are rewarded, you'll cut your throat." He finishes off his drink and reaches for the bottle. "Find other ways to get money." He fills his glass again. "Steal coins from blind men's cups. Rent out your sister. Murder a wealthy friend and marry his widow."

"Write for the movies?" Nathan says.

Hawker raises a hand in horror. "No, no. I would never suggest such depravity to any young man."

On Monday, Abou Bekker, shopping at T. Smollett for Christmas gifts to mail to friends in the service, learned that Nathan was alone and jumped to invite him to Thanksgiving dinner. It feels odd to ride again in the wooden-sided station wagon, as Nathan so often did before the war, with so many lost friends. There are only the two of them rattling along in the holiday sundown traffic toward Fair Oaks, but the car seems crowded with ghosts, his younger self among them, someone he hopes he'll never be again. Crossing the porch with its striped canvas swing and clutter of flowerpots and stepping into the dowdy little Bekker house is like entering a dream. Nothing has changed. Not a book has been shifted on the crowded shelves. Van Gogh's self-portrait in a straw hat still looks down blue-eyed from above the piano. Abou and his mother moved everything out in the summer of 1941, but it's all back as it was. And he wonders dizzily if he ever did see it empty. Maybe he was dreaming that awful day. Because to believe they would ever leave here was absurd. They never will. They'll live here together till they die. No. Stop. Premonitions are Alma's business. He shakes his head to rid it of the notion.

"A flea in your ear?" Abou asks, smiling.

There's no time to answer. Lucille Bekker comes through the curtain from the kitchen to put her pudgy little arms around him and give him a breathtaking squeeze. She is hot and damp with steam and smells of sage and onion. "Adonis," she cries, and stands on tiptoe to kiss his chin. "Oh, I am so glad to see you." She steps back, holding his hands, and glows at him. "Dear child, I do believe you're handsomer than ever." She turns to her son, who is grinning with his gorgeous Arabian teeth. "Bobby, isn't he beautiful?"

"I hope he's hungry," Abou says. "I almost fainted when we came in." He lifts his head, tests the air with his splendid nose. "The smells are sheer torture."

"It won't be long," she carols, and hurries back into the kitchen. "You'd better have your cocktails while there's time."

The cocktails are Manhattans. Icy. But sweet. With maraschino cherries. Nathan is happy there's time for only one. Then Lucille calls them. There is room on the screened back porch next to the dark little kitchen only for a table, three chairs, and a set of the collected plays of Eugene O'Neill. Under a hanging pierced brass lamp shade steam plates loaded with turkey, dressing, yams, cranberry sauce, mashed potatoes, gravy. All American. Except for one touch. Hidden by a napkin in a basket is fresh-baked bread in small, flat loaves. The butter melts when it touches the hot bread. Nathan finishes off one and reaches for another.

"This is the best bread I ever tasted."

"It's Lebanese. My father was a baker," Lucille says, and adds with a wry laugh, "My husband was an acrobat."

Nathan looks at her, startled.

Abou tells him, "It's true."

"Bobby began life traveling with the circus."

"In a carved crimson wagon trimmed with gold," Abou says, "baroque as a Bavarian church."

His mother has a mouthful of turkey and a dreamy look in her eyes. "Al G. Barnes. Sels-Floto. Ringling Brothers." She swallows, dabs her mouth with a napkin. "Of course, the age of traveling from town to town drawn by horses was long past. The wagons were loaded on flatbed railroad cars. Mostly, performers' wagons were kept together, but sometimes a wild-animal wagon would be put on next to us. Lions hate railroad travel. They grunt and grumble all night. The lions were the worst."

"It ended before I was six," Abou says. "My father was killed in a fall."

Lucille is silent for a moment, eating away, sorrow in her round face. "Not from a high wire," she says suddenly. "It's the high-wire and trapeze artists that usually die in falls. No, Sam was part of a tumbling team—the kind that vault into the air from teeter boards, you know, and land on each others' shoulders. He flew too high, lost control in the air, and landed on the back of his neck." She shudders and closes her eyes. "I can still hear the crack of the bones. He died instantly." She opens her eyes and looks at Nathan. "Twenty-six years old. A beautiful young man."

"You were beautiful yourself," Abou says to her, and to Nathan, "About ninety pounds in spangled tights with gossamer butterfly wings, twirling on a rope, light as air, high above the crowds—you shall see the photographs."

"It sounds like a wonderful life," Nathan says to her. "You should write about it. The circuses are dying out."

"Hmm." She gives him a mechanical smile. And they eat in silence. Suddenly, she says in a hard voice, "No, it was not a wonderful life. It was brutal and sordid. It wouldn't make a nice book, Adonis. People would be shocked. Behind all that gaiety and glitter there's pain and squalor. And terror. The clowns are the worst."

Nathan is startled and blinks at Abou. "They are?"

"Mother," Abou says, "it's Thanksgiving. Can't we—"

She ignores him. "Horrid and vicious and deadly. Sick men who hate the world, hiding their bitterness behind painted smiles and silly costumes."

"Bitterness?" Nathan says.

"Mother," Abou says again.

She glares at him. "You know who killed your father. You know it was no accident."

Abou sighs and rolls his eyes at the ceiling.

She lays a plump hand on Nathan's arm. "It's funny, when they get themselves up, the clowns, as women, isn't it? Huge breasts and hips, carrying piglets and little dogs dressed up as babies. Well"—she leans toward Nathan and lowers her voice—"it's because they want to be women. They're not—normal. That's why they hide from the world."

Nathan looks at Abou. Abou's head is bowed. He has covered his eyes with a hand. His mother's fingers tighten on Nathan's arm. She leans closer.

"And, of course, it's men they want. Handsome young men like Sam. They hated it that we were married and had a child. They couldn't keep their hands off him. And when he laughed at them and pushed them away—that's when they formed their bitches' circle and put the curse on him that killed him." She draws her head back, tilts it, studying Nathan's expression. "You don't believe it? Well, it's the absolute truth. They came to me and bragged about it afterward, giggling and gloating."

"Mother, they knew how superstitious you were. They were teasing you. It was an accident. The police said so."

"They killed him as sure as I'm alive to tell about it." She turns to Nathan again. "They're vicious people. I don't mean only clowns. Homosexuals, all of them. You're handsome like my Sam. They'll be after you. They're everywhere. Beware of them, Nathan." Maybe he's losing his struggle not to smile, because she adds, "I mean it. They're no joke."

"I'll be careful," Nathan promises.

Silence falls. That's fine with Nathan. It's easier just to eat, and everything tastes wonderful. When the plates are empty, and the bread basket too, the fat little woman rises and takes them away. It is growing dusky on the porch. Abou switches on the brass-shaded light. It casts lacy shadows. Lucille comes in with pumpkin pie on two plates that she sets in front of Nathan and Abou. Then she brings what appears to be tar in small cups.

"Now, you'll have to excuse me." She takes off her apron. "My ride will be here any minute." She pats Nathan's cheek. "Thank you for coming, Adonis. It was so good to see you again." She kisses her son. "Don't bother to wash up." She goes out. "I'll do it when I get home."

"I never had such a great Thanksgiving dinner," Nathan calls. "Thank you. You putting on nursery rhymes tonight?"

"At the Presbyterian church," she calls back in her tuneful voice. "Not nursery rhymes, no. *Aladdin and His Wonderful Lamp.*" From the tiny living room come thumps—her big case full of marionettes, the fold-up frame of the stage they caper on. "It's everyone's favorite." The screen-door spring twangs. The door slaps shut, and her footsteps fade down the long driveway.

Nathan's mouth is full of pie. He blinks at Abou. "You came to the Black Cat as a clown," he says.

"Who'd have believed me as an acrobat?" Abou says. "With my figure? Try the coffee."

Nathan drinks from the tiny cup. It's thick and sweet as syrup. He nods, forces a smile, quickly puts it down.

Abou says, "My father's brothers in Morocco sit in circles on the floor drinking that all day long." He gives Nathan a cigarette and fits one into his ivory holder. "They can't talk about anything without their coffee."

"What shall we talk about?" Nathan lights the cigarettes.

Abou smiles through smoke. "We don't have to talk. We can just lie down quietly together. In the dark."

Nathan tilts his head. "Who was it you came looking for at the Black Cat?"

"The boy from the mail room at Paramount who lived with me in Hollywood. For a few weeks. While mother was away in New Jersey visiting relatives. Keith. I'm always looking for him. I don't know how he could vanish so completely."

"Maybe the Army got him," Nathan says.

Abou leans across and kisses Nathan's mouth. "You must be as lonely as I am these days. Who would we be hurting?"

" 'Whom.' " Nathan lays down his napkin, pushes back his chair, stands. "You know the answer—you, me. Thanks for dinner. You don't have to drive me home." He pushes into the dark kitchen. "It's too far. I'll catch the bus."

He climbs the stairs with his head down and doesn't notice the lamps glowing in Hoyt's place, his place. Not till he steps inside. There are smells of cigarette smoke and coffee. His heart leaps in his chest. He shouts "Hoyt?" and runs for the kitchen, smiling so hard it hurts his face. And there is Hoyt, all right, at the kitchen table. And he looks up and he is smiling too. But he doesn't jump up and hug Nathan and kiss him and start undressing him right then and there. His smile is the kind reserved for when others are present. And there is another present, all right. It's Frank. In a travel-rumpled suit he's owned for years. Nathan can't get his breath to say anything. He can only stare in disbelief.

"Where have you been?" Frank says.

"Fair Oaks. For Thanksgiving dinner," Nathan says. "Why didn't you write you were coming? I'd have met the train." He looks at Hoyt. "You too."

Hoyt shrugs. "I hitchhiked. I didn't know how long it would take. It didn't take long."

"I'm glad you're back."

"Me too," Hoyt says.

Between their two coffee mugs, drawings are spread on the table. Still too shocked to make conversation, Nathan sorts through them. Grain elevators, scruffy horses, an old flivver, men in straw hats seated side by side whittling on a storefront porch, studies of tumbleweeds, farm wagons, a bleached cow skull, a wasted old man lying on a narrow bed, eyes closed, gnarled hands folded on his chest—Long Tex Stubblefield? Nathan picks this one up and looks at Hoyt.

"Is he gone?"

Hoyt shakes his head. "I couldn't wait."

Frank nods at the drawings. "Beats a Brownie," he says, "by quite a stretch. Good work."

"It was the Bekkers who invited me." Nathan finds a mug, pours himself some coffee, and sits down. "You remember Abou Bekker? You always said he looked like he ought to be leading a camel?"

"What's he doing now?" Frank says.

"Building airplanes," Nathan says. "P-38s."

"War makes it tough to get a place on a train," Frank says. "Full up with servicemen, going, coming. I wanted to come for Christmas, but I expect by then nobody out of uniform will stand a chance."

Nathan lights a cigarette. "I'm glad to see you."

"I guessed the only way to bring that about," Frank says with a faint smile, "was for me to come here. I played some extra funerals to raise the money for the fare."

"I appreciate the sacrifice," Nathan says. Hoyt touches his hand that has the cigarette pack in it. The touch makes Nathan dizzy with lust. His voice wobbles. He says to Frank, "I know how you hate the smell of cut flowers." He gives up the pack to Hoyt and lights the cigarette Hoyt takes. "You don't like Sensations."

"They beat Bull Durham," Hoyt says, and pulls from his shirt pocket a little cloth sack and waggles it on its string. "You can't buy anything else in Amarillo."

"I went through Army training in 1917 in Texas," Frank says. "All I remember is heat, dust, and wind."

"Nothing's changed," Hoyt says. He looks at Nathan. "He'll die just the same without me there. Never once opened his eyes in all this time and looked at me. Or anybody else. Place is full of Stubblefields and Hoyts. Eating up the food. Money I brought went fast. After that I was no use."

"Your mother?" Nathan says.

"Her idea was for the old man and me to part on friendly terms. Could never happen anyway, but certainly not with him dying in a coma. After a while she admitted it, at least to herself. I could tell. She begged me to stay, of course, but I doubt she misses me. It's Tex she loves, and I was always a trouble to her, fighting with him that way."

Nathan looks at Frank. "What about Alma?"

Frank's laugh is brief and wry. "I'm to bring you back to Minneapolis with me. No ifs, ands, or buts. Those were her conditions for turning me loose at Thanksgiving."

"What did you do for dinner?" Nathan says.

"There's a big drugstore on Hollywood Boulevard. They had a banner in the window—Thanksgiving dinner with turkey and all the trimmings for seventy-five cents. I ate there. It was darn good. It really was."

Feebly, Nathan says, "Are you staying with us?"

"Hell, no. No offense, but staying with people, you can't call your soul your own. No, there's a little hotel a block or two below the Boulevard—the Mark Twain. Clean. Private bath. I've stayed in worse in my time. It's cheap. And I like the name." He smiles, and Nathan realizes how much older he's grown. He still has his thick thatch of white hair, but there's more stoop to his wide shoulders. His face is thinner. And his eyes don't twinkle as they used to. They're sad. "Don't worry about me. I'll be fine."

"I work all day," Nathan says. "I can't get time off. It's the Christmas shopping season."

"We can't take you sightseeing," Hoyt says. "No car."

"I'll get around by trolley. I'm used to it. Spent half my life alone in strange towns." He raises his eyebrows at Nathan. "Lots of good jazzmen playing your barrooms."

Nathan cheers up. "We can go together."

"You don't mean tonight!" Hoyt yelps.

Frank looks at him curiously. "They're closed tonight," he says.

They keep too busy in the dark for talk. For a long time. What they do naked to and for and with each other feels so good Nathan thinks he will die. They do sleep at last. From exhaustion. Hoyt, after all, has come a long journey today and yesterday and the day before. He has a rightful claim on sleep. For a time, propped on an elbow, Nathan watches him sleep, feels his warm, slow, regular breath on his chest—they are that close. He never wants to be any farther away than this from Hoyt again. The leaves at the window rustle in the cool night breeze. Moving carefully so as not to wake him, he fits himself against Hoyt, lays a leg across Hoyt's legs, an arm across Hoyt's chest, nuzzles Hoyt's hair, and he too sleeps. He hasn't slept well since Hoyt left, and this sleep is a good sleep. When they waken it's not quite morning and they don't quite waken. Slow-moving as underwater swimmers, they please each other awake, then lie side by side, smoking cigarettes.

"I thought you missed him," Hoyt says.

"He used to be my god," Nathan says. "But something's happened. I'm not a child anymore, and he's become a tired old man I feel sorry for. And why did he have to come just when you got home? Why not last week, the week before? Now I want to spend my time with you—what little time I've got."

"What are you doing working? I left money."

Nathan tells where the money went. "Reggie's trying to pay it back. Ten dollars a week. Only you know he can't. I was lucky Mr. MacKenzie let me have my job again."

"But what about your book?"

"The hell with it," Nathan says.

"Ho. Sounds like the publishers wrote," Hoyt says.

Nathan tells him what they said. "I asked James Hawker what to do. He said ignore them. But he was drunk." Nathan snubs his cigarette in the ashtray that lies on Hoyt's flat belly. "Connie's right. I'm too young to write a novel."

"I'd take Hawker drunk over Connie sober, anytime. And what about me? I've read the book, they haven't. It's a fine, funny, truthful book. I've told you over and over. Nathan, what the fuck's the matter with you?"

"Don't go and leave me again." Nathan grabs him and clings to him. "Nothing's any good for me without you."

Hoyt strokes his hair. "I'm back now. Everything's going to be okay. Don't cry."

"I'm not crying," Nathan says.

"Sure." Hoyt reaches Kleenex and mops Nathan's face. "Blow your nose." Nathan blows his nose. Hoyt tosses the wet tissues into the shadows and kisses him. "Just finish the book. Everybody will love it. You'll see."

"When? Finish the book when? What about the rent?"

"Leave it to me," Hoyt says.

He takes Frank to the City of Paris—in a basement across the boulevard from T. Smollett—to hear Kid Ory, to the Suzie-Q for

Jack Teagarden, and upstairs to the Montmartre to hear Jimmy Noone and to spend the time between sets talking over the 1920s with Noone and his bass player. He used to jam with them privately after hours in New Orleans and other river towns when he made his living playing with vaudeville orchestras. There is a lot of laughter among the old men. It makes them all younger for a time, and Frank leaves at two A.M. smiling. Nathan walks him back to the Mark Twain Hotel, and when they part, Frank hugs him and laughs. Nathan has made him happy.

For a few hours. Mostly, when Nathan's with him, he's quiet, keeping inside himself, worried about something. Nathan has to work all day Saturday, but on Sunday he and Frank travel on the big red car to the beach. They walk the amusement piers at Ocean Park, at Santa Monica. There are crowds of soldiers, sailors, and marines and their girlfriends. The rides wheel against the blue sky, their spinning pods filled with shrieking thrill-seekers. The roller coaster rattles and roars. Screams fall from on high. The scaffold is rickety, its white paint peeling. Ice cream cones, candied apples, popcorn are in all hands. Frank stops at a stand enveloped in greasy heat and buys hot dogs and bottles of soda pop. They lean on the rail over which ragged old men and women bend, holding fishing rods.

"Pretty seedy," Frank says. "Must be the war."

"It looks the same as ever to me," Nathan says.

And his arm is nudged, and he turns and looks into the face of Amour from the Captain's Cabin—shiny brown eyes, chestnut curls, dimples. The boy smiles, careful not to show his spotty teeth. He is wearing skimpy swim trunks and that's all. His body too is like an academic eighteenth-century French painting. Too smooth, too perfect. "It's you again," he says.

"Do you live down here?" Nathan says.

"Coincidence," Amour says, and cranes to look past him at Frank. "Don't tell me this is your rawhide Texan."

Frank crumples up his hot-dog wrapper, tosses it into a wire-mesh trash basket. "Friend of yours?" he asks, and holds out a hand. "Frank Reed. I'm Nathan's father."

Amour makes a quick little sympathetic grimace at Nathan, smiles, bad teeth and all, at Frank, and shakes Frank's hand. "André Langlois."

"French Canadian?" Frank says. "So's the girl I married, Nathan's mother. Family named Du Bois."

Langlois bats his long-lashed eyes at Nathan. "Perhaps we're cousins," he says.

"Could be." Nathan squints at gulls circling over their heads and tosses the last bite of his hot dog into the air. A gull catches it on the wing. Nathan wishes André Langlois would go away. Instead, the boy gets chatty with Frank.

"Do you live out here, Mr. Reed?"

"Minneapolis," Frank says. "This is just a short visit." His glancing smile at Nathan doesn't seem to mean to be a smile. "To check up on my pride and joy."

"Don't worry, he's doing just fine," Langlois says. "He's the talk of the town." Tongue noticeably in cheek, he gives Nathan a sly sideways glance. "Didn't he tell you?"

Frank's eyebrows go up. "Tell me? What?"

"About the sensation he created Halloween night?"

"Shut up, André," Nathan says. "Go away."

André dodges him, grinning. "At the costume ball?"

Frank says, "I didn't hear about that."

"Well, it seems he and his cowboy friend"—André is backing away now—"went wearing nothing but stars painted all over their bare skins, and—" He bumps into a bull-necked marine and knocks the bag of peanuts out of his hand.

"Hey, pansy, look where you're going," the marine says, and swings at him. His girlfriend catches his arm. André yelps, takes to his pretty heels, disappears into the crowd.

Nathan watches him, and turns back to find Frank staring at him. Asking for an explanation. Though not with words. Nathan says, "You want to ride the bumper cars?"

"We did that in nineteen thirty-nine," Frank says. "Our first week in California."

"That's why I thought of it," Nathan says.

They walk to the pavilion in silence and buy tickets and wait in line. From this place, they can hear the wheezy music of the merry-go-round.

"Was what he said true?" Frank says.

"There was no harm in it," Nathan says.

"You used to have better sense. I don't think you're ready to be on your own. Noble was right. You pick the wrong friends." Frank looks away for a minute, at the crowd moving along the pier. "That André, for instance."

"He's just somebody I met once," Nathan protests.

"I'd like to know where you find them," Frank says. "I warned you that time about Desmond Foley and next thing anybody knows you're at his place and in trouble."

"I explained about that. I was curious."

Frank smooths the little red ticket in his fingers, studying it. "Back when I was your age, on a Sunday, I'd take a girl to the beach—the lake."

"I took you," Nathan says.

"I'd feel better if I met your girlfriend sometime."

"Hey, our cars are ready." Nathan moves off. "Which do you want—the blue one or the yellow one?"

"Only you have to pose for both of us this time."

"No, Hoyt, damn it, I won't."

"Nathan." Hoyt tries to unbutton Nathan's shirt. "It will get you the money to finish your novel."

Nathan drops onto the couch. "I don't want to get it that

way." He picks up a book. He doesn't know what book it is. It doesn't matter. "I'll keep on at T. Smollett, thanks." He scowls up at Hoyt. "What happened to your three hundred a month?"

"I was away for weeks. I missed a lot of meetings."

"Well, you're back now."

"Not with them." Hoyt takes the book gently, turns it right side up, gives it back. "It'll read easier that way."

"Hoyt, there has to be decent work. What about advertising agencies? They use artists. Magazines?"

"They'll want to see a portfolio." Hoyt drops down beside him. "It will take me weeks to work up a portfolio. Then I'll have to make appointments and tramp around from office to office. That will take more weeks. Nathan, I can do this painting in a few days if you'll—" He reaches for the buttons again. Nathan grabs his wrists.

"No, damn it, Hoyt. It makes me feel filthy."

"That's unreasonable. We do it all the time. It's beautiful. I'll paint it that way."

Nathan jumps up. "I don't want you to paint it that way. I don't want you to paint it at all. For some jaded old crud to drool over and show off to his disgusting old friends?" He runs into the kitchen. He doesn't know why. He opens the refrigerator and stares into it. "Hoyt, what do you want to ruin it for? It's good. It's the best thing there ever was in this world." He slams the refrigerator door. "What makes you want to turn it into shit? It's love, Hoyt. It's us." He shuts his eyes, raises his fists, and howls at the ceiling. "Can't you understand?"

"You keep explaining in that voice"—Hoyt puts his arms around him from behind, lovingly, with a soft laugh—"and the whole neighborhood will understand. Nathan, the faces won't show. No one will know it's us."

"Let me go." Nathan fights free. "I won't do it."

Hoyt sits down and studies him. "You know what's wrong

with you? You figure it's time to settle things with Frank. He's old. You might never see him again. And you want to do the right thing and tell him you're queer. But you can't."

"Don't change the subject," Nathan says.

"I'm not. What scares you about the picture's the same thing. You think it would put a seal on the truth. And deep down, you still don't want to admit it—even to yourself."

"Come to bed with me." Nathan takes his hands and tugs. "I'll show you just how wrong you are."

He takes Frank on the streetcar out Sunset to Benbow's and they spend the evening together in the empty house at the top of the hill, playing the piano. Nathan plays—stumbles around, rather. Frank plays as if he practiced every day. They find in the piano bench an arrangement of tunes from *Carmen* for four hands and bumble through that, alternately glaring at each other and laughing. At last, they get to laughing so hard, they're not playing anymore, only trying to play, and they have to stop.

"Where's the bathroom?" Frank says, wiping his eyes.

Nathan points. "Through that bedroom."

Frank goes. Nathan shuffles scores on top of the piano, finds a simple Bach piece, sets it on the rack, starts on it cautiously, and, after a page, senses Frank in the room again. He turns. Frank looks pale. "I'm going," he says. And when Nathan starts to rise, "No, no. You stay here and work. You need all the practice you can get."

"Are you sick?" Nathan says.

Frank shakes his head and turns away. "Just tired."

Nathan stands up. "I'd better come with you."

"I don't want that," Frank says sharply, and starts up the stairs to find the door they came in by. "Thank you."

Nathan goes to the foot of the stairs. "There's something wrong," he says. "Frank, what is it?"

"Nothing." Frank drags his big-boned old frame to the top and vanishes. Puzzled and hurt, Nathan hears floorboards creak overhead. The house door opens and closes. Frank's heels thump on the long zigzag of outside stair flights.

Nathan wants to run after him. He doesn't run after him. There was a time, but that time is past. Why isn't Frank just tired, as he claims? He's not used to late nights, treks to the beach, all that. But they were having a good time here, making music—like the old days. Frank seemed happy. And all of a sudden—what? What happened? Frowning, Nathan goes back to the piano in its island of light, sits down, puts his hands on the keys, and focuses on the Bach piece again. He plays it, not well, but not so badly as last time, replays the bollixed passages, finally gets to the end. And right behind him Benbow says:

"Well done."

Nathan turns. "I didn't hear you come in."

Benbow picks up a score from the piano top. "Hah. 'Piano Four Hands.' You've got someone with you." He looks around.

"My father was here," Nathan says. "He's the musician in the family."

"You said he lived in Minneapolis."

"He came for a visit," Nathan says. "I didn't think you'd mind if I brought him tonight."

"I'm delighted," Benbow says. "Why didn't he stay?"

"He said he was tired," Nathan says. "He's old, you know. Most times people think he's my grandfather." Nathan closes down the keyboard cover and gets up. "He enjoyed himself, but then he went to the bathroom, and when he came out he said he was going. And now it's time for me to go."

Benbow is staring at him. "The bathroom?" He walks to the bedroom door. "You mean the one through here?"

"He's a little crippled up," Nathan says. "He doesn't climb stairs too well. Wasn't it all right to use that one?"

Benbow says, "All right with me? Of course. But there are fathers and fathers." Benbow looks grave. "Nathan, does he know about you?"

Dismally, Nathan shakes his head. "I knew how he'd take it —hurt, disgust, anger. I never had the nerve. But it's time. I'm going to tell him before he leaves."

"I suspect I have spared you that embarrassment." Benbow steps into the bedroom. "You'd better see this."

Nathan feels a chill. He goes into the room. Hoyt's big smoky portraits hang on the wall, side by side, Nathan naked, Hoyt naked. "How did they get here?"

"Dr. Marriott's garage proved leaky in the recent rains. He asked me to store them while the presumptive nephew stays on as his house guest."

"Oh, shit," Nathan says.

When he gets home it's early morning. The outside stairs are damp with dew. He starts up them wearily and sees Hoyt sitting at the top. Asleep. Head tilted against an upright. He has on a navy watch cap, sweater, corduroys, so maybe he isn't cold, but Nathan is afraid he must be. He shakes him. "What are you doing out here?"

Hoyt winces at him. "Waiting for you. Where the hell have you been?"

"The Mark Twain Hotel, the Union Station. Looking for Frank. He didn't come here, did he?"

Hoyt shakes his head.

Nathan sits down beside him. "I didn't think so. Cigarette? The machines are empty at the station."

Hoyt digs out Dominos and they light up, cupping the paper match against the chilly little morning breeze. Out on Highland cars and trucks begin to pass. Someplace up in the hills in back, a dog barks.

"You been at the damn station all night?"

Nathan tells him why. "He wouldn't stay and call me dirty

names. He'd just go home. He doesn't like facing unpleasant facts. Never has. The streetcar put me an hour behind him at the Mark Twain, and he'd packed and gone. In a taxi, the desk clerk said. But I couldn't find him at the station. It was crowded, five thousand people milling around. I looked and looked, but somehow he dodged me. Then when the Chicago train finally left and it was no use looking for him anymore, the streetcars had stopped running."

Hoyt gets stiffly to his feet. "Let's make coffee. I'm about frozen to death out here." In the kitchen, Nathan sitting at the table half asleep, Hoyt runs hot water into a kettle, sets it on the stove, turns the blue flame under it up high. That's the last Nathan remembers when twenty minutes later Hoyt shakes his shoulder. He's slept with his head on his arms. Yawning, he pushes upright, smells the coffee, stretches, smiles. Then he remembers Frank.

"I'm sorry I worried you," he says. "It was childish of me to run after him, wasn't it? I told myself that, but I ran after him anyway. In a panic. I wanted to explain, to change what he was thinking." The red-and-black pack lies on the table. He takes a cigarette from it and laughs bleakly at himself as he lights it. "But what he was thinking was the truth." He shakes out the match. "So that was even more childish, wasn't it?"

Hoyt shrugs, sipping at the steamy coffee. "Natural. For most of your life, his good opinion was everything to you. You wanted to shine in his eyes. It's no use anymore—you've changed, he never will. But old habits die hard."

Nathan smokes, sips at the scalding coffee, broods. "He knew, anyway. It wasn't the paintings. He knew way back in Fair Oaks when I got into that mess with Desmond Foley." He looks at Hoyt through the smoke. "I told you about that, didn't I?" Hoyt nods. Nathan says, "I made some lame excuse, and he pretended to accept it, but looking back I think he guessed. But he's told himself all this time it wasn't so. Then that bastard Noble writes to him. And he comes here. And even in a dress he wouldn't mistake you for a blushing bride. And there's Reggie, the grande dame. And all those shrill middle-aged aunties nibbling chicken Kiev at Drossie's. God, his face was a study that night."

Hoyt nods. "Then somebody tells him about Halloween."

"That malicious little faggot André," Nathan says.

"On the pier at Ocean Park." Hoyt grins. "That's right—you told me."

"Not funny," Nathan says. "Frank's really hurt. And I hate that." Tears blur his eyes. "I really do."

Hoyt lights a cigarette from the coal of the one he's burned down. "You hate it enough to change? Find a girl? Get married? Give him grandchildren?"

Nathan makes a face. "Are you crazy?" He drinks more coffee. "Did Benbow tell you the paintings were there?"

"I guess he was saving it for a surprise," Hoyt says.

"That worked out." Nathan shivers and hugs himself. "It's going to be a sad world without Frank."

"He'll always be funny in your book," Hoyt says.

Nathan is stacking new books on the counters—at least he's trying to. Customers crowd the aisles. They bump into him. He bumps into them. Angus MacKenzie's red hair is ruffled. He dances like Ray Bolger from customer to shelf to cash register in a happy daze. Business has never been so good. As Mr. Constance keeps moaning to Nathan, a toothache is killing him, but there's no chance for him to get to a dentist—not today. Annie MacKenzie's voice and hair are brassy behind the counter, where she is all thumbs, wrapping books in Christmas paper, getting her fingers stuck together with Scotch tape, dropping rolls of colored ribbon that whiz along the floor. Mr. Constance has taught them all how to tie pretty bows, but she hasn't learned. She's always yelping for him or Nathan to come help her. The telephone rings and rings—everyone's too busy to answer it. At last, Nathan makes a dash for it.

"T. Smollett Books," he says.

"Nathan Reed, please."

"Hoyt?" Nathan stares at the receiver in surprise. Hoyt never calls him here. "Is that you?"

"It's Steve," the voice says. "Steve Schaffer."

Nathan's heart bumps. "You're alive. You said you'd write, but you never wrote, and I thought you were dead."

"They never laid a glove on me," Schaffer says.

"Where are you? Do I get to see you?"

"Right now. I'm across the street at the Christie. Room 703."

"Jesus," Nathan says. "It's awfully busy here. They'll never let me go."

"Sneak out," Schaffer says. "Nathan, I've only got two hours until train time."

MacKenzie taps Nathan's shoulder. "Nathan, no personal calls. You know that."

Then he prances off to take a stack of books from a woman in a fur coat, and Nathan says softly into the phone, "I'll be right there." He hangs up, and tells Constance at the cash register that he's going to the washroom. But the real reason he struggles up the crowded aisles to the back is to get his jacket. On the workbench, tall stacks of books in gay paper wait for him to wrap them for mailing. He ignores them and, looping a muffler around his throat, ducks out the back door. He doesn't know why his heart is racing. He doesn't know why he is so happy.

He steps out of a creaky elevator that's carried him all alone and rather jerkily to the seventh floor. The hallway here is murky. The light bulbs are weak. Is the Christie saving electricity for the war effort? He takes a couple of wrong turnings before he locates room 703. He is trembling as he knocks. "It's Nathan," he says, and has to repeat it because it isn't loud enough. "It's Nathan."

"Door's unlocked," Schaffer calls.

Nathan opens it and steps inside. To his right a door stands open, letting out steam and light and the smell of soap. He looks in. Schaffer stands naked at the washbasin, leaning to the mirror, shaving. He throws Nathan a grin, wipes lather off his face with a washcloth, comes and takes Nathan in his arms, and kisses him. Openmouthed, urgent. It makes Nathan weak in the knees, but he keeps his mouth closed, and Schaffer stops trying. He lets Nathan go and studies him, head tilted, not frowning, smiling curiously. His gentle brown eyes are more beautiful than Nathan has remembered them—and he's remembered them often.

"Why did you come, then?" he says.

"Why didn't you write to me?" Nathan wanders into the room, where the bed is made up, fresh underclothes lying on it. The duffel bag is in a chair. A fresh uniform is on a hanger on the open closet door, corporal's stripes on the sleeve. "I worried about you—that if you weren't wounded or dead, you'd forgotten me. That hurt too."

"I couldn't get you out of my mind." Drying his face, Schaffer follows him. Still naked. He is beautiful naked. He goes to the dresser, tosses away the towel, combs his dark curly hair. Nathan leans against the windowsill, a brick airshaft at his back, and watches him. Schaffer sees that he is watching. He says with a dry laugh, "I did write to you, but I didn't mail the letters. They were"—he makes a sheepish face—"you know what they were." He touches his cock. It is erect. "You can see how I feel."

"I can see." Nathan sits dolefully on the side of the bed. "You're forgetting there's Hoyt."

"I wish I could." Schaffer tucks the comb into a ditty bag on the dresser. "I wish you could." He picks up khaki boxer shorts from the bed, puts them on. Nathan watches this bleakly. Schaffer says, "I saw him this morning. Where you live. I had to tell him something." He buttons the shorts. "I left a carton of Camels, but he still doesn't like me."

"He thinks I like you too much," Nathan says.

Schaffer laughs wanly. "I wish he was right."

Nathan asks, "Tell him what?"

Schaffer pulls on a skivvy shirt. "That my mother's death was no accident—she was murdered. Friends of hers told me last week in New York."

"Hoyt always believed that," Nathan says. "He spent months trying to find who did it."

Schaffer frowns. "Why didn't he tell me on the day of the funeral?" He flaps into a starchy suntan shirt.

Nathan shrugs. "I suppose because he hadn't any proof. Do your mother's friends know who did it?"

Schaffer buttons the shirt. "Not yet—but they will."

Nathan has a cold. He has crept his way unwillingly to T. Smollett Books every morning, coughed and sneezed and ached his way through endless hectic hours with customers who have their own problems and don't care how he feels—and dragged himself up the steps of home every evening, sure he'll never survive another day. At last it's Sunday, and he can stay in bed, reading *Lafcadio's Adventures*, piled with covers when he chills, throwing the covers off when he burns up with fever, though it's cold, and the windows can no longer be closed—the tree branches have grown too strong to be pushed back outside.

Smoking those PX Camels of Schaffer's—he's never told Nathan where they came from, and Nathan has never asked—Hoyt works away doggedly at his portfolio, seated on the old couch, little paint jars beside him, drawing board on his knees, feet propped on the coffee table, brushes held waiting in his teeth while he carefully lays in color with a brush in his fingers—working from photos torn from old magazines he brings home from thrift shops, pictures he calls his morgue, pictures he can study to get the details right.

He breaks off every hour or so to fetch Nathan hot lemonade with honey, or aspirins, or Reggie's preferred brand of cough syrup laced with ether, each dose of which makes Nathan feel wonderful, at least for a short, blessed while. He is in one of these happy states, asleep but not asleep, when he hears heavy footfalls on the stairs.

He dreams for a few seconds of an elephant coming up here, putting its huge gray head in at the door. Then he hears a querulous female voice and opens his eyes. He knows that voice. It's Flora Belle Short's voice. Linnet's mother, Rick Ames's landlady. What's she doing here?

"No, Hoyt," she's saying, "no excuses. I can't come back without you both. Where is he?" And the next thing Nathan knows, Flora Belle is looming beside the bed, massive, hair bound in a gypsy scarf, over her shoulders a ratty fur cape, her dress swaths of gaudy mismatched fabrics. She glares down at him as if he were a dog. "Runny nose, coughs, fever?" she jeers. "It's all in your mind."

"I don't think so," he wheezes.

"I'll prove it to you," she says. "You've had bad news lately. And you can't decide what to do about it. Am I right?" Nathan doesn't answer. He's used to this kind of rubbish from Alma. Flora Belle nods briskly. "Your silence says yes. And so does your cold. You watch and see. Make up your mind to do one thing or the other, and the cold will vanish." She bends and throws the covers off him. "You're dressed. Good. Put on your shoes and come along. Percy Hinkley wants to see you. Home is the sailor, home from the sea, and he is extremely upset."

"Upset?" Groggily, Nathan sits up, wiping his nose on his sleeve. "With me? I never even met him."

Hoyt is in the bedroom doorway. "You can't drag this boy out in the cold. He'll get pneumonia. He's prone to pneumonia. It nearly killed him once."

"All he has to do is settle the confusion in his mind." Flora Belle heaves toward him, and he jumps back from the doorway so she can pass. In the green-shingled living room she stands and waits, hands folded across her vast bosom, rings twinkling with glass jewels, while Nathan shuffles to the bathroom. He braces himself with trembling arms on the washbasin, studies his face in the mirror. Plainly he's dying. If she can't see it, he can. Feebly,

he brushes his teeth, washes his face, combs his hair. "We're waiting, Nathan," Flora Belle calls. He leaves the bathroom.

"I can't go," he says. "I can't walk that far."

"If you don't come with me, today, now," Flora Belle says,
"Percy will file a lawsuit against you tomorrow morning downtown
at the Hall of Justice."

Nathan stares. "What? He's joking."

"Percy Hinkley never jokes." She twists the knob, pulls open
the door. "As I can testify to my sorrow."

"A lawsuit?" Hoyt says. "What the hell for?"

"He's forbidden me to reveal that." She lumbers out. "He
prefers to tell you himself. Come along, please."

Hinkley waits at the top of the house, the king in his high tower.
Nathan nearly faints climbing all those stairs. He has to sit on the
floor at the top to get his breath. His heart is laboring. While Flora
Belle barges off down a narrow, crooked, makeshift hallway where
there is almost no light, Hoyt stands over Nathan, looking worried.
"Go ahead," Nathan pants, and waves a hand. "I'll be there in a
minute."

Hoyt glares after Flora Belle. "Rhinoceros."

"I deserve it," Nathan coughs. "I took advantage of her, and
of dumb Linnet. Person should never do that."

"You didn't hurt them," Hoyt says.

Nathan shakes his head. "That's not the point."

"You're delirious. What is the point?"

Nathan gasps, "I guess Percy will tell us, won't he?"

Down the hall, a male voice yelps, "What are you doing here
alone? Didn't you bring them?"

"They'll be along in a minute," Flora Belle says. "The Reed
boy is sick or thinks he is. The stairs were too much for him. He's
collapsed."

"What? Oh, poor Nathan." Linnet comes running out of nowhere to kneel beside him. "Oh, poor Nathan," she says again, and, looking up at Hoyt, "Can't you do anything?"

"You've done pretty much everything already," Hoyt says. "Don't you think?"

Linnet bursts into tears. "I couldn't help it."

"Hung you up by your thumbs, did he?" Hoyt says. "Gave you forty lashes across your beautiful behind?"

"You're mean," she says, jumping up.

"Give me a hand." Nathan struggles to stand, but there's no strength in him. "Let's get it over with."

And Hoyt and Linnet help him along the Dr. Caligari hallway and into the fabled tower room. Hinkley swivels in his chair to face them from a patchwork panel of dials and knobs and tangled electrical wires. He's a skinny, white-skinned man with a thin, high-bridged nose, a blue lantern jaw, a built-in sneer curling his lip.

His sanctum is no more than eight by ten, and it's jammed with junk—not just radio bits and pieces in and out of cardboard cartons, but stacks of tattered science fiction magazines, ragged math and physics textbooks, phonograph records in and out of albums, chess pieces scattered around. A poster is peeling off a wall—Bela Lugosi in *Dracula*. Dusty models of spaceships hang on wires from a ceiling stained by rain. Daylight waits outside grimy windows. Loudspeakers crackle with bursts of static and with far-off foreign voices crying that the world is on fire.

A fierce bulb lights the radio control panel. It glares into Nathan's eyes so at first he doesn't see the monster in the corner. "This," Hinkley says with a wave of the hand, "is my friend Jukes." Jukes shambles up out of his chair. He is lumpish, with a straggly pirate mustache, long mangy hair, a slack mouth, a cracked green celluloid eye visor. "Jukes is not only a brain who can play three-dimensional chess in his head," Hinkley says, "but he is a paradigm of Homo sapiens in that he also possesses great physical strength." Jukes laughs mindlessly and sits down again in his dim corner, like a storm subsiding. Nathan coughs.

"Can't you see Nathan's sick?" Linnet says. "Will you get on with it, Perc, please?"

"Gladly. Hand me the coats." From somewhere Linnet produces the overcoat and raincoat Nathan and Hoyt wore to the Black Cat on Halloween night. Hinkley peers into the shadows from his blaze of light. "Stubblefield, Reed, you want to step over here and look at these?"

They stumble between the stacks of junk. Percy turns the coats inside out, holds them up to the light. The linings are smeared with gold and silver paint. Sequins are stuck to the paint—too much paint, too many sequins.

"We didn't do that," Hoyt says.

"Then who did?" Hinkley says mildly. "Babe—aren't these the coats you lent these men on Halloween?"

Eyes downcast, Linnet mumbles, "Yes, Percy. I told you."

"I wanted you to tell them," Hinkley says. "They seem to have forgotten." He squints at Nathan and Hoyt. "You went to a party wearing nothing but spangled jock straps, with gold and silver stars painted all over your bodies."

Nathan peers into the shadows at Linnet. "I never told you that." He looks at Hoyt. "Did you?" Hoyt shakes his head. Nathan says to Hinkley, "Who told you that?"

"A tenant of mine," Hinkley says, smirking, "one Richard Sheridan Ames. A fat old pansy wino war regulations forbid me to evict. But it turns out he can still be useful. He heard all about you from somebody who was there. There's an underground party line, did you know? Of pansies?" He throws the coats aside. "I guess you know, all right."

Hoyt makes a sound and goes for Hinkley with clenched fists. But in his corner Jukes rumbles and surges up out of his chair. "Touch him and I'll break you in two," he says. Hoyt decides not to touch him. Jukes grins at Hinkley like a small boy. "That okay, Perc?"

"Perfect," Hinkley says. "Thank you."

"We didn't leave those coats all smeared with paint like that."
Nathan peers around for Linnet and sees dimly the glow of her
blond hair. "Did we, Linnet?"

She shrugs sheepishly. "I guess I didn't notice at first," she
says.

"According to the dry cleaner, they can't be saved. Anyway,
you rowdy girls practically tore the arms off. Both coats will have
to be replaced. I've been shopping. The raincoat will run fifty
dollars, the overcoat ninety-five. That's one hundred forty-five dollars you owe me."

"Shit," Hoyt says. "You wrecked those coats yourself."

"Forget it," Nathan says. "Where are we going to get a
hundred and forty-five dollars? I only earn twenty a week. And
Hoyt's out of work."

"You should have thought of that"—Hinkley smiles—"before
you started making free with my possessions."

"We never did that," Nathan says. "Linnet—"

"Oh, yes—Linnet let you have them." He stretches out a bony
hand. "C'mere, Babe." Linnet steps sulkily out of the shadows and
takes the hand. Hinkley smiles up at her. "She's the loveliest female
I ever met in any port of all the seven seas, but she's young. You
tricked her, took advantage of her innocence." He unfolds his skeletal limbs from the chair. "Did you ever." He pushes Nathan and
Hoyt out of his way. "C'mon, Jukes. Downstairs to the garage.
Come on, everyone." He leaves the tower room, trailed by Linnet,
Flora Belle, and the hulking Jukes. Hoyt and Nathan bring up the
rear.

"What now?" Nathan says.

"The truck," Hoyt says. "Remember?"

Nathan is too hoarse to shout down the staircase, but he tries.
"We didn't hurt your lousy truck."

Hinkley calls back, "You sure didn't help it any."

The garage is gloomy and stacked with storage cartons, even
overhead on the warped rafters. Also rocking chairs, bicycles, surf-

boards, a canoe. There's barely room for the truck. When Hinkley opens the padlock and the crooked old doors that scrape the cracked driveway, and flips a light switch, the weak bulb dangling overhead still doesn't show them much. Only that he hasn't wreaked mayhem on the truck as he did on the coats. The head lamps are intact. There are no new dents, no smashed windows. Nathan breathes a sigh of relief, and then he notices the tires. They are the worst-looking tires he has ever seen, worn right down through the old gray rubber to the fabric. And three of them are flat.

"Damn." Percy crouches by the left front wheel. "Look at that. I pumped these tires up only this morning. They're hopeless." He raises his beaky face to them. Bland, blank, guileless. "You can see that, can't you?"

"Where did you get them?" Nathan says.

"You better return them and get a refund," Hoyt says.

"What do you mean?" Hinkley stands. "Those are the tires that were on here when I went to sea."

"You're a liar," Hoyt says, and behind him Jukes growls.

"The farthest we drove was Westwood," Nathan says.

"That's not what the odometer shows." Hinkley pulls open the door of the cab. "You want to check it? You ran up close to two thousand miles."

"Anybody can make an odometer say anything," Hoyt says. And, "Ouch, God damn it. Cut that out." Jukes has twisted Hoyt's arm up behind him and brought him to his knees.

"Jukes, stop it," Linnet says.

Jukes cackles his empty laugh and lets Hoyt go.

"Have you any idea"—Hinkley slams the truck door—"how hard it is to get a set of tires these days? You have to buy them on the black market. They're asking a hundred bucks apiece—did you know that?"

"You better put it up on blocks, then," Hoyt says, rubbing his arm. "Because you sure as hell aren't going to get any four hundred bucks from us."

"Five," Hinkley corrects him. "You can't drive Mexican roads without a spare. And Babe and I are going to Mexico for Christmas."

"Five, either," Nathan says. "Look. I'm sorry I borrowed the truck. I didn't mean any harm. It was just sitting here. I didn't really think you'd mind."

"You also owe me for twenty gallons of gas," Hinkley says. "I left the tank full when I shipped out. And gas isn't easy to get, either."

"Where are the real tires?" Hoyt says. "You put those old things on there yourself."

"Can you prove it?" Hinkley says.

"Extortion is a crime," Nathan says.

Hinkley snorts. "You've got it backwards. You two are the criminals, I'm the victim. But I'm not vindictive. I'm not out to punish you. I only want what's owed to me. You ruined my two best coats, and you wore out my tires. Pay me for those, and we'll forget about the gas. We'll forget about Babe's modeling fee."

"Mod—?" Hoyt gapes.

"For that picture of her you drew. As I understand it, a model is paid for her time."

"He gave her Spanish lessons," Nathan says.

"Oh, yes?" Hinkley cranes to see Linnet, who with her vast mother has hung back and stands outside on the driveway. "Say something for me in Spanish, Babe."

"I can't," she whines. "Perc, you know I can't."

"You can keep the picture," Hoyt says.

"I'm afraid I tore it up," Hinkley says, and herds them all out of the garage, and pushes the doors shut.

"You made a mistake," Nathan says. "That picture will be worth a lot of money someday."

"When it comes to money"—Hinkley closes the padlock and turns, smiling—" 'someday' isn't a word I much care for."

"When it comes to money," Hoyt says, "it's the only word we know."

"Learn another, or I'll have the court garnishee Reed's wages at the bookstore. And what will you live on then?"

"But this is a pack of lies," Hoyt says. "You can't prove any of it. It's your word against ours. And you weren't even home— you were away at sea."

"You've seen the evidence—and I have two witnesses." Hinkley nods smugly at Flora Belle and Linnet standing shivering in the gray December wind. "They weren't away at sea. They were right here. They know what you did and when you did it and how you did it. They saw it all." Clothes flapping around his stick limbs, he ambles under the porte cochere. "They'll swear to everything." And with a wave of the hand, he goes up cracked cement steps, into the house, and shuts the door.

Nathan says to Linnet, "Are you going to stand up and lie in court? You know it's not true."

"Well, you did wear those coats," she says, "and I don't know how the tires got that way. They weren't like that when Perc left. They were almost new."

Hoyt takes Nathan's arm and drags him off down the driveway. "Don't waste your breath," he says.

"I'd advise you boys," Flora Belle calls sweetly after them, "to find that money somewhere. Percy Hinkley never makes threats he doesn't keep."

And behind her, the hulking Jukes laughs.

Hesketh Kreisler is a gray-faced, bespectacled man in his fifties, ordinary-looking except for a large, lumpy nose. There's an odd pale triangle at his throat. The large house he lives in looks prosperous, but his shirt, white with narrow blue stripes, is frayed at the collar and cuffs. The necktie looks as if it had lain crushed in a drawer for a long time. At a guess, he's borrowed his suit from somebody. He nods furtively to Dr. Marriott and peers apprehensively at the boys behind him in the drizzling rain. It's dark. There's a light beside the front door, but it's not very bright. He gestures them inside with a panicky air and, once the boys have got the big painting in its thick wrappings into the hall, quickly closes the door. Then he struggles to work up a welcoming smile.

"Well, here we are," he says.

"I hope it's late enough," says Marriott. "There's not a light on in the whole neighborhood."

"Thank you. I'm sure it is," Kreisler says, as if he didn't believe it. He is eying the damp, twine-tied newspapers swaddling the painting. "Let's bring it in here. I'm so eager to see it, I couldn't eat my dinner."

"May I present Hoyt Stubblefield," Marriott says, holding back for the sake of correct decorum, "and Nathan Reed." There is hand shaking. Kreisler's grip would be the same if he were in his coffin. "Mr. Stubblefield is the gifted painter of the picture."

Kreisler's dead eyes take in Hoyt, head to toe, then Nathan. He moistens his thin lips with his tongue. To Nathan he says, "And you are his—gifted model." Then he makes a sudden lunge along a hallway. "This way, please."

They trek through a half-lit dining room, kitchen, pantries, a concealed door, and end up in an office that smells of paint and plaster and new carpeting. It has a desk, a couple of straight chairs, an old buttoned leather sofa, and a bookcase stacked with what look like photograph albums. It's a secret room. It has no windows. Kreisler slides shut the concealed door behind them and rubs his hands, this time really sincerely smiling. "I've prepared this room just for your picture," he tells Hoyt. "A sort of shrine. Please. Will you unwrap—unveil it now?" He is trembling. His eyes glisten. His mouth is wet. "I seem to have been waiting forever for this moment."

Hoyt cuts the twine with his jackknife, strips the newspaper away, starts on the waxed paper he's laid over the picture on account of the rain—and Kreisler pushes him aside and does that part himself. The picture is upside down. "Turn it, turn it," Kreisler says, hands shaking, eyes bulging. Hoyt and Nathan turn it. Kreisler's legs seem to give out on him. Dr. Marriott catches his elbow and lowers him to the sofa. "Oh, my God," Kreisler breathes. "It's beautiful. It's perfect." Hands clasped reverently in front of his chest, he sits and gazes at the painting. Enraptured. Nathan is having a hard time not being sick on the new carpet. Kreisler jumps up and gives the surprised Hoyt a hug. "Oh, how can I ever thank you! It's the picture I've dreamed of all my life."

"Yeah, well, we aim to please," Hoyt says, and pries the man off him. Laughing in delight, Kreisler hugs fat little Marriott next, thanking him over and over, pumping and pumping his hand. He turns to Nathan, who dodges behind the desk. Kreisler's mood shifts. Now he's crying. "Hang it for me," he sobs. "The hooks are already up."

Hoyt has wired the frame. It takes only a minute, and the painting—two slim, naked young men entangled in sex in that same sad, smoke-hazy yesterday Hoyt always paints—hangs big as life against the fresh white wall. Standing back, feet among the crumpled wrappings, Kreisler quavers:

"I haven't the words, I simply haven't the words."

"The words are, I fear," Marriott tells him, "five hundred dollars. These boys are starving."

"Oh, no, oh, no." Looking stricken, Kreisler opens a drawer of the desk, takes out an envelope, and hands it to Hoyt. "It's cash—I hope that's all right."

"Thanks." Hoyt turns to find the hidden door, slide it, and push Nathan out ahead of him. "Merry Christmas."

In bed, in the dark, the rain whispering on the roof, they hold each other close under all the blankets they own, and their teeth still chatter. Hoyt says, "Did you notice the church we passed on the corner?"

"What about it?" Nathan says.

"I read the signboard out front," Hoyt says. "Shall I tell you the minister's name?"

"Let me guess," Nathan says. "Hesketh Kreisler, D.D. I wondered why he looked wrong in those clothes. He usually wears a dog collar and a black suit, doesn't he?" He gives a little laugh. "He never noticed the one face that shows in the painting isn't yours or mine."

"Pity there's no way old Perc will ever see it," Hoyt says. "Teach him to watch who he calls pansies."

" 'Whom,' " Nathan says. "Hoyt—we *are* pansies."

"I should have laid her," Hoyt growls. "She was just begging for it. And she'd never have told Percy about the truck, the coats, anything." He gasps and jerks. "Hey—what's this now?"

"It's in the handbook," Nathan says. "How to get warm when all else fails?"

"Rub two Boy Scouts together?" Hoyt says.

"That's it. Don't you think all else has failed?"

Hoyt laughs. "Why wait around to see?"

He wants to give Hoyt a new pair of cowboy boots for Christmas. He has seen the pair he wants in a tiny booth crowded with hanging huaraches, handbags, belts, boleros on Olvera Street, where the smell of leather is so strong it almost blocks out the smell of simmering chili from the cook shacks. He and Hoyt have discovered Olvera Street as a cheap place to eat, even after adding in the carfare to get there. At the rough wooden tables in these booths, you can stuff yourself for two bits, founder yourself for fifty cents. And they have to eat as cheaply as they can. Percy Hinkley was gravely disappointed to get only five hundred dollars the rainy morning after they delivered the picture.

"What about the coats?" he said, rocking back in his twangy swivel chair at the radio controls, and counting for a second time the bills from the Reverend Hesketh Kreisler's envelope. "You still owe me a hundred forty-five dollars for the coats." He looked up suddenly, squinting at the ceiling, then handed Hoyt an empty coffee can. "It's started over there now." He pointed. "Put that under it." Cans and pans were perched all over the place, catching drips from the roof. Percy had moved the junk around to keep it dry. "Rain is a pain," he said.

"Not completely," Nathan said. "It's washed the windows. A little daylight's getting in."

"That'll save on your electric bill," Hoyt said.

Nathan glanced at the Bela Lugosi poster. "Or send you scurrying back to your coffin."

Hinkley made a face. "Pair of comedians. Babe and I leave for Mexico tomorrow. But that doesn't let you off the hook. You get that money to Flora Belle. I'll be phoning her. She'll tell me if you don't." Heavy footsteps sounded in the jury-rigged hallway, and he craned to peer past the boys. His face lit up. "Ah, just the man I wanted to see."

Jukes filled the doorway in a yellow slicker. His small sour eyes ran Nathan and Hoyt over. "You back?" he said.

"To pay their just debts," Hinkley said. "Only not quite." He waved the cash at the ogre, who was struggling out of the slicker. "They came up a hundred and forty-five dollars short." In a raveled black sweater and greasy dungarees, Jukes thumped down onto his corner chair and peeled rubbers off his vast feet. Hinkley said, "And if they don't get it to Flora Belle before the end of the month, I'd appreciate it if you'd include them in your New Year's Eve festivities—will you do that, Jukes?"

Jukes leered at the boys. "It will be a pleasure, Perc," he said, and laughed his empty laugh.

So Hoyt and Nathan eat pretty often on Olvera Street, where men in charro outfits—white-braided black sombreros, vests, trousers—fill the scented air with jaunty music on guitars and trumpets, and little kids in fancy costumes dance, and shoppers roam the narrow lane of crooked red tiles between the scabby white walls of tumbledown eighteenth-century adobes. Since the boys seem doomed to die horribly at the hands of Jukes before they see 1944, they waste whole evenings walking up and down and gawking.

And Nathan has seen those gorgeous boots, tooled madly all over and dyed the most awful magentas, purples, greens. There never was a pair of cowboy boots to equal them. He's privately tried them on, so he knows they'll fit Hoyt. He half hoped they wouldn't. That would have solved the problem for him. But they did. And he almost wept when he learned that. He's got to have those boots, but the way things are, how can that be? The gnomish little shoemaker, brown and crinkled as his goods, is full of apologies that sound like castanets, but he has to have fifty dollars for them. And Nathan knows they are worth it—hell, they're worth twice that. And they might as well cost ten times that, for all the chance he has of paying for them.

But they're still on his mind when, two days before Christmas, he's in the back room of T. Smollett Books, pulling on an extra sweater for the walk home, and Angus MacKenzie, pale and trembling from the excitement and exhaustion of raking in all those crazy Christmas profits, appears with Nathan's pay envelope. Outside in the bleak wind of darkening Hollywood Boulevard, where the shop windows glitter with Christmas tinsel, Nathan rips the envelope open. His fingers tremble. Besides his regular check, he's hoping for a bonus. And it's there: a crisp fifty-dollar bill. He lets out a whoop and bolts straight into traffic to cross the street. Brakes are slammed, tires shriek, horns honk, drivers curse. He doesn't notice. He wants the streetcar that will take him to Olvera Street, and it's getting away. He catches the red iron rail of the rear steps just in time and swings himself aboard. Slumped on the tough green fabric of a rear seat, while the big iron wheels rumble along the rails beneath, he scolds himself. He's acting like a child. But, damn it, even with the thirty-five they've kept back instead of paying the rent, this fifty dollars still won't satisfy the sneering Hinkley. Nathan sits straight. He's been beaten up before, and lived through it. To hell with Jukes. Let him come. Hoyt is going to have those boots.

At Benbow's urging, Nathan plays Christmas songs on the piano after dinner. Everyone stands around him and sings: Benbow; his mother, still flushed from fixing a big meal in a hot kitchen; George Lafleur, flushed from wine; Benbow's sturdy sister; her husband, the Armenian who works for the senator; rosy little Dr. Marriott; and Hoyt. In a corner a tall Christmas tree glows and glitters. Ribbons and fancy paper strew the carpet. Gift books, records, sweaters are stacked up. Boxes of chocolates and dried fruits lie ravaged on coffee and end tables. The familiar songs are used up, and most of the voices drop out. Finally only Benbow and Nathan are left, bawling away at "The Cherry Tree Carol." Mrs. Harsch serves a last round of eggnog and fruit cake, there are "thank you"s and "good night"s, and Hoyt and Nathan in the cold dark air head not quite surefooted down the hill for Sunset Boulevard and the streetcar. Hoyt sleeps on the streetcar, head on Nathan's shoulder. Nathan is too worried to sleep. He took Benbow aside and told him what they were facing and why. Benbow listened with sympathy, but Nathan of course didn't ask him directly, and he didn't offer to lend them a hundred forty-five dollars. Maybe he doesn't have it. It's a big house, but shacky. He may be powerful, but he isn't rich. Nathan dozes, and only just wakes up in time for Highland Avenue.

Hoyt comes toiling up the stairs. It hasn't rained today, just kept cold and gloomy. He's worn his new boots, his best cowboy hat, and the suit. The portfolio is under his arm. Nathan has got home from T. Smollett, where after the hurly-burly of the Christmas rush, the days are dull and give him too much time to worry about Jukes. Though Hoyt, against Nathan's protests, has cut back the branches so the windows will close, the apartment is cold. Nathan has lit the oven and left its door open, heated coffee, and got himself into corduroys, sweaters, watch cap, moth-eaten muffler, and sat down with a mug of coffee at the typewriter when he hears Hoyt's steps and goes to open the door for him. Hoyt looks sore. He slams the portfolio down on the couch, throws his hat away, jerks out of the suit jacket.

"Guess what I just saw," he says.

"You want coffee?" Nathan starts off. "Come to the kitchen. It's warm."

"Linnet's portrait," Hoyt says, following him.

Nathan rinses out a mug. "Perc said he tore it up."

Hoyt scrapes chair legs on the linoleum and plunks himself down. "Well, he didn't. And you told him it was worth money." They haven't had any cigarettes for days, but in some shop somewhere he's found a pack of Wings. He lights one. "Helpful Nathan."

Nathan sets down a mug of coffee for him. "You mean he sold it?"

"It's in a gallery back in that nest of shops off the Boulevard. Right near T. Smollett. All matted and framed. In the window." Hoyt snorts. "Sixty-five bucks."

Nathan whistles, gets his mug from the writing table, and sits down across from Hoyt. "How much do you think the shop gave him for it?"

"I don't think, I know," Hoyt says grimly. "I asked. They weren't going to tell me, but I showed them stuff from my portfolio that convinced them I was the one who drew it, and they told me. Ten dollars."

Nathan takes a cigarette. "He was robbed."

Hoyt gives a little smile. "You're sweet, you know?"

"Any luck today?" Nathan says. "Anybody hire you?"

Hoyt shakes his head. "Most of the offices were locked up, everyone gone for the holidays. Two had people in them, but nobody that could hire anyone. I never even opened my portfolio, not till I walked into that art shop."

"Wait till after New Year's." Nathan lights the cigarette. "You'll get more work than you can handle."

"Not with my arm in a sling."

"What do you mean?"

"If we don't pay for those coats in the next day or two," Hoyt says, "Jukes will break every arm we've got between us. And a couple of legs too, I expect." He points at a torn envelope by Nathan's elbow. "Mail today?"

"A Christmas card from Frank." Nathan pushes it across to Hoyt. "Late, of course. Frank's dependable that way."

Frank has folded a letter inside the dime-store card:

Busy as you were, you paid me a lot of attention, and gave me some pleasant times while I was there, and it was wrong of me to run out on you without a word of thanks. I had a failure of nerve. And it wasn't the first. You see, I paid that visit with only one thing in mind—to try to get you out of that life. It's no good, Nathan. Not only does it make you an outlaw and slam doors in your face, but in the end, when you're old, you'll have nobody. If you're honest and open about it, as I think it's your nature to be, then ordinary people will despise you. If you keep it secret, you've got to spend your life shamming and lying, and hating yourself for it. Nathan, conventional ways are conventional ways because they work. They're time-tested and, as near as man could design, foolproof. I expect that sounds simple-minded, but if you think about it you'll agree. Take the main road and you'll have a lot of company. Take the other one, and you go alone, and ten to one you'll get lost. There's a public library near the Mark Twain Hotel, and while you were working, I spent quite a few hours there trying to learn about homosexuality, but the more I read, the harder it became for me to see how you slid into this. You're a fine-looking, healthy, straight young man, not some frail, pimply, simpering sissy. Your mother never dressed you up in girl's clothes. You didn't play with dolls—you rode your bike. Swam. Skated. Nathan—you don't fit with what the books say. I don't know what to make of it. Are you still trying to get back at me for going on the road when you were little? Son, it was the only work I could get. I thought we had that straightened out long ago. You're still very young. It's not too late to break away from Stubblefield, and Poole, all those people, and start over doing things like the rest of mankind. To be a writer is a fine thing, but I never saw it carved in stone anywhere that a writer can't live a normal life with normal people. Hell, there are plenty of misfits in the music business—I know that, if you don't. But that never meant to me I had to be like them. All right, end of lecture. I'm sorry for worrying you, sneaking off as I did, but I didn't want to yell at you, and that's what it would have come to. I was feeling desperate. I might even have tried to drag you back here with me, as your mother asked. But you'll be twenty-one in six months, when I lose the right to order you around, if I ever had it—and those six months wouldn't have been pleasant for any of us. You always had more common sense than your mother and me together, so maybe you'll straighten out your life on your own before much longer. I hope so. I want it to be a happy life, because you're my son, and I love you. That's all for now, except merry Christmas and a successful 1944 with your book!

Hoyt sighs, folds the letter, puts it inside the card, tucks the card into the envelope, hands the envelope back.

"You going to change?" he asks.

Nathan nods. "Starting with the color of my eyes."

Not knowing what else to do, they spend the hours until midnight jammed into Slim Gaylord's narrow barroom on the Boulevard with a hundred other anomalies in and out of uniform—and after everybody has cheered, hugged, wept, and sung "Auld Lang Syne," they go home.

"I wish Reggie were here," Nathan says.

"I don't think he'd be good in a fight," Hoyt says.

"He could give him a brisk rap with his fan," Nathan says, and opens the door. Jukes may be only an empty threat, but they think if he is going to come, he will come up the stairs; they will hear him and can run like rabbits out the back way. They'll keep their clothes on, just in case.

But Jukes has already come. He waits inside, in the dark, in the room where Nathan writes, waits while they visit the bathroom, shed their shoes, get into bed, and switch off the lamp. Then he jumps them. He lands on them with a roar, grabs their hair, and bangs their heads together. They yell.

Jukes drives a fist into Nathan's belly. It knocks the wind out of him. He falls off the bed and lies curled up on the floor, gasping for air. He hears Jukes's fists crunching against Hoyt's face. Sick with pain, he totters upright, falls on Jukes's back, tugs at him. Jukes doesn't stop punching. He simply grunts and bucks Nathan off.

And Nathan is caught from behind and helped to his feet. Someone else has come, who sets Nathan aside as if he had no weight, grabs Jukes, and yanks him off Hoyt. Only dim light comes in the windows, but Nathan can see what happens. The someone kicks Jukes in the crotch; then, when Jukes howls and doubles over, takes both fists together and brings them down with all his might on the back of Jukes's neck. Jukes grunts and falls flat on his face and lies there as if dead.

Whimpering, Hoyt gropes out and switches on the lamp. Blood is pouring from his nose and a torn ear. It runs into his mouth, down his chin and neck, and soaks his shirt. He wipes at his mouth while he stares at their rescuer. Nathan also stares. Unbelieving. The someone who saved them and now stands over Jukes panting is Mike Voynich. He wears a nice new suit. He holds a thick wrist to a big ear and listens anxiously to a new watch. He taps it.

"You can wreck a watch in a fight," he says.

"*Quel dommage*," Hoyt says, trying to sop up the blood with a fistful of Kleenex.

Voynich grins. " 'Who would have thought the young man could have so much blood in him?' That's from *Macbeth*."

"Almost." Hoyt scrambles off the bed and bolts, hand over his nose. In a minute, water splashes in the bathroom.

Nathan says, "Where did you come from?"

"I heard you yell," Voynich says. "I was waiting in Reggie's in the dark to surprise him." He bends, rolls the inert Jukes over, grabs him under the arms, and starts to drag him off. "Where is he—do you know?"

"At Grady Sutton's?" Nathan guesses.

"Naw." Voynich shakes his head. "That's where I live. Help me here, will you?"

Nathan takes Jukes under the knees. He's heavy as well as smelly. As they stagger through the door into the living room with him, Nathan says to Voynich, "You did do well for yourself. I told Reggie you'd land on your feet."

"Yeah?" Voynich backs across the living room. "What do you want we should do with him?"

"Jesus," Nathan pants. "I don't know."

They get him out to the stair landing and roll him down the stairs like a sack of old clothes. He gets stuck halfway. Back in the apartment, Nathan locks the door.

"What's that for?" Voynich says. "He won't try it again. He never saw me. He thinks you did it to him."

"I hope so," Nathan says. "Surprise Reggie how?"

Hoyt comes out of the bathroom without his shirt, looking pale, hair damp. He has got his nose to stop bleeding and has rigged a lumpy bandage on his ear. He leans in the doorway, gingerly touching his nose. "By giving him his money back, right?"

"Him and you. I got work. Two pictures. And my old man says never start a new year without you pay your debts."

"I didn't realize you'd only borrowed it," Nathan says.

"You think I'd steal?" Voynich says. "Shit, I'm not like that." He digs into a pocket, comes out with a wad of bills, peels off five twenties, and hands them to Nathan. "I was raised a good Cath'lic. My old man would kill me if he thought I'd ever steal."

"We won't tell him," Nathan says.

Hoyt says, "What pictures?"

Voynich shrugs. "I don't know the titles. Lloyd Nolan. Chester Morris. In the first one I only drive a taxi. In the other one I'm a crippled ex-GI, trying to keep my mother from marrying my sister off to a gangster."

"Reggie will be thrilled," Nathan says.

Voynich doesn't hear the irony. "I stuck fifty bucks in one of them glass jars of his." He squints. "That about wipes me out. You think it's enough?"

"I don't know," Nathan says. "But he'll be pleased. He loved you, Mike. He believed in you. When you ran out on him it broke his heart."

"That lady up in Santa Barbara would have laughed at me. You knew that. I wasn't ready for Shakespeare. I never will be. Reg had too fancy ideas. He's a dreamer. Grady didn't try to make me over. He got me work."

"You still think you'll be a star?" Hoyt says.

"I'm better-looking than Chester Morris," Voynich says.

Flora Belle Short says, "They're in jail in Calexico."

Hoyt pokes his head forward. His eyes are swollen almost shut. The swellings are purple. "In jail?"

"And you put them there." Flora Belle nods.

She has come huffing and puffing up the stairs early. It's raining a little. Drops glitter on the mangy old fur of her cape, the greasy satin of her turban. Hoyt has gone to the door because Nathan is shaving to go to T. Smollett. Hoyt has invited Flora Belle to sit down and has offered her coffee, but she's refused with a grim shake of the head. Now Nathan comes out of the bathroom and stands drying his face with a towel in the door from the kitchen.

"We put them there?" he says. "How?"

"The border guards found guns in the truck," the big woman says, "under the seat. Military rifles. He claims someone planted them there. But the government has arrested him for gun running."

"And he told you we did it?" Hoyt says.

"As an act of vengeance. To get back at him."

"But that's impossible," Hoyt says. "We're here. If we planted them, they'd have been found on the way into Mexico, not out."

Flora Belle shakes her head. "He says you have confederates south of the border. Friends. Probably—excuse me—homosexuals. Mexico is your second home. You told Linnet."

Hoyt laughs in disbelief. "I was there a few times in my teens. Drinking, knocking around. If there are homosexuals there, I never met them. No, if Percy's gun-running for fun and profit, he's the one with Mexican friends."

"Where would we get the money to buy guns?" Nathan goes to the bedroom to find a shirt to wear to work. "We haven't got a dime—he knows that better than anybody."

"He's convinced you're behind it. And says I'm to tell you if you get him cleared, he'll give your money back and never bother you again."

Hoyt says, "We didn't put him in, we can't get him out, but if he wants to think so, his promise better include Jukes. Look what he did to me on New Year's Eve."

Flora Belle has so far avoided this. Now she gives him a quick glance, winces, looks away again. "I'm so sorry." And unexpectedly she starts to cry. "It's all my fault." Fat fingers crusted with cheap rings, she rummages in her huge bag, finds a handkerchief, blots her tears. "I should have forbidden Linnet to lend you Percy's things. He's furious with me. God knows what will become of me now."

"He's crazy about Linnet," Nathan says. "As long as he's got her, he won't do anything to you."

She blows her nose. "Thank you. I hope you're right." She turns to leave. "I just wish Linnet were a little more—dependable." Scarves fluttering, she lowers her bulk on swollen ankles down the stairs.

Through the window, they watch her go. Hoyt frowns at Nathan. "I never told Benbow about Percy."

"I did. At Christmas. The whole miserable story." Nathan goes to sit on the bed and put on his shoes. "I was scared of Jukes. It made me babble. I guess I hoped Benbow would lend us the hundred forty-five."

Hoyt grins. "He did better than that."

Nathan ties the shoelaces. "No wonder he loves power. What if the senator doesn't get re-elected next time?"

"Benbow will find another host organism," Hoyt says.

Nathan blinks up at him. "I just finished *Lafcadio's Adventures*. You know why he gave it to you to read?"

"To plant the seed in my mind that maybe somebody pushed Eva Schaffer under that streetcar just for the hell of it."

"Why didn't you tell him?" Nathan says.

"I wanted him to think I missed the point. I was sure he was wrong, and Eva was killed for a reason. See, I knew something had upset her. Very much. She'd passed me a note to meet her that night, so she could tell me about it."

"And you figured she'd already told somebody else?"

"The one who killed her."

Nathan chooses a tie, turns up his collar, strings the tie around it. To Hoyt's image in the mirror, he says, "But you aren't looking for him anymore?"

"It's no use. I got too anxious, asked too many questions, and everybody got spooked." He shakes his head. "I don't know. Before Christmas, Steve told me they were calling it murder in New York. But how could they know? Three thousand miles away?" He sighs. "It was probably an accident. I sure as hell never proved it wasn't."

Nathan loops the tie around itself. "Did Eva know you were a spy?"

Hoyt squints. "What did you say?" He lays a hand over Nathan's mouth. "No, I heard you. Nathan, she was dead. I was looking for her killer." He takes the hand away, laughing but eying Nathan uneasily. "It was afterward, all right?"

"What do you think she wanted to tell you that night?"

"Well, not about spies. That wouldn't have worried her. There's always been spies inside the CP. She knew that."

Nathan tucks the tie through the loop to make a knot. "George Lafleur—was he one?"

Hoyt stiffens. "Who told you that?"

"Nobody, but that FBI man, Noble, said George used to be a member of the Communist party, and it doesn't make sense to me. He doesn't give a damn about politics."

Hoyt makes a face. "Knowing George, he was probably just trying to get into some cute comrade's pants. A spy—George? You've got quite an imagination. You should try writing a book."

"I think of it sometimes." Nathan finishes the knot and slides it up to where the collar buttons. "But that's as far as it goes."

Hoyt says, "The *Daily Worker* warns the comrades against spies all the time, but nobody quits. America and Russia are allies in the struggle against fascism, aren't they, so the CPUSA has the biggest membership they ever had right now. But secret? Hell, the government's got all their names. I turned in half a dozen mailing lists myself. And Hitler won't last forever. Then Russia will be the enemy. Again. They're very naive people, true believers are. Not Eva."

Nathan, tired of the subject, folds down his collar, straightens the tie. "It was nice of Benbow to help us."

"Yeah, well—he'll want to be paid back. Wait and see." Hoyt watches Nathan get his jacket from the closet. "Phone him from the bookstore, will you? Thank him, tell him it worked, and he can shift operations into reverse now."

"What's the rush?" Nathan says. "I like the idea of old Perc rotting in the Calexico jail. Why not wait a week? Or a year. Are you in such a hurry to have him back?"

"Linnet," Hoyt says. "Didn't you know? I'm deeply in love with Linnet."

Nathan snarls and shows him a fist.

He has been to the leather goods booth on Olvera Street to get Hoyt's boots stretched, and with the boots in a box beside him on the bench, he is waiting for a streetcar when a black limousine pulls up to the curb. A chauffeur sits in front and doesn't even look at him. It's the back door that opens. "You want a ride, kid?" The sun is in Nathan's eyes, and he squints. The passenger is the squat, black-browed movie producer, Dryrot. He wears a dark, chalk-striped suit, a homburg hat, and smokes a cigar. He doesn't smile, but he says, "It's Reed, isn't it? Don't you remember me? Harry Dryrot. Come on, get in." And as if in a dream, Nathan steps off the curb and gets into the car and closes the door and the car rolls away. "Where you going?" Dryrot says.

"T. Smollett Books," Nathan says. "On Hollywood Boulevard. I work there."

"Yeah? I thought you were a writer."

"I have to eat," Nathan says.

"What's in the box?" Dryrot sniffs. "Hot tamales?"

"I wish," Nathan says. "No—cowboy boots. Raw."

"I read the outline of your book," Dryrot says. "Stanley Page sent it to me. I'm sorry, there just isn't a picture in it."

"Not as sorry as I am," Nathan says.

"Yeah." Dryrot laughs. "I guess you could use the money. A bookstore can't pay much."

"Why isn't there a picture in it?" Nathan says.

Dryrot sighs and taps the ashes of his cigar neatly into an ashtray in the door at his side. "It's about this little kid music genius, right? And his old man who plays all those different horns and his old lady who's the fortune-teller? And they're always broke?"

"That's the one," Nathan says.

Dryrot gives him a sly little smile. "You thought I forgot, didn't you?"

"I appreciate your remembering," Nathan says. "I appreciate the ride."

"Let me tell you what's wrong with your story," Dryrot says. "It might help you next time."

"Thank you," Nathan says.

"See, the people in your story—they're not like regular people, and regular people won't understand them, and they're not going to go to the movies to see them, and nobody's going to make any money—see?"

"Regular people aren't cowboys, either," Nathan says. "But they go to cowboy pictures."

"Am I helping you here," Dryrot says, "or are you helping me? How long have you been the head of a major motion picture studio?"

"They're funny," Nathan says.

"You mean like *You Can't Take It with You*? Nah."

"I don't mean like that," Nathan says. "There never was any family like that. It was all exaggerated. It was a farce. It wasn't realistic. Maybe my people are a little strange, but they're real."

"Ah—real." Dryrot nods. "Forget it, kid."

"Why? Isn't that what writing's all about—letting people into other people's lives, showing them what it's like to be somebody else?"

Dryrot shakes his head. "You think too much. Make 'em laugh, make 'em cry, scare 'em if you can. For most people, life is lousy. They need a couple hours off in dreamland. They don't want real people, real problems." He pats Nathan's knee, leans forward, pushes aside the glass panel, and says, "The T. Smollett bookstore, Spencer. For Mr. Reed here." The chauffeur says something. Dryrot slides the panel shut and settles back in the seat. "Anyway, your story isn't a picture story. No love interest. Nobody's rich and beautiful. A little kid gets sore at his father? Who cares?"

"You mean it's different," Nathan says. "You could try it. People might like it."

"Nah." Dryrot shakes his head again. "You never 'try' anything. You go with what you know. People want the same old stories over and over again. Why turn your back on what works? You only lose money."

"What about Hitler?" Nathan says.

"What about the son of a bitch?"

"I know a writer with a great story about Hitler." The bookstore is only two blocks ahead. Nathan hurries to get into a few sentences Reggie Poole's ridiculous plot about the Führer and Colette.

"A French lady writer?" Dryrot says. "I got a French so-called actress sitting around under contract. This Colette broad—is she young and beautiful?"

"In real life, she's old and fat and powders her face white like a clown," Nathan says. "But you could make her young and beautiful. The magic of the movies?"

"Yeah, why not?" Dryrot nods.

The limousine stops.

Nathan picks up the box with the boots in it. "Shall I have his agent bring it to you?"

"Yeah, why not?" Dryrot says.

Nathan opens the door, gets out, stands in the cold winter sunshine on the sidewalk, clutching the box. "Or would I be wasting your time again?" he says. "I'm sorry. It's different, isn't it?"

Dryrot smiles thinly. "Not if it's about Hitler."

"Good. Don't forget his name. Reginald Poole."

"Did I forget yours?" Dryrot says, and shuts the door.

If Percy Hinkley got a tan in Mexico, he lost it in the Calexico jail. He is paler even than before, and thinner. His eyes look beaten, but he still has his sneer. Hoyt and Nathan have climbed to the tower room without Flora Belle. And Linnet is in the kitchen far below. When she heard them come into the house, she peeked out. Nathan saw her.

He looks around. "Where's Jukes?"

"I didn't send for him. I'm giving you back your money. I didn't think I'd need protection for that."

"He wouldn't have come anyway." Hoyt struggles not to laugh. "Not after what Nathan did to him New Year's Eve."

Hinkley swivels in his squeaky chair to look Nathan up and down. "You cracked a vertebra in his neck," he says. "Did you know that? You could have paralyzed him for life."

Nathan shrugs. "It wasn't my idea. It was yours."

"He outweighs you two to one," Hinkley says.

Hoyt says, "We pansies are full of surprises."

"So I found out. Let's not discuss it. Here—here's your money back. Now, get out of my life, will you?"

Hoyt counts the money. "This is ten bucks short."

"What do you mean?" Hinkley says.

"You owe me for my portrait of Linnet," Hoyt says.

"Christ," Hinkley grumbles, "they know everything," and digs out another bill and slaps it into Hoyt's hand.

They run downstairs. The big house is eerily quiet—the front door, which stands open most of the year, is closed because of the cold, so the noise of passing cars and trucks on Franklin is damped—and so the moaning is easy to hear. Hoyt stops and catches Nathan's arm. They stand on the worn and gritty carpet of the hall and listen. The groans come from beyond Rick Ames's door. Hoyt frowns a question. Nathan raps gently on the door and says softly:

"Rick? Are you all right?"

There's no answer. He turns the knob, pushes the door, and with Hoyt right behind him steps into the big, handsome room. It's dim. The tan roller shades are down. They walk out of the ell where Rick has his desk and typewriter and into the main part of the room, and there is the bed at the far end, and on the bed lies Tony. It's he who is groaning. Nathan goes to him. There are strong smells of urine and something sweet and rotten. He shuts his eyes a moment, opens them, gives Tony's shoulder a gentle shake.

"What's happened? Where's Rick?"

The large brown eyes open in a beard-stubbly face that is drawn and sunken. Tony has lost a lot of weight since Nathan saw him last. "Nathan? Where did you come from? I thought it would be Rick."

"I haven't seen him. We heard you moaning."

"He went to his mother's to try to get another loan," Tony says, "and he never came back."

Hoyt has come to stand by Nathan. "Went to his mother's when? How long have you been like this?"

"Yesterday morning. I can't walk." Tony starts to cry, and rolls his head on the pillow. "I've pissed the bed. I'm so ashamed. Not fit to be seen." He paws out at the bedside table. A glass stands there. He knocks it over, but nothing spills. The glass is dry. "Water?" he says.

Nathan takes the glass to the kitchen. A big black Mexican comb pinning up her blond hair, Linnet sits at the table, drinking a Coke and turning the pages of a movie magazine. She ignores him. Nathan rinses and fills the glass at the sink. "How was Christmas in Mexico?" he says.

"You're terrible," she says.

"Then we're well met," Nathan says. "Did you know Tony's been lying in his bed sick for twenty-four hours with nobody to look after him?"

"How would I know that?" Linnet says. "We don't spy on tenants, and this isn't a nursing home."

"I guess not," Nathan says, and takes away the water.

Hoyt is sitting at Rick's desk. He hangs up the phone. "I've called for an ambulance," he says softly. "He's got to go to a hospital. Those legs of his—it's gangrene, Nathan. I've seen it before. How the hell could they let them get like that? He could lose his legs. He could die."

"That must be why Rick went for the loan," Nathan says. "He had to be desperate. He hates going to his mother's. She's rich, owns a bunch of hotels—but half the time she won't give him anything. To punish him for being a queer, a lush, a sponger. This must have been one of those times."

Hoyt says, "And he couldn't face Tony with the bad news, so he bought a bottle of wine, and he's—"

"—sleeping it off in some vacant lot?" Nathan says.

Hoyt shakes his head. "He's been gone too long for that. More likely he's in jail, the drunk tank." Hoyt gets off the chair. "I'm going to try to clean Tony up a little. You go out front and wait for the ambulance."

"The hospital will want money," Nathan says.

Hoyt pats his jeans pocket. "We've got money."

"You worked hard for that, damn it."

"I never expected to get it back, though, did I?" Hoyt shrugs. "Faerie gold."

Nathan laughs. "You could put it that way."

"If there's any left," Hoyt says, "we'll pay Rick's bail. Then he can tell Percy. Won't Percy be pleased?"

Far off, a siren wails. In the shadowy, stinking depths of the room, Tony groans again. Hoyt takes the glass of water from Nathan and carries it to the bed. Nathan goes out into the cold, to stand shivering on the curb, shoulders hunched, hands in pockets, awaiting the ambulance.

"What the hell are you doing here, kid?"

It's Stanley Page, natty as always, brown suit, dark red shirt, raspberry necktie, hat. He's come with a crowd of men similarly dressed into the bookstore minutes before closing time at nine. Fresh from dinner at Musso & Frank's. They're the same men, at least the same types, Nathan last saw Stanley with at that Beverly Hills party—on the night lawn, under the trees, in the light of the paper lanterns. Their voices are loud from drink. They stand around among the tables of shiny books, smoking, shouting jokes, laughing.

"Working, Mr. Page," Nathan says.

"You should be finishing that book," Page says. "It's good. Original. You've got talent. Don't give up."

"I didn't give up," Nathan says. "The money ran out. And you vanished. I went to your apartment and you'd left, you and your wife and baby—everybody. You threw out my novel and my contract. I found them in the trash cans."

"That was Maud," Page says. "I wasn't there. She threw me out first. That's how women are. Never satisfied. Gotta change you. But I did take your outline to Pinnacle Pictures. Dryrot turned it down."

Nathan tells about his ride with Dryrot the other day, and what the producer said. "I guess it wasn't enough like *The Human Comedy*, was it?"

Page makes a face. "There's other studios." He looks around at the shop. "Goddamn cave. All it needs is stalactites and a flock of bats." He peers into Nathan's face. "How much does MacKenzie pay you?"

"Twenty a week," Nathan says. "Forty-four hours."

"Yeah—Scotchmen," Page says. "Worse than Hebes. So when do you write?"

"Early mornings," Nathan says. "I'm too tired at night." He laughs bleakly. "Sometimes I'm too tired to get up at five."

"Come work for me," Page says. "Couple hours in the morning. Two days a week—let's say Tuesdays and Fridays, okay? That way you'll have time to write. Ten dollars an hour—that sound fair?"

"More than fair. What do I have to do?"

"Type letters, contracts, make out checks, wrap up manuscripts and take 'em to the post office. Whatever comes up. Nothing to it."

"It sounds easy," Nathan says. "You mean it?"

"Business is getting too good. I need help."

"All right." Nathan shakes his hand. "Thank you."

The men Page came in with have gathered around one table where two of them are arm wrestling. The watchers shout encouragement and wave money. There's a cry of pain. A stack of books crashes to the floor. So does one of the contestants—the one with the mustache. Nathan thinks this is William Saroyan. There are laughs, moans, jeers.

"I have to close now," Nathan says.

Page hands him a business card. "That's where to find me," he says. "Next Tuesday. Ten A.M." He walks off, shouting to his friends, who are helping Saroyan to his feet, giving him back his hat, dusting him off—"Come on, let's go someplace where we can get a drink."

They trail out, raucous, shoving each other like high-school boys, dropping their bets and retrieving them from the floor. Nathan picks up the books, puts them back on the table, gets his jacket and muffler from the back room, turns off the lights, wheels the creaky bargain cart inside, pulls down the heavy door, and locks up the shop. He hopes it's for the last time.

Page is in the Avondale Apartments in Cahuenga Pass. It's an easy walk eastward from home. Nathan opens the heavy glass-paneled door into the silent lobby early. The marble floor is damp from mopping, and a strong smell of disinfectant makes his eyes water. He presses a gummy button at the elevator shaft and waits, but nothing happens. He climbs a dark staircase to a long, dark hallway. The plaster is a grimy gray, door frames and doors dark brown, and it might as well be a house of the dead for all the sounds he hears. After a long walk on worn carpet, he finds Page's door and knocks. Hoarse phrases mumble from inside. There's a thump of heels. A chain rattles, a bolt slides back, a spring lock turns, and the door opens. Page grunts "Come in" and turns away. He has on candy-striped boxer shorts and that's all. His hair is rumpled from sleep. Nathan goes in and shuts the door. It's dim. On the single window the dusty venetian blind is closed. Page is at the dresser. In the mirror, his face looks bloated, and his eyes are bloodshot. He finds money and lays it in Nathan's hand.

"Get my breakfast, will you, kid?" He coughs.

"All right," Nathan says. "What do you want?"

"A big can of orange juice"—Page stretches out on the bed and lays an arm across his eyes—"and a half a pint of vodka. Liquor store's just down at the corner."

"Why is it so quiet here?" Nathan says.

"Hey, you're on Lysol Alley, kid." Page's wry laugh turns to another cough. "That's what Pep West called it."

"Miss Lonelyhearts? Day of the Locust?"

"We used to go deer hunting together," Page says. "He had a station wagon with a false roof. Storage compartments where we stowed the carcasses. That way you can go hunting when you want to. You don't have to wait for the fucking government to tell you it's the fucking hunting season. That was the car he got killed in, you know. Drove right out onto a highway from a country side road someplace. Never even looked. The world's worst driver."

" 'Lysol Alley'?" Nathan says. "I don't understand."

"He got peon's wages from the studios, and he had novels to write, and to save money he roomed in this neighborhood." Page lifts a hand and points. "Couple streets over. Ivar. No different from here. The apartments are all full of hookers. Lysol Alley—get it? And the reason it's so quiet in the mornings—a girl works late, she sleeps late." He lays the arm across his eyes again.

"I'll be right back," Nathan says.

Page's hands shake, so Nathan pours his breakfast for him into the tumbler from the bathroom. With a beer-can opener Page refers to as a "church key," he punctures the top of the big orange juice can. On Page's instructions he half fills the glass with orange juice, then pours the vodka in on top of it and stirs the mixture with the handle of Page's toothbrush. Page sits on the edge of the bed and drinks and smokes cigarettes, while Nathan types letters, addresses envelopes, fills in the blanks in contracts, and writes checks for Page to sign when his hand steadies. Writers are getting paid. It lifts Nathan's heart.

After Nathan has finished his work, Page is feeling talkative. "Sit down, kid," he orders. And with his second glass of breakfast in easy reach, he lies propped on pillows on the bed and spins yarns. "Hell, I give him titles all the time." He means Saroyan. *"Jim Dandy?* You know that play?" Nathan knows it. He saw it at the Pasadena Playhouse with Abou Bekker. "I gave him that title. Up in that hometown of his. Armenians. Nothing but wall-to-wall rug peddlers. And they're all related."

"That's in *My Name Is Aram,*" Nathan says. "Everybody's his cousin."

"It was on a panel truck that drove by," Page says. " 'Jim Dandy Cleaners.' I pointed it out to him."

"It's a good play," Nathan says.

"We come out of a tavern at two in the morning," Page says, "and it's deserted, the whole town, not a sign of life. We're on the moon, all right? All alone on the moon. Absolute silence. And I walk to the curb and put my hands to my mouth and shout, 'Hello-o-o out there!' "

"It's a one-act play," Nathan says.

"You think he remembers who gave him that title? Forget it. Writers don't get ideas from other people. Everything's their own idea." He drinks, and gossips on about writers, editors, publishers, movie people until the vodka is gone. Then he suddenly sits up. "Jesus. What time is it?"

There's a clock on the desk. "Noon," Nathan says.

"I have to get going." Page climbs off the bed. "Got to meet Saroyan for lunch at Musso's. Write yourself a check. I'll be out in ten minutes." He steps into the bathroom, and the shower splashes. At the desk, Nathan types a check for himself and lays it with the others on the dresser. He sits and reads a few pages of a much crossed-out and penned-over typescript—a biography of a Civil War cavalry general named Hood—until, with a damp towel around his waist, Page comes out, combed and shaven, and signs the checks, all of them, in the steadiest of hands. Nathan puts them into their envelopes and seals the envelopes while Page gets dressed. He looks bright-eyed, healthy, scrupulously neat as he steps with Nathan into the gloomy hallway and closes the door. The expensive tang of his cologne almost drowns out the reek of disinfectant in the air.

On these short, gray, rainy days, Nathan has more time to write than he thought he would. Bundled in sweaters and muffler and watch cap, he can sit with mugs of hot coffee for uninterrupted hours at the typewriter, rattling away on *The Shotgun Flat*. Because Hoyt isn't home. He has found work—as an artist for Roy Lockerby, painting watercolors. For greeting cards. Sappy subjects. The company doesn't want his ideas. Another department hands out the ideas. All he has to do is sketch and paint the cute puppies and kittens and little kids, the Easter lilies, the sleigh rides, the flights of ducks against sunset skies, the corn shocks and pumpkins. It disgusts him and makes him glum company during the few hours when he and Nathan can be together—but he smiles on Fridays when he comes running up the stairs with a paycheck. They are rich. They eat at the Chinese place, the Hungarian place, Drossie's. They buy new jeans, corduroys, flannel shirts, sweaters, even raincoats. They buy art books—Caravaggio, Donatello. And records—Beethoven by the Budapest Quartet, Bach by E. Power Biggs. They dare to talk of getting a telephone. Heady times.

And on February fourteenth, Nathan finishes his book. When he completes the scene where Nathan and Frank play a duet—the signal that all is patched up between them at last—he sits on the hard chair stunned, staring at the words "The End" and scarcely daring to believe what they say. He doesn't know whether to laugh or cry or pass out. At last, he draws a deep breath, rolls the page out of the machine, lays it with the others, and takes them to the kitchen table, where again he cuts up a grocery sack, wraps the chapters in it, seals the package with Reggie's gummed tape, sticks on the address label he typed a little too eagerly days ago, shrugs into his new raincoat, and heads down Highland.

Stepping into the post office and the smell of damp wool from the clothes of customers lined up at the two little barred windows, he runs into Rick Ames again. Red-faced, big-bellied, wearing his torn old mackintosh, he's about to leave. In his hand is a flat package he's plainly just picked up—it's dry. Nathan tells him the novel is finished.

"From the peaceful look on your face," Ames says, "Ah divined something wonduhful must have happened. Congratulations." He touches the package in Nathan's hand with awe and reverence. "Ah would invite you to repeat our earlier intimate champagne gala, the memory of which Ah shall always cherish, but Ah no longah partake of the grape."

"Seriously?" Nathan says.

"Tony barely escaped with his life," Ames says. "And that was thanks only to you and Hoyt. Alcohol had robbed me of every shred of responsibility. Ah was literally allowing mah dearest friend on earth to die horribly right unduh mah eyes, and Ah did nothing, nothing."

"You tried." The line has moved up. Nathan watches the gray little old clerk weigh his package, pushes at him the coins to pay for the stamps, then goes out with Ames into the rain. The rain sifts down, cold, indifferent; the tires of cars hiss past on the worn-out asphalt of Highland. "And Ah swore nevuh, nevuh to drink again. It's insidious, you know. You're scarcely aware it's slowly destroying you."

"How are Tony's legs?"

"They're a ghastly sight, but he'll soon be on them again. The doctuhs say he won't even limp. And, best of all, the years of pain are forevah ended. Meantime"—Ames holds up his package—"he's using his convalescence to study hotel management. A mail-ordah course."

"Who's paying for it?" Nathan says.

"Mah mother, Mrs. Scrooge. Once Ah convinced her Ah was truly on the wagon, and Tony, too, of course—"

Of course. They'd never do anything singly, would they?

"—once she accepted that, she was very generous. For her. When Tony's completed the course, she's promised to employ him at her hotel in Visalia.

"And what will you be doing?"

"Writing, naturally," Ames says stiffly. "The old ogress used to believe in mah talent. She says she's prepared to believe in it again."

Nathan smiles. "Isn't that going to make it a little hard for you to go on hating her?"

Ames makes a face. "Maybe. But it is not easy to love someone who has been right about your dissolute charactuh all along"—he begins to waddle away splay-footed through the puddles in his threadbare tennis shoes—"especially when they remind you of it every chance they get."

It seems a doubtful morning to be boarding a boat. It's cold. A fine misty rain falls. Gusts of wind blow the rain into their faces —Nathan's and Stanley Page's and Gentleman Jim Hawker's. The sky scowls. The water is steely gray and restless, heaving in long swells, hissing around the black-barnacled stakes of the pier, and rocking the boat. The boat is an old power launch, painted white, with streaks of rust running down from its rivets. The waves bump the hull against the pier and the sound is hollow. It doesn't seem much to go to sea in. Nathan wishes he hadn't come.

But Page, with a hunting rifle in a canvas-and-leather carrying case, motions him to be first aboard, and for no reason he can think of, he legs over the side and twists an ankle in the scuppers. In tennis shoes, digging his toes into loose duckboards as the ship rocks, he takes the gun case, a knapsack, and a picnic hamper from Page and steadies him as he flounders over the corroded rail in his new khaki jacket and pants and boots. Then Nathan takes Hawker's rifle and gives him a hand. Hawker is lighter, lither, and his hunting clothes are old. Both men are excited, but neither of them shows it, except that Hawker, when Nathan takes his arm, seems to be vibrating.

A beard-stubbly, middle-aged Mexican climbs down from the pilothouse to say something in Spanish to the men. They all laugh together, the pilot climbs back up the ladder, and the agent and the writer disappear below with their gear. This is a hunting trip. Twenty miles out to the Channel Islands. To shoot wild pigs. That explains the rifles. It's going to take all day, so the hamper from Musso & Frank's contains roast-beef and ham sandwiches, smoked chickens and cold lobster, and jars of fancy mayonnaise and mustard—and three bottles of whiskey. One of the bottles is no longer full: the men were into it in the car. Nathan doesn't follow them below. He is already tired of their company.

The Mexican starts the engine and shouts to a skinny brown adolescent shivering on the dock, and the kid takes his hands out of his pockets to unwind the painters fore and aft from their cleats, tosses the painters aboard, and the *Mermaid* is roaring away from land. The bow slams into the waves and the broad launch bucks, and goes on slamming and bucking. The sections of duckboard underfoot rattle and jump loosely. Nathan sits on a cold, wet bench and, in spite of the spray and the wind, finally manages to light a cigarette.

He looks up at the Mexican at the steel helm. The man laughs to himself and, every few minutes, swigs from a bottle in a rumpled paper sack. Nathan decides bleakly that he is going to die at sea with Stanley Page and James Hawker and this Mexican, none of whom he gives a damn about or who gives a damn about him. Suddenly the rain comes down as if someone had turned over a barrel. He flicks the cigarette over the side, scrambles up the ladder into the pilothouse, slams the door, and wishes he had made Hoyt come.

"Hunting why?" Hoyt said. "They're not starving. They're not going to eat them. So why kill them?"

"It's a rite of manhood, or something. Hawker writes about it all the time. Who cares? You don't have to shoot pigs. I'm not going to. I just want you with me."

"So do I. Right here. Use the phone across the street, tell Page something came up and you have to cancel."

"No, he's spent money, made all kinds of preparations. He'd never have borrowed a car if I hadn't promised to drive him. They won't let him have a license, and Hawker doesn't even know how to drive."

"They should have hired a plane. He can fly, can't he? He claims he was in the Canadian RAF in World War One."

"Well, they didn't hire a plane. Hoyt, they're relying on me. Stanley's been good to me. He overpays me like crazy. I owe him. I'm just asking you to come along."

"Nathan," Hoyt said, "have you ever been seasick?"

"The lakes in Minneapolis are pretty calm."

"Yeah, well, I hope you don't find out what it's like. I'd rather be dead than go through that again."

The Mexican gives him a smoky-toothed grin, touches the bill of his grubby captain's cap with a finger in a comic salute, and begins to sing in Spanish about his *corazón*. He has a nice voice, carries a tune well, and knows a lot of different songs, and for an hour or so Nathan sits and listens while the boat jounces roaring through the waves.

But then he realizes two things are against his staying in the wheelhouse for the whole trip. First, he was up at three this morning and had to stay awake and alert for the long drive to Santa Barbara, so now, in spite of the cold, he's sleepy. Second, he's hungry. He keeps thinking of all that glorious food in the hamper. And finally, when the Mexican pokes a dirty hand into a brown bag, pulls out and starts to devour a huge burrito as he steers—if what he is doing is really steering—Nathan can stand it no longer.

He shinnies down the ladder, parts the slatted doors, and drops down the companionway to the passenger cabin. Dim in the gray, bleary light of portholes, the low-ceilinged room smells of whiskey, tobacco smoke, and, blessedly, of food. The splendid hamper stands open on a small table that has a little railing around it to keep plates and glasses from sliding off—though no one is using plates and glasses today.

"Hey, kid, come eat," Page calls, and waves him in with a chicken leg. "This is great grub."

"Nothing like sea air," Hawker says, "to whet the appetite."

Pushing back his wet hair, Nathan drops onto a bench at the table. He gropes a sandwich out of the hamper, unwraps it, and takes a ravenous bite. The bread tastes fresh-baked; the ham is juicy, sweet, and tender. He finishes half the sandwich before he takes time out to breathe and find the mustard. He adds that.

"Wonderful," he says, mouth full. "I never tasted mustard like this."

Hawker's small mouth smiles. "Stanley has great discernment in matters gustatory."

"Why settle for less than the best?" Page says. "Dip a chunk of lobster in that mayonnaise. You never tasted mayonnaise like that, either."

"Thank you," Nathan says. "In a minute."

Hawker swigs whiskey from the bottle and pushes the bottle at him, but Nathan shakes his head. Early this morning, he scavenged a vodka bottle from Stanley's wastebasket, filled it with water from the bathroom tap, and stowed it in the hamper, and he locates it now and drinks from it. Does the water really taste of Lysol? He's imagining it. Just the same, he hurries to get rid of the taste with the last bite of his sandwich, then tackles the lobster. He has never met lobster before. It is so good, he is ready to faint.

"How can I ever eat regular food again?" he says.

"We sell that book of yours to the movies"—Page takes his turn at the bottle—"and you won't have to." As he makes to set the bottle down, the boat pitches. The bottle falls over, gurgling out whiskey into Page's lap. Page paws at the bottle, trying to right it, cursing all the while. Nathan stretches across, gets the bottle, sets it straight, and corks it.

Hawker says, "I once sold a book to pictures, and look at me. I dine daily on pheasants' tongues. In my lavish Italian palazzo. With forty servants to tend to my every whim." He gets up suddenly. His little sunken eyes are glazed, his small body rigid. "I believe I will take a postprandial turn around the deck." He starts up the companionway, unsteady on his feet, tripping on the narrow, steep steps. At the top, he pushes open the doors, and a gust of fresh, damp, cold air washes down into the cabin. It sounds to Nathan as if the sections of duckboard up there have come loose and are sliding over one another. Hawker calls, "Anyone care to join me?"

"Later," Page says. He is already rolling fully clad into a bunk. "I need a snooze."

"I can't keep my eyes open," Nathan says. "Sorry." The doors above clack closed. Numbly he packs away the leftovers from the meal, peels off his wet jacket, and crawls into an empty bunk. The noisy engine drones. The hull slams and hisses through the waves. And Nathan sleeps.

He opens his eyes, turns over in the bunk, and blinks up at the porthole. The light has changed. Not its fogginess, but its angle. The round, thick glass is still bleary with spume, but the gray light comes in steeply. It must be noon. And still cold—maybe colder than before. He shivers, gets out of the bunk, goes into the tiny head to piss, comes out and puts on his jacket. The boat still plows the waves. It hasn't slowed. The motor hasn't given out. The Mexican's voice has. He's no longer singing. Stanley Page snores in his bunk. Nathan feels lonely and, ducking his head, climbs the companionway to look for Hawker.

There's no need to look. Hawker lies on the deck. The duck-boards have piled themselves against the taffrail. Water sloshes around the deck. He is up to his ankles in it, and Hawker lies in it facedown. Nathan yells "Help!," grabs at the old hunting togs, and rolls Hawker over. He looks green. Water runs out of his mouth and nose. He is inert, and he doesn't make a sound. "Oh, Christ!" Nathan shouts. "Help, God damn it!" He kneels in the bilge water, gets purchase, and heaves Hawker into a seated position. More water runs out of his mouth, but his head lolls. Nathan touches his face. It's cold. Jesus, he mustn't be dead. "Help!" Nathan yells. "Stanley, wake up! Something's wrong with Hawker!" Page doesn't come. Nathan raises his eyes frantically to the wheelhouse, but the Mexican doesn't come. Nathan tells himself he can't do it, but he does it—he lifts the limp Hawker out of the water. He holds him from behind, arms locked just below the writer's ribcage, and squeezes suddenly and hard. Water comes jetting out of Hawker's mouth, along with whiskey, everything he ate for lunch, and a set of false teeth. Hawker shudders, moans, and feebly lifts his head. Nathan laughs with relief. The doors of the passenger cabin slam open.

Page winces in the rain. "What the fuck's going on?"

"It's all right," Nathan says. "He's alive. Help me."

They carry him below, stretch him on the bunk Page just vacated, get the clothes off him, and wrap him in blankets.

The Mexican comes down the stairs. *"Qué pasa?"*

"Man almost drowned," Nathan says. "Where were you?"

"I am worried," the Mexican says. "There are many ships ahead. They look like warships."

"Some navigator," Nathan says. "Fell asleep, didn't you? We're probably coming into Long Beach Naval Station."

Page hustles the Mexican up the companionway ahead of him. "I want to see this."

Hawker catches Nathan's sleeve. "A moment," he croaks. "Listen. I owe you twice over now for saving my life. I am deeply in your debt. If ever, in days to come, you stand in need of help —you must call on me."

"But it wasn't Long Beach," Nathan tells Benbow. "We'd got to the island, all right. And was that ever a mistake!"

Come to practice the piano, he has met Benbow at his door, professorial in tweeds and a cable-knit sweater, briefcase in hand, on his way to the university to lecture yet another batch of intelligence officers on the history of German culture. But he doesn't rush off. Holding the door open on the cold night, he waits, smiling, to hear the end of Nathan's story.

Nathan says, "The Navy does gunnery practice out there. It's off limits to civilians."

"And the boatman didn't know that?"

"He was so surprised it almost sobered him up."

"Were the Navy firing their guns? That would certainly have sobered me up."

Nathan laughs. "They started right about then. We were in the wheelhouse. Stanley and the Mexican dropped to the floor facedown, arms over their heads. 'Hit the deck, kid!' Stanley yelled. 'They're shooting at us.'

" '*Madre de Dios,*' the Mexican said, 'it's the Japs!'

"But if it was, they were out there for the same reason we were—to shoot pigs. It was foggy, but you could see the shells exploding on the island. And then here comes this cutter bearing down on us. Big bright light glaring on the front. I was glad the Mexican couldn't see."

"The Coast Guard?" Benbow says.

"The waves were so high, I don't know how they boarded us, but they did. Bristling with guns. And were they sore? Jesus. I really thought we'd be shot for high treason on the spot. If the lieutenant in charge didn't explode first. He'd lost his hat and a shoe over the side. Fat guy, red-faced, just screaming at us. Stanley was in shock. A convict? On parole? With a rifle in his gear? He couldn't even mumble. The Mexican sat on the floor and cried."

"That would have been my solution." Benbow laughs. "I take it there was a better one?"

"Hawker. He came up the ladder, still looking like a drowned rat, still wrapped in blankets, no teeth, but every inch the aristocrat. All it needed was a lift of his chin, an icy glare, and a quiet little speech. 'Gentlemen? My name is Hawker, James Hawker. Kindly explain, if you will, this truculent and cacophonous intrusion.' "

"The uses of fame?" Benbow asks. "The lieutenant knew his books?"

"I hear from a friend in the Coast Guard. They have a lot of time to read." Nathan grins. "So—the great pig hunt was canceled.

The Mexican lost his license. But we got off with a warning. And an armed escort back to the mainland. Page and Hawker sulked like kids. I felt lucky to be alive."

Reggie Poole is giving a party. It's afternoon. His small living room is filled with pretty sailors, willowy, artistic young and not-so-young civilians, and withered old women in heavy makeup and too much jewelry. One of them, seated in a corner, reads aloud in a fake French accent, batting sooty false eyelashes, waving a skinny arm so her bracelets clash. Her hair is fuzzy as a dandelion gone to seed. Her face is powdered white. In painting her mouth, she's smeared lipstick on her teeth. This is Fay Bower, pretending to be Colette. Reading from Reggie's play.

Three of the willowy types, and a dwarfish boy Reggie claims is the next Jascha Heifetz, sit on the floor at her feet, listening enrapt. But most of the guests take no notice except to talk louder to one another. Her voice is raised. She projects well. Since she was a silent movie star, Nathan wonders where she learned the trick. Reggie takes his arm in a warm grip. He wears a new suit and looks splendid, if a little flushed from champagne. He has been in a state of elation since Dorcas Blaufisch, one of the old women here today, rang him at Drossie's a few days ago to tell him Harry Dryrot was buying his play for Pinnacle Pictures.

Reggie says, "Isn't she perfect? Absolutely perfect for the part. I am so thrilled. Think of it. Fay Bower a star again, after all these years."

"Reggie," Nathan says, "no."

"What?" Reggie lets go his arm. "What do you mean, no?"

"Harry Dryrot's already cast the part," Nathan says. "She's French and young and beautiful and she's under contract."

"But—but—" Reggie turns pale. "But I wrote it for Miss Bower." He steers Nathan into the hall. "You're sure of this? Who told you?"

"Mr. Dryrot himself, the day I told him your story. I'm sorry, your idea is the right one. I mean, she does look like the real Colette."

"That's the whole point," Reggie says.

"Right. And it will be a lie, the way he does it, but your friend's a crone—she's got a figure like a fireplug. He wants curves, Reggie—glamour, sex appeal. He doesn't care about reality. All he cares about is money."

"Money? The money will pour in. Fay Bower is a legend. She'll make him a fortune."

"Reggie," Nathan says, "until you introduced us that day, I'd never heard of Fay Bower. I mentioned her to Steve Schaffer. He'd never heard of her, either."

"I didn't write the play for children," Reggie snaps. "Oh, God—this is a catastrophe." He wrings his hands. "I promised her the part."

"Promised? How could you? Reggie, you've worked in the business. Even I know writers have no say in casting."

"I wanted it that way," Reggie says tearfully. "It was my dream. To bring her back in triumph to the screen again. Nathan, she's old—it was her last chance. What will I tell her? How will I ever explain?"

"Let Miss Blaufisch explain," Nathan says. "She should have warned you right away."

Reggie snorts. "So should you."

"How could I? You never said a word about Fay Bower."

"Well, you had no right to tell Harry Dryrot about my play. That Philistine. Now look at the mess you've made."

Nathan is stung. "I was only trying to help. Do you like picking up dimes off crumby tables for a living?"

"Oh, no, no, no." Reggie enfolds him in a bear hug and rocks him side to side. "Forgive me. I've been a romantic fool again and I'm furious. With myself—not you, not you. I'll be grateful to you forever. You've given me back my career." He kisses Nathan's forehead and glances toward the party. "It will be all right. Dorcas and I will simply tell her. She'll make a scene, but it won't last." He straightens his shoulders. "We'll pour a couple of stiff gins down her, and she'll soon be smiling through her tears." He takes a deep breath and starts for the noisy room. "She knows as well as I do how heartless Hollywood can be."

It's the sixth day of March. Rainy. He's glad to have his raincoat but tired of the rain. Gloomy, wondering when if ever Craven & Hyde are going to write to him about his book, he trudges eastward along Franklin under dark, dripping trees. At the corner of Cahuenga, he pushes inside the liquor store, where if not warm it's at least dry. The bony blond woman always behind the counter at this early hour has a cold. She's put on an old cardigan sweater too big for her. She wipes a red nose with tissues and asks him what she can get him. She ought to know by now what he's come for. It never changes. But he tells her again. And she gets him the can of orange juice and the flat bottle of vodka and puts them into a sack and takes his money.

"I don't remember such a wet winter," she says.

"It must be the war." Nathan pushes out to the sidewalk. And a horn toots. A car waits at the curb. Its door swings open. Nathan bends and squints. The driver is John F. Noble. Nathan steps around puddles on the sidewalk, looks into the car. "What do you want?"

"To talk to you," Noble says. "Get in."

"I have to get to work," Nathan says.

"That's what I want to talk to you about. Don't worry. It will only take a few minutes."

Nathan gets in and slams the door. "I haven't seen you in months. I thought you were gone for good."

"Obviously I was gone too long." Noble rolls the car slowly along the street. The windshield wipers swing and creak. "Did you know Stanley Page is an ex-convict?"

"He took the blame for his partners," Nathan says. "Anyway, it wasn't a crime. It was a mistake. He republished an old humor book. Chick Sale. They told him it was in public domain. But it wasn't. It was still copyrighted."

"You know why he did that?" Noble says. "To try to raise money to pay off his creditors. He owned a bookstore. It went bankrupt."

"He told me," Nathan says. "Mr. Noble, why don't you leave me alone?"

"It went bankrupt," Noble says, "because he gambled all the profits away. On racehorses. And what he didn't gamble he drank up. He's a drunk, Nathan."

"He's always been kind to me. Where are we going?"

"Just for a short drive," Noble says, and turns down Vine Street. "He's not a proper person for you to be associating with."

"Have you got the right to watch me this way?"

"I'm trying to protect you," Noble says.

"I don't need protection," Nathan says.

"That's not what the Coast Guard tells me," Noble says.

Nathan grabs the door handle. "Let me out."

"That was a close call," Noble says. "Page is going to end up back in prison one of these days, and he could very well drag you with him. Don't let that happen. You're an intelligent boy. I've seen your IQ scores. Talented too. At the school, they showed me those pieces you wrote for the paper. They think you'll be a successful writer."

"And Stanley can help me," Nathan says. "He knows all kinds of editors and publishers and movie people."

"And they know he's a terminal alcoholic going nowhere but the morgue," Noble says. "I've told you before—we're judged by the company we keep. With you, first it's Communists and homosexuals—now it's Page. Don't you see, you're ruining your chances. Nathan—will you please go home to your parents?"

"And that's another thing," Nathan says. "What right did you have reporting on me to my father?"

"You're underage," Noble says, shifts down, brings the car to a careful halt at a red light. "He's responsible for you. But he was in Minneapolis, and you were out here. He needed the facts. I had the facts."

"All your damn facts did," Nathan says, "is destroy the love between us. Does that satisfy you?"

"But not between you and Stubblefield," Noble says. "You're still with Stubblefield."

Nathan opens the door. "And I always will be."

"I don't think so. He's in danger, Nathan. Deeper than he knows."

Nathan snorts. "What danger? You're just trying to scare me."

"Not scare—warn," Noble says. "Go home, Nathan."

Nathan gets out in the rain. "Where Hoyt is," he says, "that's my home." He slams the door. And steps into deep water in the gutter. In his hurry to get out of it, he trips on the curb and sprawls across the sidewalk. The orange juice can rolls away unharmed. But he's going to have to buy vodka all over again.

He lays the letters and checks he's typed on the dresser and sits down to read about General Hood, and Stanley Page comes out of the shower shaven and combed and with the damp towel around his waist, and Nathan looks up:

"This is my last day, Mr. Page," he says.

"How come?" With a pen Nathan has laid on the dresser Page signs the letters and checks. "Did Craven & Hyde finally pay for your book?"

"It's not that." Nathan puts the manuscript down and stands up. "The FBI is watching me. And that means they're watching you too. And I don't want that."

"Shit." Page stares at him. "I don't want it either."

"I didn't think so." Nathan gathers up the signed papers. "So I'm getting out of your life."

Page hands him the pen. "What the hell are they watching you for?"

"They say my friends are Communists." Nathan folds the letters at the little desk and inserts the letters and the checks into envelopes he has already addressed and stamped. "It started last year. But I haven't seen the agent for a long time, and I thought he'd given up. Then he came around this morning. That's why I was late."

"Jesus," Page says. He steps into clean undershorts. "I thought you were a mouse."

Nathan is licking the glue on the flap of an envelope. He stops and stares. "A mouse?"

"You know." Page sits to pull socks on. He doesn't seem at all disconcerted. "That you liked boys."

" 'Mouse'?" Nathan laughs.

"As in 'man or mouse.' " Page flaps into a plum-colored shirt. He scoffs, "Who ever heard of a Communist mouse?"

"He knew all about our trip to shoot pigs."

Page squints. "The hell he did."

"And all about your—uh—past," Nathan says.

"What the fuck for? I'm no pinko."

"If I leave," Nathan says, "maybe he'll forget you."

Page hands him his coat. "So long, kid." He pulls open the door, pats Nathan's back. "It was nice knowing you."

Naked in the dark bed, holding Nathan close, Hoyt says, "He was bullshitting you. The danger is past. I told you. I'm not hunting for Eva's killer anymore."

Nathan lies quiet, watching the dim windows, the leafy silhouettes outside. "You loved her, didn't you?"

"Be serious. You said it yourself—I'm a pansy."

"I guess not. I guess you were her lover. That's why you went on and on trying to find who murdered her. You were her lover, right here in this room, in this bed."

Hoyt pushes up on his arms, gazes down into Nathan's face. "All right. For a while. But I was too young. That's what she said. She ended it."

"Why didn't you tell me?" Nathan says.

Hoyt sighs and lies down again. "I didn't tell you because it connected to everything I was doing, and none of it was safe for you to know. Benbow recruited me because Eva was a top Communist.

With luck, she'd tell me important things. George had been his agent, but the Party found out he was a flit and threw him out. Benbow asked me at that time to take his place and I said no. Then, when he learned Eva and I were lovers, he blackmailed me."

"A spy for what, who?" Nathan says.

"A U.S. Senate special committee on wartime internal security," Hoyt says. "If you believe Benbow Harsch."

"And you don't?"

"I've checked. There's no such committee."

Nathan whistles softly. "Blackmailed you how?"

"Eva and I had written letters. Benbow got hold of them. And said unless I helped him, when the government jailed her for subversion, he'd see I went with her."

"But she was killed," Nathan says. "Why did you—?"

"I was deep in the Party by then. He still had me."

"But he fired you when you got back from Texas."

"I told you—the comrades had gotten leery of me. Anyway, somebody else was stepping in to run things. Ol' Benbow is leaving UCLA for a desk in Washington, D.C. In a tailor-made uniform, with gold braid on his hat."

"What a nightmare." Nathan shudders, and clutches Hoyt against him. "And you had to keep it all to yourself." About to cry, he swings his feet to the floor and reaches across to the chest of drawers for cigarettes and matches. "I was no good to you. You should have had somebody else—somebody older, brighter, stronger."

"I didn't want somebody else," Hoyt says, takes the cigarette and matches from him, and kisses him hard and deeply. "I wanted you. Then. Now. Forever."

And they make love, and to Nathan it is the best they ever were together—because now, at last, Hoyt has no secrets from him. Now, at last, Hoyt is as naked as he is.

Craven & Hyde write:

We are sorry to have disappointing news for you. As you know, everyone here fell in love with the first chapters of The

Shotgun Flat, *and we were all eager for it to fulfill its promise.
You write well, have a fine, dry sense of humor, and a shrewd
but always gentle gift for character.*

*However, we're afraid that all these talents do not in this
case add up to a publishable novel. Frank's absence for so long
in the middle of the book still seems to us a serious mistake, but
even were you willing to correct that, thornier difficulties would
remain.*

*Your delightful opening chapters led us to overlook in the
outline you sent with them warnings of the central problem—
that* The Shotgun Flat *is basically a protracted anecdote, and
while the amiable and honest material might be enough to flesh
out a short story or even a play, it's too frail to sustain a full-
length novel.*

*Of course, you will be upset by this decision, and we
ourselves are grieved that things have not worked out. But we're
certain you don't want to make your publishing debut with a
flawed entry, and it would be wrong of us to encourage you to
do so. Please believe us when we say we have not lost faith in
your outstanding talent, and are looking forward with high
hopes to your next book.*

He waits on the sidewalk in the long afternoon shadow of the
Highland Hotel. The manuscript of *The Shotgun Flat* is in his hand.
He leans against the white stucco wall and smokes and looks up
the street toward Cahuenga Pass for the dark blue De Soto of the
writer who shuttles Gentleman Jim Hawker to and from Warner
Bros. As on the three previous days, it doesn't come. He never
looks down the street, so when Hoyt, who walks home from work
that way, touches him, he jumps, though it's the fourth time it's
happened. Hoyt says:

"This is crazy. Why don't you just leave it for him? At the desk?"

"I told you—I have to talk to him."

"Attach a note. Tell him to send it to his publisher. He

said he'd help you when you asked, and now you're asking."

"What if he doesn't like it?" Nathan says.

"What's 'like' got to do with it? Did you 'like' saving him on that fucking boat? You just did it, didn't you?"

"That was different. What are you trying to say?"

"Don't ask him to read it—tell him to send it."

Nathan gapes. "Would he do that?"

"That's what Sherwood Anderson did for Hawker's first book. Come on." Hoyt takes his arm and hikes him up blue steps to the hotel door. "You don't even have to write the note." He pushes inside. "I'll write it."

It's Sunday and the weather is fine. With mugs of coffee growing cold on the floor beside the bed, cigarettes burning down in the ashtray, Mozart on the radio in the next room, they find things to do with each other naked that are always good and always new no matter how often they've done them before. Sun shines on the bed. And up the hill a typewriter rattles. Nathan doesn't know how long it's been rattling, but suddenly he hears it.

"What's up?" Hoyt says.

"Hawker's home." Nathan scrambles out of bed, tries to look up the hill through the window, but the tree branches are in the way. "He must be outside working." He kicks into jeans, snatches up a shirt from the floor, pokes his arms into it. "I have to talk to him."

"You better wash up first," Hoyt says. "While you do that, I'll fix breakfast."

"Afterward." Nathan shucks the shirt and jeans and runs for the bathroom. "I'll eat afterward."

But when he comes out, Hoyt has cooked, so Nathan eats before. So as not to hurt Hoyt's feelings. The ham and eggs, anyway, and a gulp of coffee. The toast he takes with him as he runs down the stairs. He darts past the rubber tree to look up. The typewriter is no longer tap-tap-tapping, but Nathan can see Hawker's straw hat above the edge of the balcony. He's out there all right, seated at the table where he works. Nathan trots down the street, finishing off the toast. Wiping his buttery fingers on his pants, he pushes into the dim lobby of the Highland Hotel and hurls himself at the stairs. After a few flights he has to slow down, and he's panting and his heart is hammering when he reaches Hawker's door and knocks. He doesn't hear typing. He doesn't hear anything. So he knocks again and calls:

"Mr. Hawker? It's me. Nathan Reed."

Nothing.

He knocks again. "Mr. Hawker? Can you hear me?"

Still nothing.

He tries the door. It isn't locked. He pushes it and steps inside. Across the cluttered room the glass slide door is open to the sunlit balcony. And Hawker is out there in his straw hat and a Hawaiian shirt. But his hands are not on the typewriter. His hands hang down beside the metal-and-canvas chair he sits in. And his head rests on the typewriter. He has passed out drunk again. Nathan sighs, and picks his way through the bottles and books on the floor, and steps out on the balcony. He touches Hawker's shoulder.

"Mr. Hawker? Are you all right?"

And Hawker tips away from him. Dark glasses were hanging off one ear. Now they fall with a delicate clatter. The slight form of the great writer leans against the balcony parapet. His hat sails out and downward on the breeze. With a shriek, the chair legs slip. Nathan catches at Hawker's arm, but he can't keep him from slumping to the floor. A sharp leg of the chair jabs Nathan's leg. He kicks the chair aside, kneels, and shakes Hawker.

"Sir? Mr. Hawker. Wake up."

He begins to panic. Is Hawker even breathing? He grabs the writer's limp arm and tries to find a pulse in the wrist. He has never done this, so maybe he doesn't know how, but he can't feel a pulse. He drops the arm and lays an ear to Hawker's chest. He can't hear any heartbeat. He straightens, banging his head on the rusty underside of the table. He stares helplessly at the famous pinch-nosed face with its white beard stubble and small mouth.

"Say something," the boy begs. "Wake up. Please."

But Hawker just lies there, eyes shut, chin on chest.

Numbly, Nathan goes to the telephone on Hawker's desk. Among tobacco pouches, briar pipes, and scripts, *The Shotgun Flat* lies there. He lifts the receiver. He doesn't know what to dial. Anyway, the numbers blur because he's crying. He starts to hang up, but then:

"Desk," somebody says.

"I'm calling from James Hawker's," Nathan says.

"Oh, God," the voice says. "What's he done this time?"

"This time," Nathan says, "I think he's dead."

Mr. Constance is on vacation, so Nathan is working nights for two weeks. When he climbs wearily up the dark stairs of the green-shingled house at ten-fifteen, the door to Reggie Poole's rooms is open. And Reggie in shirt-sleeves is packing his books. The room is almost bare. He's moving to fancier quarters, a house in the hills—white stucco, red tile. It isn't big, but the address is good, and so is the view of Lake Hollywood, the reservoir. And Reggie now has a car to get him up the steep, winding streets among the trees.

Nathan leans in the doorway. "I'm going to miss you."

Reggie straightens his back and gives him a smile. "Bless you, child. But we're not going to be strangers." With a tuft of feathers, he whisks dust off books and lays them in a carton. "I'm only a few blocks away."

"How's working for the Philistine?" Nathan says.

"The pay is excellent." Reggie carries the carton into the hall, switches off the light. "One must not kick against the pricks." He closes his door. "I'm off. Good night."

"Good night." Nathan crosses the hall, opens the door, closes the door, and sees something that makes his heart bump. A duffel bag lies on the couch. But no one's in the room. He doesn't hear voices. The kitchen is alight, but no one's there. He turns back, frowning.

"Hoyt?" he says. "Steve?"

No answer. He looks into the bedroom. Because of the half-glass door, he doesn't have to light the lamp to see that the bed is occupied. He feels the way he felt when Jukes knocked the wind out of him. Only this time his brain can't catch its breath, either. What's the matter with them? Has the clock stopped? In the excitement of the chance for sex with beautiful Steve, has Hoyt forgotten when Nathan gets home these nights? What happened to Hoyt's dislike of Schaffer? What's the attraction? Is Steve so much like Eva? These questions tumble in his head. He is hurt and angry, but more angry than hurt, so that he steps into the shadowy bedroom and says:

"Excuse the hell out of me, but—"

And sees that there's only one in the bed, not two.

"Hoyt?" He reaches across and switches on the lamp. But it isn't Hoyt. It's Schaffer, who stirs, mumbles, then opens his eyes wide and sits up sharply. He is unshaven, tousled, and Nathan can smell his sweat. His uniform lies in a crumpled heap on the floor. It has sergeant's stripes now.

"Time is it?" he croaks.

"Ten-thirty," Nathan says. "Where's Hoyt?"

"Can I have some coffee?" Schaffer swings his legs to the floor. He is naked. Again. "I have to get out to the air base—if I miss that midnight plane I'm sunk."

"What are you doing here?"

"I came to warn Hoyt." Schaffer reaches wearily for his skivvy shirt. "I faked a twenty-four-hour pass." He pulls the shirt on over his head. "And caught an Army cargo plane to L.A. Really deluxe accommodations. Not even seats. Certainly no bunks." He hikes his butt to put on shorts. "Have to be on the docks in New York by noon. Big doings coming up in Europe. Wouldn't want to miss the boat, would I?" He tugs socks on. "Please, Nathan. Coffee?"

"Warn Hoyt? About what?"

Steve picks up his shirt and stands. "That my mother's friends in New York have finally determined who killed her." He gets into the shirt, buttons it.

"Determined?" The drawers of the chest are open. Hoyt's stuff is gone. Schaffer is putting on his pants. Nathan steps past him to the closet. Hoyt's hang-up clothes are gone. So is the dark blue suit. So is the suitcase. He stands staring. When he turns back, Schaffer is tying his shoes. Nathan says, "Steve, where did he go?"

"He wouldn't tell me." Schaffer makes for the kitchen, shrugging into his tunic. "Least of all."

Nathan follows him. "But why? I mean, why did he go?"

Schaffer peers into the coffee pot. "Because he did it, and they're sending someone to get him."

"Did it? Killed her? Hoyt? Oh, come on, Steve. He hunted for months for her killer, while your mother's friends here pretended it was an accident. He knew it wasn't."

"Thou sayest it." Schaffer lights a burner under the pot and turns the flame up high. "Nathan, he faked looking for the killer so no one would suspect it was him."

" 'He,' " Nathan says numbly. "Can they prove that?"

"They can prove that Eva found out that this boy she'd loved, who'd been her protégé"—Schaffer rinses out mugs under the hot-water tap—"was a spy. She arranged to meet with him that night on a dark, deserted street downtown to confront him with the evidence." He turns off the tap, takes a ragged dish towel off the back of a chair, dries the mugs. "And he pushed her under that streetcar to shut her up."

Nathan sits down because his legs won't hold him. "Do they know who he was spying for?"

Schaffer sets the mugs on the table and shrugs. "Yup. Old California types. Moneybags. Hate Communists, Chinese, Japanese,

Mexicans, Jews, Negroes. The Save America Foundation? Some name like that."

"Why would Hoyt kill your mother to protect them?" Nathan says. "You don't really think he did it."

Schaffer turns to get the coffee pot. "I don't? Why?"

"Because you let him run away," Nathan says.

Schaffer fills the coffee mugs. "He can't run forever."

"But why break your neck to come and warn him?"

"Because you haven't got a phone, and the man they send won't waste time." Schaffer clatters the pot back on the stove, pulls out a chair, and sits down. He is pale under the beard stubble, plainly exhausted. He slurps at the half-heated coffee. His bloodshot eyes look into Nathan's. "I didn't want to save the son of a bitch. I wanted to kill him. I could have. The Army teaches you how." He takes his tie out of a side pocket and puts it on. "I should have. She was my mother. But someone will—it's only a matter of time. And if I'd done it, you'd have hated me." He pushes heavily to his feet and puts a kiss on Nathan's mouth. "And I don't want you to hate me. I want you to love me."

"When? You'll forget about me."

"Never." In the living room, Schaffer slides a carton of Lucky Strikes from the duffel bag, lays the carton on the table, buckles the bag, and picks it up. He pulls open the door and smiles. "Read the casualty lists. If I'm not on them, I'll be back." He goes down the stairs, and Nathan stands on the landing and watches him. In the dark at the foot of the stairs, Schaffer remembers his cap and puts it on. He looks up. "You're well rid of him, Nathan."

"He didn't do it," Nathan says. "Not Hoyt—I know him."

"His kind nobody knows," Schaffer says. "Goodbye." With the lift of a hand, he trudges off into the night.

"I know him," Nathan shouts in tears. "I know him."

But this time he's the liar, isn't he?

———

"Nathan, wake up. Do you hear me? Wake up."

A hand shakes his shoulder. He mumbles thickly, "No, go away," squeezes his eyes shut, pulls the blankets over his head. He didn't get to sleep until sunrise. It was the worst night of his life. He is so tired it amounts to sickness. "Leave me alone." But now the hand yanks the covers halfway off him and says:

"Nathan, where has he gone?"

Since he is naked, he sits up and snatches the covers back. He screws his face up, blinking against the morning sunshine. It's Flora Belle Short, massive in a flower-print muumuu, the same one she wore the first time he saw her. The big scuffed leather bag hangs from her shoulder. Nathan says hoarsely, "What's the matter?"

"Where is Hoyt Stubblefield?"

"I don't know, Miz Short. I wasn't home from work yet when he left. And he didn't leave a note." He squints. "What do you want with him?"

"The truck is gone," she says. "When Percy went back to sea, he left orders with Jukes to check on it every morning. And he does. And this morning the garage doors are wide open, and the truck is gone."

"Well, I haven't got it. Not this time. Those days are over." Nathan swings his feet to the floor and tries to keep a blanket across his wake-up erection when he stretches for the pack of Luckies on the chest. "You don't see it anyplace around here, do you?"

"No, and I wouldn't expect to," Flora Belle says. "You're not the sort to steal another man's wife."

"What?" Nathan coughs on cigarette smoke. "What are you saying?"

"Linnet," Flora Belle says. "She's not in her room. Her clothes are gone. She's run off with Hoyt Stubblefield."

"Jesus Christ." Nathan stands up in surprise, and the blanket falls.

Flora Belle claps a hand over her eyes and cries out, like a shocked virgin, "Cover yourself!"